MURDER TIMES TWO

Santa Fe 2019

MURDER TIMES TWO

Maxine Neely Davenport

To Ginny

Enjoy!

Maxine Neely Davenport

Lance Publishing
Santa Fe, NM

Murder Times Two
Murder Mystery

By Maxine Neely Davenport

First Edition

Printed in the United States

Published by: Lance Publishing
                 1205 Maclovia Street
                 Santa Fe, New Mexico 87505

ISBN: 978-0-9892431-0-0

1. Fiction.   2. Crime.   3. Murder Mystery.

Cover art by MediaNeighbours.com, copyright ©2013

This book is dedicated to the many friends, neighbors, teachers, and professors who influenced my life positively at Latta High School and at East Central University in Ada, Oklahoma. Beautiful friendships create wonderful memories.

It is not the place we occupy which is important,
but the direction in which we move.

OLIVER WENDELL HOLMES

ONE

October 31, 1964

In muggy Chicago, Detective Tracy Hunter ripped her letter of resignation from the typewriter and headed for Captain Carson's office beyond the investigators' cubbyholes. She stormed in without knocking, leaving the door open so that their conversation could be heard by the entire unit. She hurled the missile onto his desk.

"I'm leaving, without a forwarding address!" She controlled the pleasure she felt at hearing the gasps coming from members of her unit.

Captain Carson bolted from his chair. "You can't do this, Tracy. My hands were tied. The decision was made upstairs." He sat down, lowering his chin, staring upward through his bushy eyebrows. "Shelby's been here longer than you have."

"Plus, he's the mayor's nephew, right?" She slapped both hands on top of his desk and leaned forward. "You know that was my job. You could have twisted some arms, but you sat on your fat ass, letting the boys upstairs dictate the moves." Straightening to her full five-foot-ten-inch height, she lifted her chin and pointed a finger in his direction. "For your information, I don't care. I have bigger plans for my life." She whirled and headed for the door.

The captain flushed. "Tracy, don't leave. It was all politics, and besides, the mayor ordered me to find a different desk for you—windows overlooking the lake—anything you want. Just don't leave. We depend on you to make this place look good."

Tracy glared. "I didn't graduate from beauty school, Captain. I'm a cop! And don't waste your time looking for another position for me. There aren't any desks big enough, the windows overlooking the lake aren't wide enough, and I don't like the coffee in this two-bit joint. Save your promises for someone who'll settle for a dead-end street."

"Wait a minute, Tracy. The job as department head isn't the only possibility for you around here. He leaned forward, whispering. Lucy just kicked me out of the house. Maybe you and me—us?"

"Don't even think about it, Captain. There is no us. There is *you* in bed with the mayor, and there is *me* looking out for myself. Notice my new wings. I'm flying out of here right now." She lifted her arms, flapped them like a swan, and slammed the door behind her. As an afterthought, she opened his door and picked up a large cardboard box left for the cleaning crew. She saluted the captain. "Thanks for the U-Haul."

The door closed this time to the applause of her colleagues standing at their desks. Tracy bowed, swished her blond curls from her face, and flipped the bird at Shelby and his friends. She found it freeing to dump the junk from her desk into the cardboard box, to wave goodbye, to sprint downstairs, and to gun her beat-up Karmann Ghia convertible out of the basement parking lot for the last time.

For a thirty-two-year-old woman with one marriage behind her and no prospects in sight, with an occasional silver strand showing up in her hair brush, and with no job on the horizon, Tracy admitted her exit performance rated a grade of BS—Brash and Stupid. But who cared? She was liberated.

To tell the truth, the idea of quitting police work had begun appearing in her daydreams from the time she suspected that a woman would never be promoted to head the investigations unit. Men had trouble accepting a woman in pants telling them what to do. For years, she had fooled herself into believing she was the exception. She dreamed of running the unit, living out her working days in the same office, in the same town, with the same friends, and at the end, being buried in the city cemetery with a police escort. The alternative, niggling at her subconscious, urged her to quit the safe job and search for new adventures. Today, for sure, she had given up the police escort to the cemetery.

This seemed like a good time to realize her fantasy of becoming a private investigator. With *Tracy Hunter, P.I.* printed on the door, she would be head honcho from day one. No doubt about it, the position of Top Dog appealed to her.

In the past, her thoughts of going independent always got sidetracked when she tried to imagine where she would open that office. Smart people hung their shingle where longtime friends could send them clients. For her, that meant Chicago. But she had moved to Chicago from Oklahoma because Aunt Rose had promised to send her to a good school, not because she loved the noise, the dirt, or the homeless bums sleeping outside her door. Let's face it, she loved sunshine, open prairies, horses, and cowboys. However, the very thought that she might move back to her hometown caused her to hiccup a laugh. What would a private investigator do in the small, quiet town of Ada?

One didn't need twenty-twenty vision to maneuver the streets between the police station and her apartment. She unlocked her mailbox and pulled out the usual stack of advertisements. After dumping mail into the U-Haul box with the pencils, note pads, and the stapler (which a super-honest employee would have left on her desk), she carried the box inside, where she poured José Cuervo over rocks, took a sip, and shuffled through the bills, throwing away ads and donation pleas. She whooped upon discovering a response from the Bureau of Vital Statistics, Oklahoma State Board of Health. Her birth certificate, at last. Thank goodness it had arrived before she vacated her apartment, or it might never have resurfaced.

Receiving this birth certificate could very well qualify as a cosmic happening in her life, allowing her to apply for a passport at a time when she found herself footloose and free to travel wherever a passport could take her. She opened the envelope, spread out the document, and frowned. How weird. This certificate belonged to someone named Brigitte Cerise Hunter. She squinted, surprised to find that Brigitte had been born to her parents. Huh? No way. Neither of her sisters bore the name Brigitte Cerise, and she did not. The certificate spelled the mother's name S-a-r-a, not S-a-r-a-h. No big deal. That error often appeared in documents. Her father's name and the family address were correct.

Tracy shook her head, sloshing the tequila up her nose. Her sneeze baptized the certificate with sprinkles of alcohol. Disgusted, she brushed

4 Maxine Neely Davenport

the drops away and pressed the paper flat. She knew her original birth certificate, lost somewhere in her move to Chicago, listed her name as Tracy
Hunter. How in the world could this certificate have become a part of her
family history? It must belong to someone else. There were cases where
babies were switched at the hospital, and that would explain why she
lacked the dark hair and tanned skin tone her sisters inherited from their
parents. Her hair was blondish, and freckles spattered across her light,
creamy complexion, much to her dismay. But she knew she could not
have been switched at the hospital, because the stork had dropped Tracy
in a log cabin in Oklahoma on a snowy February day. Plus, if her parents
had had the privilege of selecting one baby over another, they would have
gone for a boy.

Tracy rose from her chair, drink in hand, and stared out the window.
Lake Michigan lay calm and dark, except for the reflected lights near the
shore. Despite her ravings to the police captain, this view would be hard to
replace. Maybe her crazy drama-queen exit from a secure job ranked right
up there with being stupid. It was okay to be called too brash, too sexy,
and a loud mouth, but "stupid" was something else.

A heaviness settled over her and she slumped to the couch. The day's
happenings left her feeling discombobulated. First, she had given up her
identity as a Chicago police officer, and second, this birth certificate questioned whether the name she had used for thirty-two years belonged to
her. José began soothing the rough edges of her tensions. She refilled her
glass, determined to find a logical answer to this mistake.

She knew a correct birth certificate rested somewhere in the Oklahoma state records, and if the bureaucracy couldn't unearth it, this one
could be amended to read "Tracy Hunter." No problem. Another sip of
tequila was calming, but why did the idea of an amendment not make
her feel better? Snorting in an unladylike fashion, she reached for the telephone to call Ruth, who could always come up with a sensible, down-
to-earth suggestion for how to resolve Tracy's personal problems. Advice
from big sister came as a perk she would not allow this Brigitte girl to take
without a fight.

A busy signal disappointed her. Oh, well. She laid the birth certificate
aside and listed the need to amend the thing as another reason to visit
Oklahoma before job hunting, traveling, or opening an office. She looked
forward to a vacation in Tulsa, surrounded by Ruth's hunk of a husband

and their three teenage football players. Tracy loved fighting her way into table discussions at their home.

She set her drink aside. The nicest part about an Oklahoma vacation would be spending time with Nora Smeltzer, her former college roommate. Their frequent telephone conversations always cheered Tracy, but it had been years since they'd shared some downtime together. Her watch indicated that Nora might still be at her medical clinic, handing out pills, and maybe Dr. Jordan, who had screwed up Tracy's birth certificate, would also be available to take a call. She needed to know whether he had purposefully added the wrong name or whether it was a sloppy accident. Neither answer would make her happy, but with the help of her friend José, she felt challenged to find the answer. Who better qualified to unearth the doctor's motive than a past member of a great police department, where her interrogation skills had been honed to perfection? She smiled. Depending upon what Paul Jordan revealed, Tracy might find herself engaged in her first private investigation case. Pro bono, wouldn't you know?

While Tracy was dissolving her relationship with the police department in Chicago, patients crowded into the old Hodges Medical Building in Ada, Oklahoma, coughing and sneezing. Most were unaware that their doctor, Paul Jordan, had arrived in town over thirty-three years ago, a drunken bum, dumped from a train passing through town on the way to California. Those who remembered did not care; that was history, and everybody in the West has a history.

The telephone kept ringing in the front office, and Paul cursed under his breath. "Where the hell is Tillie?" His nurse knew not to ignore the phone beyond the first ring, because it irritated him. He took the tongue depressor from the mouth of his young friend and patient, Hal Montgomery, and waited to see if the ringing would stop. It didn't.

"Damn." He threw the stick into the wastebasket, which seemed to have the effect of lifting the receiver off its cradle. Hal grinned as the doctor relaxed and reached for a new tongue depressor.

"Try not to hit my appendix this time, Doc."

Paul ignored Hal's needling. Despite the difference in ages, they were best friends and rivals on the tennis court. On weekends, after exchanging wins and losses, Hal would drop by for lunch at the Jordan home, and Paul's wife Kit would sit with them to hear the replay of their game. To their dismay, Hal's chronic sore throat had interfered with tennis games all summer.

Tillie appeared at the door. "Some lady from Chicago wants to talk to you."

"I'm busy," Paul said.

"I can see that." She shrugged at Hal as if to say, *I have to put up with this all the time*. Out loud she said, "When shall I tell her to call back?"

Paul stopped poking in Hal's throat. "Who is it?"

"She said her name was Tracy Hunter." She paused, frowning. "Dr. Hodges used to see some Hunters. This may be their youngest, all grown-up."

"Humm," Paul murmured, his pulse throbbing. Was it possible that one of Sarah's daughters was contacting him? He did not remember a Tracy. His heart raced faster.

Hal sat straighter on the examination table. "Tracy Hunter?" he asked, with an element of disbelief. His voice softened. "You can bet I knew Tracy. We were high-school sweethearts." A smile flickered beneath his mustache.

"No kidding?" Paul hesitated. That meant she was now in her thirties and could be the baby he delivered to Sarah Hunter that many years ago. He turned away to clear his throat.

"When shall I tell her you'll be free?" Tillie asked.

"After six." Paul's voice was harsh and impatient.

Tillie uttered a disapproving *huh*, and went back to the office.

"She hates missing out on long-distance calls. We don't get that many," Paul said. "Open your mouth." He pushed a new tongue depressor far back into his patient's throat, and Hal responded with a choking sputter.

Paul's mind refused to concentrate on Hal's sore throat. "How could you have dated one of the Hunter girls in high school? They moved to Oil Center when Emily and Ruth were young—even before Tracy was born."

"Yeah, but they came back. Josh got tired of rough-necking in the oil fields. Wanted to farm, so they bought one hundred twenty acres just south of where I lived. Tracy and I were freshmen together in high school and rode the same bus. We dated even before I could drive, because Mother would take us to movies when Dad wasn't home—which was all the time. Then, in my junior year, Mother transferred me from Latta to

Ada High—for a better education, she said, but I figured out later she wanted to break us up."

Paul followed the story like a cat waiting for a mouse to make a mistake. According to this story, Sarah had been living no more than fifteen or twenty miles from Ada during the last years of her life. And he hadn't known it. After Dr. Hodges's death, she must have gone to another doctor, and that's why he'd never seen her again after the baby was born.

Hal coughed. "Are we through here?"

"No." Paul pushed aside his worries about the call from Sarah's daughter and concentrated on his patient's problems. "This looks like another strep infection. If so, it's the third one you've had this year. Those tonsils have to come out. I'll run tests, and if it's strep, you'll have to go on a penicillin regimen again. As soon as your throat heals, you should schedule a tonsillectomy in Tulsa or Oklahoma City. These operations aren't easy on people your age." He ran a swab across the back of Hal's throat and placed it on a side table for Tillie's attention.

"I don't have time for this, Paul. We're getting ready for the cattle auction, and as soon as it's over, we have to start moving the herds into the winter pastures. That'll take weeks."

"We can't operate anyway until this infection is healed. Then you can spend a couple weeks recuperating from a tonsillectomy or risk serious heart damage caused by the rheumatic fever that sometimes follows these recurring infections. Makes no difference to me, but it might to your mother and Brandon."

While Paul made notations in the file, Hal slid off the examination table and reached for his shirt. He was tall, handsome in a cowboy way, and his blue eyes could laugh spontaneously or cut his enemies to ground level. Mumbling to himself, Hal recovered his wide-brimmed hat and scattered dust when he flicked his middle finger against the brown leather band. Worry lines deepened between his eyes as he slapped the hat against his thigh.

Paul thumbed through the file while his patient grumbled to himself. "Did you take care of that other problem we talked about?"

"What problem?"

"You know what I'm talking about. You're too young to be having sexual problems. Could be hiding something serious. I told you to go see Dr. Tuttle in Tulsa."

"I did. He didn't find anything wrong. Thought I should be examining something higher up." He grinned and pointed to his head.

Paul ignored the effort to make a joke of the matter. "What did he suggest you do?"

"Gave me the name of a therapist who specializes in male dysfunctions. I called and that guy wanted to talk every week until it starts working again." Hal stopped grinning as he reached for the penicillin prescription.

"Are you seeing him?"

"No. After one session, I figured it out myself. There was never a strong sexual attraction between me and Muffy. After a few years of marriage, it became more work than fun. We finally decided to split, and I haven't wanted to find myself in that embarrassing situation again. Maybe someday. Besides, I have more important things to do than screw around with head doctors."

"I doubt that," Paul said and threw the file on his desk.

Hal frowned. "You really think these tonsils have to go?"

"Rheumatic fever can be serious."

"I thought that was a kid's disease."

"Not if you hang on to bad tonsils into adulthood."

"Well, we'll see how it goes. I'll call Tillie when I have some free time." He took the prescription and started out the door. "You and Kit are coming out to the auction Sunday, aren't you?"

"Is it this Sunday?"

"A week from Sunday. Louie's barbecuing a side of beef. Bob Wills and the Texas Playboys will be performing for the square dancing, and Gene Autry's coming to bid on a bull and some heifers for his ranch."

"No kidding?" Paul remembered hearing Autry sing "Red River Valley" over the radio years ago, while he struggled to forget a traumatic birth delivery earlier in the day. It would be interesting to see the movie star in person, but Paul shook his head. "Kit will be out of town, and I'd have to come by myself. I'm not much for social doings without her."

"Don't worry. I'll have Mother or one of the girls hold your hand. Brandon will be there, too. You can talk to him." Hal turned. "And if Tracy calls again, get her telephone number. I may decide to go see that head doctor after all." He winked at Paul and disappeared out the back door.

Paul grimaced. He'd always envied Hal's ability to appear disinterested in the women attracted to his good looks and money. This reaction to a call from Tracy Hunter made Paul suspect that, out of the public eye, Hal succumbed to temptations like most men. His philandering may have caused his separation five or six years ago from his wife Muffy, the daughter of Senator Fortenberry. For some reason she had moved off the ranch and gone to live with her father in Oklahoma City. Paul shook his head. Philandering didn't jibe with impotency. His suspicions must be off base.

At any rate, Paul didn't like the idea of being a go-between for Hal and one of Sarah's daughters. Their association might lead to a meeting between Paul and the girl, and that was to be avoided, if possible.

Hours later, Paul pulled a Coke out of the refrigerator and sat down to decompress from the day's stresses. He hated soft drinks, but Tillie had already emptied the coffee pot. Coke was not a good substitute for the wine he used to rely on at the end of the day, but he admitted that sobriety had its merits. He was no longer pale, emaciated, or depressed. In fact, he enjoyed being the opposite—healthy, suntanned, happily married, and the proud father of two grown children a few years younger than Hal. The telephone rang and he answered, "This is Dr. Jordan."

"Hello, Doctor. This is Tracy Hunter. Your nurse said I might reach you about this time."

Paul leaned back in his chair, afraid to relax but anxious to get this conversation behind him. "Yes, ma'am. What can I do for you?"

"I've discovered some mistakes on my birth certificate, and I thought you might be able to explain them."

Paul sucked cola down his windpipe and covered the mouthpiece to hide his coughing. He had expected that she might have questions about her birth, but not the birth certificate! Could she have uncovered the bogus form he'd filed after her birth? Unbelievable. He had been sure that document would lie forever undetected, because there was no Brigitte Cerise to ask for it. He cleared his throat. "What seems to be wrong with the certificate?"

"It has the wrong name on it. I'm Tracy Hunter. This certificate says 'Brigitte Cerise Hunter.'"

"You're sure?" He was buying time.

"Of course I'm sure. It's right here in front of me. You did substitute for Dr. Hodges at my birth. Right?"

Paul didn't answer and Tracy continued. "It's been thirty-two years come February. Perhaps you don't remember."

She must think I'm senile, Paul thought. *Perhaps I should pretend to be, because I'd rather not answer these questions.* He'd prepared a story to cover all eventualities concerning the birth of that child, including a challenge by Sarah's husband, and even his wife's potential interrogation. What he had not allowed himself to consider was the possibility that Brigitte Cerise Hunter would appear on his doorstep, questioning her paternity. He could see his whole world collapsing.

"I do remember your parents," he said. "They were Dr. Hodges's patients."

"But you were the one who delivered me, and I assume you filled out the information on the application for my birth certificate."

Paul didn't answer.

"Brigitte Cerise is not my name."

The information hit Paul like a bullet. This was no longer a friendly interview. He felt like a criminal being interrogated in a courtroom. He needed a lawyer. He tapped his pencil on the desk. He was not ready to rake around in the mucky slough of his mind, where long ago he buried the traumatic memories of his own daughter's death, along with the duplicity involved in the birth of the Hunter baby.

"I can't say I remember that. I've delivered a lot of babies since that time." Is that what a lawyer would want him to say?

Tracy's questioning picked up to a staccato pace. "You were there because Dr. Hodges was sick that day."

"Yes. Dr. Hodges had pneumonia. I agreed to go with your dad because he said your mother was suffering from high blood pressure. That can be dangerous to a pregnant mother, and to the child. I couldn't take chances."

"Was there just one baby born that day?"

Paul sat straight in his chair, shocked at such a question. "One? Of course there was just one. Why do you ask that?"

"That could be the reason we have two birth certificates, couldn't it?"

He shivered. The conversation was spinning out of control. Maybe he should beg off answering questions until he had talked to a lawyer. Better still, he'd better squelch this interview right now.

"Look. I was there. I should know how many babies I delivered."

"Then why do I have two birth certificates? One with my name and one for another baby born to my parents that same day?"

Paul wiped perspiration from his upper lip. He felt lightheaded and closed his eyes as he recalled writing "Brigitte Cerise" on the application. "I'm sure there's a logical explanation," he said.

"And what might that be, Doctor?"

Paul was used to a modicum of respect from his patients, based on his professional standing. His patients loved him and would never have questioned his actions this way.

"It's true. I filled out an application for a birth certificate even though your folks hadn't picked out a name. The law requires the application be sent in within forty-eight hours of the birth, and I was trying to meet that deadline. I suspect your father brought a name in the next week, and Dr. Hodges filled out the second application, not knowing I'd sent one. That's an easy mistake to make. There were two birth certificates, not two babies."

"And which name did you write on the application?" He knew it was a rhetorical question. She knew the answer. It must be a trick. If he admitted he had written his dead daughter's name on Tracy's birth certificate, that would lead to questions about whether he was drunk when he did it. Medical malpractice tort suits were becoming common. Could she be fishing for evidence to support a law suit?

"I . . . I don't remember the name. Did you say 'Tracy'? I suppose that's what I put down."

"No. No, you did not."

Paul closed his eyes to stop the dizziness surrounding him, but the darkness served as a movie screen reflecting scenes from that snowy day. He remembered his medical bag sliding out of the car when they arrived at the farm and his falling on top of it, so drunk he had trouble rising. He learned later that the grandmother had told her granddaughters that the doctor was bringing them a baby brother. Four-year-old Ruth, arms akimbo, stood inside the door accusing him of dropping the baby in the snow. She was a smart little girl. He sighed. Ruth must be thirty-six or older by now. Would she also remember the earlier times he stopped by their house, while she and Emily were playing in the yard? Would she recall that he sat on the porch swing with their mother? Had Tracy heard these stories and was feigning ignorance to see what he would let slip? Was she looking for information beyond a screwed up birth certificate? He shuddered and wondered how to put a stop to this interrogation.

Her voice interrupted his thoughts. "'Tracy' is the name my parents gave me. At one time I had a birth certificate with that name on it, but I lost it, and the replacement I have in front of me says 'Brigitte Cerise.'" Her voice now carried a touch of anger and frustration.

Perspiration ran from Paul's armpits. He rubbed his hand over the offending trickle. *Damn*, he thought to himself, then back to her, "You seem to have the information you need. Why are you calling me!" He wanted to say, "Why the hell are you calling me?"

Tracy's voice softened. "If this birth certificate is mine, I want to know why the name is wrong. It's a little shocking to discover this late that I'm Brigitte Cerise and have been for thirty-two years."

Those words sent chills over Paul's body. Tracy's voice was little more than a whisper, no longer a strident prosecutor's. "Truth is, I'm having an identity crisis," she said. "I always suspected there was something different about me. I'm not much like my sisters or my father. This birth certificate makes me think I'm not one of the Hunter girls at all. Maybe I have another family somewhere, and if I do, I want to find them." Paul suppressed a groan, cut short by Tracy's follow-up. She resumed her prosecutor stance. "For your information, I'm an investigator by profession, so I should have no trouble getting to the bottom of this."

"An investigator?"

"Yes. I just quit my job with the Chicago Police Department, where I investigated crimes. But I expect to open my own P. I. office soon. Maybe this will be my first case."

Paul sat speechless. Ada didn't need a private investigator. True, the police department was a joke, but the town managed quite well with what it had. He tried to laugh. "Don't you think you're overreacting a bit?"

"Maybe. But as I said, it's disconcerting to discover you may have relatives you don't know about. Things like that happen."

"I think you have it turned around. Why don't you assume that you are Tracy Hunter and that the certificate isn't what it seems to be?"

"I was hoping you could help me with that, Doctor."

"What can I do?"

"Tell me who Brigitte Cerise is. Why did you put her name on my birth certificate?"

Paul sat for the space of several breaths. "This isn't a good time for me to go into that discussion, Tracy. Maybe later. Take my word for it. You are Tracy Hunter."

"I'm sorry to bother you at the end of a busy day, but I must find out why I feel so disconnected from my past—as if I'm somebody else." She paused. "I'm coming to Oklahoma to visit my sister. Maybe we could follow up on this subject while I'm there."

Paul wondered how to avoid such a meeting. "I should have written 'unnamed baby girl' on the application," he said and grimaced. He was admitting guilt. His stomach complained so loudly that he feared the rumble could be heard over the telephone.

The phone was quiet as Tracy considered being called "unnamed baby girl." "Brigitte Cerise is a beautiful name," she said, "but I'm sure my parents would never have thought of it."

"As a matter of fact, I suggested it to your father, but your mother was upset that day. Nothing I mentioned would have pleased her." *Please don't ask why your mother was upset*, he thought. They waited, connected by unasked questions.

In the quietness, Paul decided he wanted to see this girl in the flesh. Would she look like her mother? She had said she didn't resemble her father or sisters. He heard her mother's voice across the line, but instead of Josh Hunter's lineage in her eyes, her hair, her manner, it was possible she would look like the daughter of Paul Jordan.

"When are you coming down?" he asked, knowing he was diving into untested waters.

"I'm taking the train to Ruth's in a few days, then drive from Tulsa to Ada before the following weekend. I'd like to see some of my friends while I'm there. You must know Dr. Nora Smeltzer?"

"Of course." Paul's heart did a flip flop. What other distressful associations could she be attached to? First it was Sarah Hunter, then Hal, and now Nora.

"We were roommates in college. She went to med school on one of those scholarships where you promise to set up practice in a rural area for a few years. I told her about Ada. She found it on the list of towns needing a women's clinic, so she decided to set up practice there. I'm dying to see her."

"She's a very special doctor. I guess you know she's been plagued by a local element bent on running her out of town?"

"She told me a little about that. I can't understand why the police don't intervene."

"The police chief has no reason to intervene because he believes the same thing the troublemakers believe   that the husband and God, in that order, make family propagation decisions.

"It sounds like Ada needs someone to point out that women have constitutional rights that trump the husband's, and maybe even God's, when it comes to procreation. I could do that. It might take more than a week."

Paul shuddered. Nora needed friends, but this lady's rhetoric would be dangerous in the local setting. Her mouth could get the whole community riled up. "You need to understand that people around here defend their presumed rights with guns and nooses. A challenge to their religious beliefs could end in a blood bath."

"Is that supposed to scare me?"

"No, just make you cautious."

"You're making me think I may be needed there. Who's standing up for Nora?"

"Her friends are hoping these problems get resolved without a pitched battle."

"Friends like Hal Montgomery? What is he doing to protect her?" Tracy's voice rose an octave. "Nora told me about meeting Hal and being invited to poker parties at his lake house."

"I'm sorry," Paul said. "I don't keep up with that relationship." That was a partial fib, since Hal had brought her to the Jordans' home on more than one occasion. However, he had never mentioned that she attended poker parties at the lake house.

Tracy paused to snort her disbelief. "Nora says he's still living on the Lost Creek Ranch."

"As a matter of fact, he owns it." There was a long pause while Paul debated whether to tell her of Hal's request for her telephone number. The sharpness in her question convinced him to leave sleeping dogs under the porch.

"He owns the Lost Creek Ranch?"

"I'm surprised you didn't know. His family made a fortune in wildcat oil drilling. Black gold, they call it. Ranching is just a hobby." Paul found himself uncomfortable talking about Hal's good fortune at the same time he was explaining his own foul-up with the birth certificate. He searched for a way to end the conversation.

"A rich man's hobby. Is that right?" Tracy's confidence had changed to icy sarcasm. "Why am I not surprised? Of course, herding cattle wouldn't leave a lot of time to help friends." She paused, then added "I'd better let you go. I'll call you when I get to town."

Paul heard the phone click on the other end of the line. So much for helping friends get telephone numbers or saving them from harassment. He held his head with both hands. He had controlled his urges for alcohol for years, but the sound of his daughter's name and Tracy's voice, which sounded so much like Sarah's, had recreated frightening images that reverberated against his skull, leaving him dizzy. He wondered if his mind and body could survive a sober revisiting of that graveyard of memories. Wiping his eyes, Paul hoped he would be able to answer Tracy's next barrage of questions without involving Tillie, Hal, or Kit.

As Paul hung up his office phone, Nora Smeltzer filled her medical bag with research papers and telephone numbers for calls she'd had no time to return. The day had been hectic, and she had had no time to comb the long strings of red hair back into the bun at her neck. Her rosy complexion needed no makeup to compliment her wide, inquisitive eyes that engendered trust in her patients. She was too thin, worked too many hours, and worried too much on her off hours.

Alone in the office after closing hours, she began to worry about her safety, wishing she had followed her employees' advice and left the clinic with them. But she'd had to meet with a late patient whom she couldn't ask to reschedule. Women who came to her clinic were often in desperate circumstances, and Nora never considered delaying a diagnosis or medication. Even those who were not seriously ill needed to be reassured that they were not pregnant, or that they did not have a sexually transmitted disease. Many of them needed information about contraceptives, like this last patient, who already had four children.

The telephone rang, sending chills through Nora's body. She debated whether to answer. As she lifted the receiver, heavy breathing swished through the earpiece. "Bitch, we told you to get out of town! It's too late now." The phone clicked dead. Her breath shuddered and she gritted her teeth to keep them from chattering. The increased frequency of the calls frightened her. Maybe leaving town was the best answer. There was no way to fight the rumors that she was running an abortion mill unless the silent women she helped took to the streets against the noisy opposition. That would never happen.

Tracy's advice had been to report the phone calls to the FBI and to relay to them the information she had gotten from one of her patients about money laundering and prostitution going on at Hal's ranch. She wished she hadn't followed Tracy's suggestion, because the FBI agent admitted they could do nothing about illegal activities on the ranch unless a connection could be made to a federal crime, such as tax fraud. And, the agent said, it would be almost impossible to prosecute a money-laundering case against Hal's father-in-law. How could the government prove that the poker parties were not a pleasant gathering with friends and family? And prostitution was not a federal crime unless the victims were taken across state lines. No crime, no case.

The agent's advice was to contact the local police about the harassment. She knew that was pointless and tried to ignore the threatening calls that increased in frequency and viciousness after her report. *My life reads like a psychological whodunit,* she thought.

She laid down the receiver, and the telephone sat like a time bomb on her desk. She eyed it, imagining it was ticking. Paul and Kit Jordan were the only people in town who might be available to escort her home, but their telephone rang ten times, and she hung up. Her best bet was to stop at Walgreens for a can of mace.

She moved to the door, but another ring from the telephone stopped her. It could be the Jordans getting to the telephone late. Or it could be another threat. She returned, lifted the receiver, and waited.

"Nora? It's Tracy. Are you there?"

Relieved, Nora expelled a deep sigh. "Thank God it's you, Tracy. I've been getting those threatening telephone calls again, and I almost didn't answer. How are you?"

"Umm. Not so good. I quit my job today. Remember I told you I'd applied for a promotion? I didn't get it, and I blew up when I learned they gave the job to the mayor's nephew."

"That doesn't sound like you, Tracy. You've always been the kid with the cool head."

"I know. But it hurt—being passed over."

"I know what you mean. We've both been butting our heads against ceilings for a long time. I don't see an end to it, do you?"

"Not any time soon. I've decided to follow your example and open my own office. But first, I need time to clear my head and make some plans. Ruth wants me to come visit her family for a week or two before I get tied down again."

"Oh, good. You can come see me, too."

"Actually, I called to invite myself. Is this a good time?"

"You bet. Things have been dicey here, but I could use your advice and support. When are you coming?" Her hand shook as she jotted the date on her calendar.

Plans completed with Tracy, Nora hung up the phone. Strange clicks on the line made her wonder if their conversation was being recorded. She shrugged. *I'm getting paranoid.*

The anticipation of having a friend to confide in—an experienced police officer, no less—made her forget for a moment the threats to her life. She smiled to think how Tracy would react to those telephone calls. She wouldn't bother notifying the FBI. She'd take Chief Mayfield on by herself.

Nora pulled on her jacket and closed her medical bag. Noise blasted from the street as cars raced past the clinic toward the football field for the Friday night game. Punching in the code that opened the back door, she hurried out and the door clicked shut behind her. Clutching her car keys, she surveyed the parking lot. Her car should be the only one there, but an old, white pickup sat near her Volkswagen. Who could it belong to and why was it parked next to hers when all the other spaces were empty? She took another step and saw movement through the back window of the truck. Without pausing, she turned and ran back to the office door. A warning alarm would sound when she opened the door and the police would come. She fumbled with the key and it fell from her hand. "Oh, God," she whispered as she stooped to retrieve it. Heavy footsteps ran toward her. The door gave way and she tripped over the door sill, sprawling head first into the office as the alarm screamed. A man's body landed on top of her, knocking the breath from her lungs as a gloved fist smashed against her mouth. She tasted blood as she rolled to one side and reached her nails toward the man's eyes. He swore and slammed her head against the floor. The security alarm faded along with her consciousness.

TWO

Five days later, at her sister's home in Tulsa, Tracy rifled through her briefcase. "Look here, Ruth. I sent off for my birth certificate, and this is what I got."

Ruth laid aside her knitting and took the envelope. Tracy watched as she examined it with a puzzled look. "This isn't yours. Where'd it come from?"

"That's what I've been trying to figure out. Remember Momma said Dr. Hodges was sick and this young doctor, who helped out at the clinic, came to deliver me? He was late, and Momma was angry because I got there before he did. Grandma said he smelled like a wino."

"Sure, I was there. I remember the whole thing. But why the wrong name?"

"I don't know. I talked to him last week when I got this thing. He said Daddy promised to bring in my name for the certificate, and when he didn't, Dr. Jordan just made one up, because it was supposed to be registered within forty-eight hours of my birth. He's guessing that Daddy brought my real name in later, and Dr. Hodges sent in a second application. I tried to get Dr. Jordan to tell me where he got the first name, but he didn't want to talk about it. Darn it, I need to be convinced there's no Brigitte Cerise Hunter floating around somewhere."

"That seems unlikely, but something fishy is going on," Ruth said.

"I'm glad you agree. I was beginning to think I'm nuts."

"Look, kid. I was there the day you were born. I remember Momma was in the bedroom making a lot of noise, so Grandma sent Daddy to get the doctor. She told us the doctor was bringing us a new baby brother. When Daddy got back, Emily and I were looking out the window and we saw Dr. Jordan fall out of the car into the snow. He dropped his medical bag, and we thought he'd dropped the baby. We were pretty pissed off."

Her story had the desired effect. Tracy bent over with laughter. "That story gets funnier every time I hear it," she said, but this new birth cer tificate makes me wonder if there isn t a grain of truth to the story that he snuck another baby into the bedroom inside his medical bag. It would explain the extra birth certificate."

"Get serious, silly. I can swear that you were the only baby in our house that day. If Momma's moans and groans meant anything, it was that she gave birth to you, and you didn't get delivered in a medical bag. Take my advice and dump this birth certificate. The state must still have a copy of the one with your name on it, and if they don't, you can get a new one."

"I guess so, but I still want to hear the story from Dr. Jordan. I think you should hear it too. Wouldn't it be fun to drive down together and go see the old place while we're there? I'd feel so much better if you went with me. We could look up old friends. What do you say?"

Ruth screwed her face into the comical, childlike mask she had always used to hide her real feelings. It made her inquisitors laugh, and Tracy suspected it gave her time to think of a clever answer to questions she hoped to divert.

"Admit it," Tracy said. "You've never gone on a vacation without Howard and the boys."

A conspiratorial gleam sparkled in Ruth's eyes, and her face muscles relaxed. Her lovely smile, carried over from her attractive teenage years, brightened the day, but she was many pounds overweight. Obese was the word. Marriage to a tall man whose body needed frequent refueling had turned her into a plump chef for him and their three teenage boys. She did a lot of tasting while she cooked, and she accepted the rolls of fat bulging over her waistline as Howard's favorite doughnut. But hidden somewhere in her obesity were her dreams of being a thin Miss Marple. She found it difficult to hide her envy of Tracy's career, even though she knew she wouldn't trade her husband and sons for anything similar.

Ruth squinted, deep in thought. "Maybe I could get away for a while. Howard's mother could come and cook and get the boys off to school. She likes me, plus she'll drive Howard crazy, and he'll appreciate me more when I get back."

"You said it." Tracy pumped her arm, surprised at how easy it had been to talk her sister into joining the venture.

Ruth laid aside her knitting. "Are you sure you want me to come? I don't have a thing to wear."

"That's the most worn-out excuse in the world. Besides, shopping is one of the fun things to do on a vacation. The important thing is that you can help me interview this doctor. Since you were there when I was born, you may come up with questions I wouldn't think of."

Ruth nodded. "Come to think of it, I do have a few questions of my own."

"It's hard to tell how much he remembers. Isn't it unusual that he decided to name a stranger's baby?"

Ruth's knitting needles clicked faster. "He and Momma weren't exactly strangers."

"What do you mean?" Tracy tilted her head as if this might be an unexpected clue in her identity search.

"Nothing particular. Before you were born, I just remember that he used to walk past our house when we lived near Ada, before we moved. He stopped and talked to me and Emily every time he found us out in the yard playing with our puppy. He even brought us suckers sometimes, so we looked forward to seeing him. I don't know how well he knew Momma, but they sat on the porch swing when she came out of the house to check on us." Ruth paused, deep in thought. She unraveled a row of her knitting, then continued. "After we moved back to Ada from Oil Center, we only saw him again on the day you were born. By then, I hardly remembered him."

Tracy picked up the certificate. "So he did know Momma, even though she was Dr. Hodges's patient? That's interesting. He didn't mention it when we talked on the phone." She stared at Ruth. "I've been confused ever since I got this second copy of my birth certificate. It's logical to believe that Brigitte Cerise was the real baby born that day, and that I'm an outsider—maybe adopted."

Ruth sighed. "Oh, Tracy. You're always so dramatic. Of course you weren't adopted. I was there. Daddy and Emily were there. And Grandma was in the bedroom helping the doctor. Daddy was so relieved that Momma didn't die, I think that's when he started to love you best."

"Don't be silly. Daddy was crazy about all of us. Giving more attention to me was his way of making up for the fact that they wanted a boy so badly."

"Being reared as a boy didn't hurt you any. In fact, your willingness to get into a fight with the boys no doubt helped you get him police work, didn't it? And your feistiness won't hurt if you become a private investigator."

"What do you mean *if* I become a private investigator? You don't think I can do it?" Tracy propped her feet up on the coffee table.

"I think you can do anything you want to. You've proven that since Daddy died."

"Thank you. And you're positive I'm Tracy?"

"You're Tracy, and get your feet off my furniture. You're worse than the boys."

"Sorry. Daddy didn't teach me good manners, and Momma didn't have a chance to."

"Yeah. Blame them. You never were one to admit you were wrong."

"That's because I never am!" Tracy threw a pillow at her sister. Ruth dodged it, and the pillow sailed across the room.

"Can we get away by Friday? I should be able to see the doctor on the weekend, when he doesn't have patients." Tracy slipped the birth certificate inside her briefcase.

Ruth giggled and her knitting needles clicked even faster. "I'll go throw a load of clothes in the washer as soon as I get to a stopping place on this sweater. I can't believe I'm agreeing to do this without first talking to Howard. What do you suppose he'll say?"

"He'll think it's great. If not, we'll shame him into it." Tracy lay down on the couch and stared into space. "You know, while we're down there, I'd like to see Hal Montgomery. Dr. Jordan said he's now the owner of the Lost Creek Ranch. He made it big in the oil fields. How's that for luck?"

"Not just luck. He was pretty smart too." Ruth laid aside her knitting. "I never understood why you two broke up. You had such a crush on each other. Momma was afraid you'd get pregnant before you got out of high school. She was relieved when he transferred to the school in town."

"She shouldn't have worried. His mother made sure we were always chaperoned. I must say that experience, plus a few other breakups, have convinced me that my life is filled with nothing but major rejections. First, Momma wanted a boy. Second, Hal's mother didn't think I was good enough for her son, and he must have agreed, because he never called me again after he started to school in town. Now Captain Carson doesn't think I'm qualified to head the investigations unit. I can understand Momma's position, but some insults I can't forget or forgive."

"I don't think Momma rejected you. She just never understood your independent drive. And you know your captain's decision on your promotion wasn't based on a lack of qualifications. I'll bet he lives to regret your leaving. And if Hal's mother could see you now, she'd be sorry—a college grad, and you get prettier every year. You would be a great catch for any mother's son. I'll admit it. I'm jealous of you, Sis."

"Don't be. I gave up believing I could have everything I wanted in life a long time ago." Tracy's eyes softened as she looked at her sister. "If I were blessed with a husband like Howard and three teenage football players to cook for, I wouldn't have time to stay in shape either. Instead, I have a college degree and skinny legs."

Ruth had grown up as the caretaker in their family. She put everyone's needs before hers, even their mother's. After their dad died, it was Ruth who nursed their mother through her depression. It was Ruth who stayed in Oklahoma instead of accepting Aunt Rose's invitation to go to college in Chicago. Tracy vacillated between feeling sorry for her sister and envying her.

Ruth laid her knitting aside. "I betcha hooking up with Hal is doable. We can find a way to run across his path while we're there. If all else fails, you can give Dr. Jordan your telephone number to pass on."

"The question is, what I'd do with him if I caught him. I've always felt we parted with unfinished business between us." She rolled over to face Ruth. "Did you and Howard have sex before you married?"

Ruth gasped. "What a nosey thing to ask! It's none of your business. For heaven's sake, why are you asking?"

"That's what I meant by 'unfinished business' with Hal. Back then nice girls didn't even talk about sex. Don't ask me how I could watch it going on every day with the farm animals and not relate it to people. I was either very naïve or my hormones hadn't started pumping. In college, I made the mistake of marrying the first guy who turned me on. As soon as the newness wore off, we discovered we had nothing else in common and got a divorce. That's when I began to wonder how it would have been with Hal. The more I think about it, the more I'm inclined to pursue a little revenge."

"I don't know what you have planned, kid, but the man is married. You'd better be careful."

"So what? A little thing like marriage won't stand in my way. Besides, that's his problem. It would make the conquest sweeter.

I must say this conversation astonishes me. My baby sister has turned into a piranha."

Tracy sat up and pounded her fist on the couch pillow. "You're right. I've been swimming with sharks long enough to know how to survive." She pointed her finger at Ruth. "The secret is to draw blood first."

"Are you talking about his blood or his wife's?"

"His. My conquest will be subtle. He'll never know what hit him."

"Knowing what a heel he is, I'm surprised you'd want to find him."

"It's the 'first love' thing. He broke my heart, and he should have to answer for it."

"Just be careful your heart doesn't get broken twice."

Tracy smiled at Ruth. "It won't. I'm less vulnerable now. He's the one who should be on guard."

Ruth reached for a newspaper on the coffee table. "I saved this article for you. It's about Nora Smeltzer—she's missing. Isn't she your friend?" Ruth pushed the paper toward Tracy.

Tracy looked at the date on the paper. "My God. This can't be true. I just talked to her Friday night. I was going to see her when I got down there." Tracy scanned the article, and then began pacing around the living room. "We've talked every week since she moved to Ada. She told me some weirdoes were using the Thalidomide controversy to stir up demonstrations against her clinic, even though there haven't been any deformities in Ada. In some places, mothers are being advised to end the pregnancy once they know the baby will be deformed, and that's set the anti-abortion fringe on fire."

"Was she doing abortions at all?"

"Not illegal ones. But the people are against all abortions and are accusing her of running an abortion mill as an excuse to close down her clinic."

"An abortion mill? In Ada?"

"All lies, but she was worried that she'd have to close the clinic." Tracy sat down and covered her face with her hands. "In police work, you see so much bad stuff that you get anesthetized." She walked over to her briefcase and fumbled through it. "Here are some pictures of her that I took last summer when she came to see me. I brought them down for her."

"How nice. You're a really good photographer, Tracy. Did you get a new camera?"

"Yes, I splurged and bought a good one. I took a class in criminal photography and that hooked me."

"I'm beginning to wonder if it's safe for us to go to Ada."

"Why wouldn't it be?"

"Because you're a friend of Nora. I don't want to get involved in riots or demonstrations."

Tracy's face muscles tightened. "There's no way I won't get involved. She wouldn't turn her back on me." She looked at Ruth. "But I understand if you don't want to go."

"Are you kidding? Every Sherlock Holmes needs a Dr. Watson. I can even grow a mustache if I'd be more convincing."

Tracy shook her head. "Sorry, I can't laugh about this. I hope she shows up before we get there. How soon can you be ready to go?"

Ruth laid down her knitting. "Let me call Howard and his mother. If they agree, we can leave Friday morning."

"Good. I'll make some reservations. Let's stay at the Palace Hotel. I've always wanted to know what the inside of that place looks like."

"Do you know how expensive that is?"

"Yes, I do. But I've been saving up for years so I could splurge on a vacation. Looks like this is it. I'll have to call Dr. Jordan to find out when he can see me. He might have more recent news on Nora's disappearance too." She set his number down near the telephone and poured a second cup of coffee. Uncovering her true identity or taking revenge on Hal seemed minor compared to Nora's disappearance. She felt her ten years of detective training falling into place like a mantle over her shoulders.

THREE

Paul Jordan looked up when Tillie walked into his office at the close of business on Wednesday. She tossed a memo onto his desk. "Tracy Hunter called and said to tell you she'd be in town Friday about noon. She wondered if she could see you Saturday." She waited for Paul's reaction, but he said nothing.

"I asked her if she had a medical problem and she said 'No.' I told her I wasn't your social secretary and had no idea what you were doing on Saturday, but you preferred not to have appointments on the weekend."

She cocked her head and looked over her glasses for Paul's approval. Long braids circled her head like a halo, with beads shining like stars in the blackness of her hair. She had been an important part of Paul's life for over thirty years. As Dr. Hodges's nurse, she nurtured Paul back to life after the emotional and physical crash that landed him in Ada. She introduced him to Kit, her best friend, who became his wife. Shortly after that, Tillie was left alone when her husband Raymond was killed in a rodeo accident. Two months pregnant, she became dependent upon Kit and Paul for emotional support. She and Tommy became like family to the Jordans.

Paul knew Tillie wouldn't be happy without a full explanation of why Tracy Hunter wanted to see him. He'd stopped lecturing her long ago about doctor-patient confidentiality, and he'd come to terms with the fact that if Tillie knew it, most of the people in this small town would know it before the week was out. He was careful about what he passed on to her, but her unhampered access to the office files and her talent for wringing information from Kit, who trusted her not to tell, meant she knew almost everything that transpired in their lives.

"So, did she say anything else?" he asked.

"She said to contact her at the Palace Hotel." Tillie's eyebrows lifted, and her eyes widened behind her glasses. With her hands resting on her hips, she stood in front of Paul's desk, waiting for an explanation. He let her stand.

"So, what am I supposed to tell her?"

"Tell her I'll contact her at the Palace Hotel." Paul tried not to smile at Tillie's frustration. He began shuffling papers to let her know the subject was closed.

"Humph." Tillie started out the door, but turned to ask over her shoulder, "And how is Kit enjoying her stay with her mother?"

Paul paused and gritted his teeth. Tillie loved intrigues. Nothing would make her happier than to tell Kit he was seeing another woman. He'd have to squelch the story before it became real in her mind and dynamited his marriage.

"Tillie, this young woman is a member of the Chicago Police Department. She's coming through town on business. If you start some gossip and upset Kit, I'll fire you. Do you understand?"

Tillie smiled and headed for the door. She'd been "fired" a number of times, but she'd never left the office. Tillie and Kit were Chickasaw tribal sisters. They chatted daily about their family affairs, including stories about Paul. He was sure they had been on the telephone every day since Kit left for Tulsa. Tillie knew how Kit was enjoying her stay with her mother, even more than Paul did.

Paul admitted to himself that he was glad Kit was out of town. He'd never talked to her about the circumstances of his first marriage, except to acknowledge that both his wife and child died in a car he was driving while drunk. He could think of no circumstances under which he would reveal his affair with Sarah Hunter the summer he was recuperating at Dr. Hodges's clinic. His walks in the country had led him past the small home where Sarah's daughters were playing in the yard. Stopping to admire their puppy was his downfall. Barefooted, Sarah came out of the house, damp hair curling around her face, so like Colette's. Over time, "Hello" led to "I love you." A few weeks later, the family moved, with no forwarding address. Nine months later, her husband came to the clinic, pleading for help with the delivery of her child.

Today Paul was confused and irritated to discover how nervous he was about meeting Sarah's daughter. He reached for the telephone to call his wife.

"Hi, princess. How are things going?" He tried to sound cheerful.

"Oh, hi, honey. Momma's doing fine. The doctor says her heart sounds much stronger, but it will be a couple of weeks before she can be on her own. Are you home already?"

"No. But it's time to close up." He paused. "I called because I miss you so much. I hate going home to an empty house."

"Oh, Paul, I'm glad you miss me. But you do have Charley." They both laughed.

"Believe me, a dog's no substitute for your warm body in bed. Besides, he misses you, too."

"I'm glad to hear that. What have you been doing to keep busy?"

"Nothing much. Trying to keep Tillie in line." He hesitated. Now he realized why he'd called. He needed to confess his guilt about filing the false birth certificate. "Do you remember a family named Hunter that used to live in Ada? They had three girls." Despite his faith in her love and forbearance, Paul felt his chest tighten and was afraid she would recognize his stress.

"Oh, sure. We went to the same church. Why do you ask?"

"I, uh, I got a call from Tracy Hunter. She's going to Tulsa to visit her sister and plans to come down here."

"Why did she call you?"

"She says I screwed up her birth certificate."

"How could you have done that, for heaven's sake?"

"I put the wrong name on it."

"You put the wrong name on a birth certificate? Must have been back when you were drinking." There was dry disapproval in Kit's voice, but she soothed the edge by adding, "I'm sure it's no big deal."

"It seems to be to her. She says she's suffering an identity crisis."

"Really? What name did you give her?"

Paul could feel his pulse pumping in his ears. He'd hoped she wouldn't ask about the name. He lied. "I don't know. Something French. I had just come from New Orleans and loved the names I heard. Using one of those names was a way of going home, I guess." His excuse sounded better than he anticipated.

"I can't believe it. Remember how hard I tried to get you to suggest a name for Becky?"

"Yeah, I know. Maybe I still felt guilty from my earlier mistake."

"You say Tracy's just now finding out that her birth certificate has the wrong name on it?"

"Yeah. She got one years ago with the right name, the one Dr. Hodges sent in, I guess. She lost it and needed a new one to get a passport. Instead of the one she had before, they sent her a copy of the one I'd filled out. She finds it very confusing."

"That's understandable."

"Really! I told her to write back for the correct one. If they can't find it, she can amend this one. Seems simple enough to me."

"A man would say that. Names are important to women. However, lots of births weren't even recorded in those days in the Indian Territory, so it isn't shocking that one got recorded twice. When did you say she's coming?"

"This weekend, I think. Tillie took the message."

"Too bad. I knew her family. I'll bet she'd remember me. Tell her I said hello."

"I will."

"What else are you doing this weekend?"

"Hal wants me to come out to the cattle auction on Sunday. Says Gene Autry may be there."

"Are you kidding? Just my luck. He was my hero when I was a kid. I'd love to meet him."

"You should come home."

"I wish I could. I hope Tracy isn't angry. Is she?"

"A little."

"Poor Paul. Don't let it upset you. The Hunters are a nice family. She won't be vindictive. Call Sunday night and let me know how your meeting goes."

"Okay. Come home as soon as you can, honey. I need you to keep me out of trouble."

"I will. I love you, Paul."

"I love you, too." Paul hung up the telephone. His marriage was the most important thing in his life. He would never be unfaithful to Kit. He prayed she never learned of his brief affair with Sarah Hunter before their marriage.

FOUR

On Thursday, Paul arrived at the clinic to find Tillie at her desk, wiping mascara off her cheeks. This emotional storm didn't bode well for the day.

"What's the matter?"

"It's Tommy. He has a new girlfriend, and I'm worried sick. I think they're sleeping together."

"That's all?"

"What do you mean, 'that's all'?" Tillie howled, and Paul regretted his statement. He walked to her desk and patted her on the shoulder. She spoke through her sobs. "I've worked my butt off raising that kid by myself. I won't have him getting a girl pregnant and ruining his whole life. He'll lose his football scholarship for sure."

"I'm sorry, Tillie. What can I do?"

"Talk to him. He won't listen to me. Make sure he's using rubbers. Tell him about syphilis and gonorrhea. Scare the hell out of him."

"Okay. I can do that. Get him in this afternoon after school. I need to see both of them, either together or separately. You work it out."

Tillie put her Kleenex away and Paul sighed. As a surrogate father, Paul had taken Tommy to little league games and thrown footballs by the hour. He felt he had earned a personal stake in that college scholarship.

"Thank you, Paul."

"Go fix your face. Take the morning off, if you need to. I can handle things here."

"No, I'm fine now."

Paul went to his office, worrying that the problem might be bigger than either of them could handle.

In the afternoon, as Paul sat puzzling over a file in his small laboratory, Tillie came to the door and pointed the long, red nail of her index finger toward his office. There he found Tommy and a beautiful blond girl, holding hands as they sat in front of his desk. Tillie followed him into the office.

"Please close the door when you leave, Tillie," Paul said. Tommy grinned at him.

Tillie stopped. "The lady from Chicago called again. Said she'd be in town tomorrow, and she wants you to return her call as soon as possible." She pointed the same finger at the three of them. "So this meeting better be short and to the point." She glared at both teenagers and slammed the door behind her.

Paul and Tommy slapped hands. Paul sat on the edge of his desk. "How are you, buddy?"

The boy was taller than Paul, with huge arms and hands. He wore his shiny black hair cut just to the top of his ears, with a front flip that fell across his brow. His shoulders were broad and his waist as narrow as a girl's. Real quarterback stock, he had the intelligence and strength to be one of the best.

"So, what's the latest about your scholarship?"

"I'm to check in for training camp this summer. Guess you'll have to mow your own lawn."

"I should have thought of that before I wrote a recommendation for you." Paul smiled and turned to the girl. "I'm afraid I don't know you."

"This is Carolyn," Tommy said, as she threw her long blond hair over one shoulder. Her eyes were a startling blue. Heavy mascara clumped her thick lashes. Red lipstick made her mouth large and too sexy for a girl her age. It was, in fact, hard to determine her age.

"Your last name?" Paul asked the girl as he sat down and leaned back in his chair, placing his hands behind his head.

"Pittman." Her voice was so soft that Paul had to strain to hear it. The name and face bore no resemblance to anyone he knew—and he would have remembered this young lady. Her sweater stretched across a full bust. She sat with her long, tanned legs crossed, allowing her short skirt to expose her thighs up to her panty line. He leaned further back in his chair to block the leg display and addressed Tommy.

"Tillie says this relationship is pretty serious. Maybe we need to talk about it."

The girl bit her lip and looked down. Tommy sat straighter in his chair and looked at Carolyn, then back at Paul. "You gonna tell Momma what we're talking about?"

"Of course not. Have I ever given away our secrets?"

Tommy smiled and looked at Carolyn. "Just once," he said, but Carolyn ducked her head and her hair slid forward, covering her face.

"You know your Momma's worried, don't you?"

"Who cares? She thinks Carolyn will get pregnant on purpose, so we'll have to get married." Tommy looked at Carolyn. "She wouldn't do that." His smile pulled one side of his mouth downward, and to show how silly his mother's worries were, his eyes shot upward.

Paul looked toward the girl as tears spilled down her cheeks. Maybe she wasn't as mature as she pretended to be.

"Are you pregnant, Carolyn?" he asked.

Tommy sat bolt upright and squirmed in his chair as Carolyn pulled her hand from his.

"No," she said to Paul, but she looked at Tommy. "I'm afraid, though. I don't think we can keep on like this without something bad happening. My daddy's gonna kill me, and Tommy too, if he finds out."

Tommy's jaw jutted forward and his lips clenched over his teeth.

"It's none of our parents' business," he said. "Momma thinks we should act the way she did when she was in school. Times have changed, man."

Paul jumped up and paced near his desk. "Tommy, times may have changed, but babies are still made the same old way. And it is your mother's business if you bring a baby into this world. Who's going to foot the bill? And don't forget the time she'd have to put in, helping to care for it—if that happens, it becomes my problem, since she wouldn't be able to work full-time." Paul sat down. "You know your mother's life dream has been to get you through college."

Tommy's eyelids squinted. "I *am* going to college. I'm *not* getting married, and Carolyn knows that. I'm playing football next year." He nodded his head toward the girl. "We've talked about it."

Paul looked at Carolyn. "There you have it, Carolyn. Tommy wants the pleasures that go with being an adult, but he doesn't intend to take responsibility for his actions. That means the consequences fall on your shoulders."

He looked at Tommy. "If you don't want to be a father, I assume you're taking precautions. Are you using condoms?"

Tommy looked at Carolyn out of the corner of his eye while shaking his head. "I pull out. That's just as good." His nostrils flared, daring Paul to disagree. Instead, Paul noted the star football player's admission to more than one sexual encounter.

"Pulling out before you ejaculate is like playing Russian Roulette, Tommy. It may work five times out of six, but the next one will get you." He waited for the information to sink in. "Take my advice. Either stop having sex or use protection every time." He reached into his desk drawer and threw a handful of condom packages on the desk in front of Tommy and others in front of Carolyn. "Make sure he uses them."

The room was quiet and Paul leaned back in his chair, ready for the discussion which he hoped would fulfill Tillie's demand that he scare them to death.

"You know, babies aren't the only things you get from having sex. There are a lot of diseases from which condoms will protect you."

He looked from Carolyn to Tommy. "Has it ever occurred to either of you that your partner may have been sleeping with other people? If so, the chances are good that one of you will have contracted syphilis or gonorrhea and will have passed it on to the other." He looked at Carolyn. "And if you get one of those diseases, you may never be able to have a baby."

Tommy glared at Paul. "I don't sleep around and I don't have diseases. If I did, you'd know about it. She doesn't either." He stood. "I've had enough of this shit. Let's go." He ignored the condoms.

"No," Carolyn said.

"He's just trying to break us up because that's what Momma wants." Tommy's face flushed, and he grabbed Carolyn's arm. She winced and pulled away.

"I need to talk to him about something else," she said, looking down.

Tommy's eyes shifted to Paul. He slammed his fist against the desk. Surprised at Tommy's violence, Paul stood, and Tommy turned to leave. "You can walk home," he said to Carolyn over his shoulder, and he slammed the door behind him.

Paul and Carolyn stared at each other. "I need some medicine," she said. "I itch something awful."

Paul found it hard to speak. He felt like a failure. Tillie had trusted him all these years to help Tommy become a man in the absence of a father. He'd failed somewhere.

"That sounds like a yeast infection, which isn't too serious. But I'll have to examine you. We also need to talk about how your life is going, Carolyn. All those things I said about diseases are true. The only sure way to protect yourself is to stop having sex."

"But I love Tommy. He'll go to someone else if he can't get it from me."

"That's okay. Let him ruin some other girl's life." Paul looked at her for a long moment.

She reached over and took the condoms lying on the desk. "How do I make him use these?"

"Tell him it's either or. Better still, stop having sex until you're both older, and he's ready to commit to a family." Paul regretted that his voice took on a worried father's sternness. "I don't examine teenagers without a parent's consent. Bring your mother in tomorrow, and we'll talk some more about diseases. As I said, you probably have a yeast infection, but we can't be sure without checking." Paul stood, dismissing her.

Carolyn frowned. "I don't think Momma will come."

"You tell her I insist that she come. I'll have Tillie call her, too. Can you get a ride home? If not, wait around for a few minutes, and I'll have Tillie drop you off when she leaves."

"I'll call Momma," Carolyn said, before she hurried down the hall and out the back door.

Paul watched as she crossed the alley and climbed into Tommy's old Ford. She had known he would come back for her. Paul shook his head. He was afraid they had wasted an hour of everybody's time as far as sex education was concerned.

Tillie walked up behind him. "Well?" she asked.

Paul didn't answer.

"You sure as heck made Tommy mad. What did you say?"

"I told him what you wanted me to."

"Maybe you scared him so much he won't see her again."

"I wouldn't count on it. He picked her up in the alley after she left here. Call and tell Mrs. Pittman that I want her to come in with Carolyn tomorrow. Find a time after school."

Tillie turned and went up the hall muttering to herself.

Paul looked up the police chief's number and waited while it rang. He wondered how the investigation into Nora's disappearance was going. The secretary apologized. "The chief won't be in for a day or two, Dr. Jordan. They found Dr. Smeltzer's body over in Arkansas. He left to go out there about noon."

FIVE

The next morning, while Tracy and Ruth were packing their car in Tulsa, Paul reached the office late. Tillie was in a panic. She met him as he parked behind the clinic, grabbed his arm, and led him toward the door.

"They're in there," she said. "I put them in your office so the other patients wouldn't know they're here."

"And who are *they*?"

"Carolyn Pittman and her mother."

"Why are we hiding them? I thought they were coming after school."

"They couldn't wait. And I don't want the whole town knowing she's been here. They'll be talking about her and Tommy getting into trouble, you know how."

"Okay. I'll see them first."

"Send them out the back door when you're through, okay?"

Paul grimaced and pointed to the front office. "Go back to your desk and calm down," he said, then knocked on his office door and entered. Carolyn and a woman who looked young enough to be her sister were sitting in front of his desk, grim, looking away from each other. He set aside his medical bag and introduced himself to Mrs. Pittman.

He looked at the girl. "Good morning, Carolyn." She wore no makeup today, and there were dark rings under her eyes as though she had not slept. Without the makeup, she looked younger, more vulnerable, and sad.

Paul looked at Mrs. Pittman. "Thank you for coming. Did Carolyn tell you why I wanted to see you?"

"You're going to fix her itching."

Paul stared at the woman. She looked no more than thirty years old, which meant she would have been no more than fourteen or fifteen when Carolyn was born. Her blond hair was dull, but it was long like Carolyn's, tied back with a ribbon. She wore no makeup. Crow's feet were already tracking beside her faded eyes.

"Yes, we can take care of the itching," Paul said as he glanced at Carolyn. "We should do more than that, though. Carolyn needs a contraceptive."

Mrs. Pittman's eyes narrowed, and she glared at Carolyn. "No, she don't. I can solve that problem by keeping her home."

Paul turned to Carolyn. "Have you told your mother about Tommy, or shall I?"

Carolyn shook her head.

Paul sat down behind his desk. "This may take a while," he said.

During the next several minutes, Paul counseled the mother and Carolyn about birth control, and then sent Carolyn into the examination room with Tillie to prepare for a vaginal examination. He entered that room afraid of what he would find.

Following the examination, he walked out, telling Carolyn to get dressed and to wait for him.

When he returned, she was standing at the window, with her back to him.

"I'm pregnant," she said.

"Yes, you are. When did you have your last period?"

Carolyn turned around and glared at Paul. "What difference does it make?"

"It will tell us how far along the baby is."

"July, I think."

"Four months or more? Is it Tommy's?"

She dismissed his question with a quick "No. How do I get rid of it?"

"I'm sorry, Carolyn. You're too far along. Abortions are very dangerous after twelve weeks. If it happened in July, you may be sixteen weeks along. Besides, it against the law to do abortions in Oklahoma, unless the mother's life is in danger."

"Then I'll take care of it myself." She picked up her purse from the chair.

"Carolyn, please don't do that. I told you, abortions are dangerous at this stage. You could die."

"I may be dying anyway. I've been bleeding. I thought my period was starting." She looked at him with desperate eyes, waiting for confirmation.

"I saw no sign of bleeding today, but even if it's true, it doesn't mean you're dying. You just need to be very careful. A little bleeding won't kill you or the baby, but it indicates you could have a miscarriage."

She relaxed "How?"

"What do you mean, how? "

"How do I have a miscarriage?"

"Are you asking me how you can legally get rid of your baby?"

"Whatever."

"I'm sorry, Carolyn. You surely don't expect me to give out that kind of advice. I can tell you that if you're bleeding, you're at risk of losing the baby. Be careful of any trauma to your body. That includes lifting, athletics, and sex. I'll talk to Tommy again. If you continue bleeding, it's possible you'll have to stay in bed after six months or so."

"Yeah. Like that's gonna happen."

"If the baby isn't Tommy's, whose is it?"

"I don't know."

"The father should be told, Carolyn. He can help you. And I need to tell your mother."

"No. I'll do that."

"Be sure you do. A yeast infection is causing the itching. Here are some samples of a medication which should help. If the itch doesn't clear up in a week or two, come back. Tillie will set up regular appointments to monitor how you and the baby are doing."

Carolyn gave him a pitying look, snatched the tubes of salve, and walked into the hall. She passed the office where her mother sat smoking and left the building through the back door. Paul went to his office.

"She has a yeast infection. I gave her some medicine which should take care of it. Carolyn said she'd talk to you about other problems. Be sure she does. I need to see her again in two weeks. Please see Tillie at the front desk to set up the next appointment."

Mrs. Pittman stared at him, unable to speak. Paul saw the truth reflected in her eyes. She left the clinic without speaking to Tillie.

He closed the door and sat down behind his desk. He felt weak and helpless. He shuddered to think of how hypocritical his advice had sounded. Why wasn't he wearing a condom when he visited Sarah thirty-two years ago? He could have avoided the confrontation coming up with Tracy Hunter.

Tillie knocked at the door and entered without being asked. "Is she pregnant?"

Paul bowed his head. There was no way he could keep the truth from Tillie, since she would read it in Carolyn's file. He'd have to take the risk she would not reveal it to other people, even Tommy. "Yes, but she says it isn't Tommy's, so we'll have to leave it up to Carolyn to tell the father."

Tillie's eyes closed. She sank into a chair, then slipped to the floor, as if her bones had dissolved.

Paul forgot his own distress and hurried to revive her. She struggled to sit up.

"Thank God it's not Tommy's," she said. "Is she sure?"

"How long have they been dating?"

"He met her when school started. Late August."

"Then it's not his. I'm worried, because she wants an abortion."

"Oh, she shouldn't do that," Tillie said. "There were lots of times after Raymond died that I didn't think I could make it alone, but with your help we survived, and now I'm so glad I have him."

"Girls have more options now."

"God knows an abortion is not a good one. Maybe I should talk to her."

"Tillie, you know this is privileged information. You have to keep it quiet. Carolyn will no doubt tell Tommy, but he may not want to discuss it with you."

"I can keep it quiet, but it may kill me."

"I'm afraid the patients who've been waiting for an hour may kill us first. Let's get going." He helped her to stand, and she went to the front desk to call the next patient.

SIX

Late Friday morning, Tracy and Ruth headed south from Tulsa in a rented Thunderbird. Ruth scolded Tracy for splurging on such a ritzy car, when Ruth's old Ford would have served them fine.

"Nope, we're on vacation," Tracy said, feeling free and happy for the first time in years. She had learned to be frugal on the farm after her father's death and was happy that her savings would allow her to live for two years without an income, while she developed a new career. Plus, she had budgeted for a vacation, which she had dreamed would be overseas. But forget that. Today was the day, and if she had to do a little work while she was on vacation, that was fine. She could deduct the expenses on her taxes.

Ruth hummed a deep sigh and fell asleep on the Thunderbird's soft leather reclining seat. Her vacation had begun. Tracy smiled at the soft snores and turned her attention to organizing the problems lying before her. The meeting with Dr. Jordan would be short and to the point. She had already found out how the extra birth certificate got filed. Now she just wanted to hear why the wrong name was placed on the application. She would call him when they arrived and perhaps have lunch on Saturday.

The next problem was finding Nora. Dr. Jordan could give them some background on the events surrounding Nora's disappearance. If she hadn't returned, Tracy knew how she would spend the rest of her time off.

As she watched the colors of the landscape deepen, she hoped that she and Ruth could cruise the countryside, visiting the old farm where they lived after moving back to Ada. Her life, her future, had been molded there, and she felt a need to return.

Today Tracy was happy, intoxicated by the shocking colors splashed along the roadway. Fall was her favorite season in Oklahoma, but her memory was pallid compared to the psychedelic splash of red and yellow hues embellishing the oaks, maples, elms, and cottonwoods along the creeks and rivers that crisscrossed this east central part of the state. The beautiful Hereford cattle grazing in the pastures reminded her of the Lost Creek Ranch, where she and Hal had spent so many happy afternoons before he moved to a school in town.

Ah ha! she thought. *That should be another goal on my agenda. Not only will I meet Hal face to face, I will lure him to the lake house.* She wasn't sure what would happen there, but an apology for the way he had left her would bring a resolution to what had been a traumatic episode in her teenage life. Anything else? She felt embarrassed to acknowledge her longing to consummate their high-school infatuation. Doing so would move her out of the "nice girls don't do that" category. She turned the radio on and hummed to accompany Roy Orbison singing "Oh, Pretty Woman."

Two hours later, the car passed a sign reading "Ada. Population 15,422." The population had been 10,000 when she left. She stopped at a railroad crossing where clanging bells warned of a coming train. Ruth jerked awake. "Where are we?" she asked.

"Ada. You slept the whole way."

"I got to bed late last night. Did laundry till midnight."

"Why don't the boys do their own laundry?" Tracy was shouting over the train's noise.

"Are you crazy?" Ruth's voice lowered. "No real man does his own laundry."

"Not if he has a mother trained to do it for him."

"Let's not get into a discussion of stay-at-home moms versus working moms. I always come away feeling inferior." As the train passed, the word "inferior" rang out in the silence following the rumble.

Tracy patted her sister's thigh. "Let's make a pact. On this trip, I'm not inferior because I'm divorced, and you're not inferior because you're a stay-at-home mom. I am Tracy Sherlock Holmes and you are Dr. Ruth Watson, best investigators, bar none."

"I like that."

Tracy found herself engrossed in downtown traffic, astonished at the many new businesses that had popped up at the east end of Main Street. Shops now extended to the gateway of the small teachers college. She slowed near the school and let pedestrians cross the street. "Look at that," she said, pointing to a line of people waving signs in front of an old Victorian house, one block from the college. "Do you suppose that's Nora's clinic?"

Ruth nodded. "Could be. The sign that lady's carrying says *baby killers*. She slipped lower in her seat. Let s get out of here.

Tracy was familiar with lines of protesters in the North, but she was surprised that a small town like Ada was the focus of demonstrations. Before she had heard of Nora's disappearance, she expected to see the same casual approach to life she had experienced here fifteen years ago.

As she drove past the clinic, she scrutinized the marchers. There were two college-age students, several women in their fifties or sixties, and one man carrying a Bible. A young mother led a preschool toddler. Pretty innocuous. They did not look dangerous. She drove to the end of the street and made a U-turn in front of the college.

"You aren't going past that clinic again, are you? We'll be on the side close to it." Ruth's criticism sounded like an order.

"We have to go back that way to get to the hotel, my dear. These demonstrators are harassing the women who want to go inside the clinic. They're not after us."

"Ha," Ruth said and slid further down in her seat, hands hiding her face from the demonstrators.

Several blocks past the clinic, Tracy turned left on Maple Avenue and came to the Palace Hotel sitting on a rise. Built by oil barons, the Palace was still the grande dame of hotels in that part of Oklahoma. Tracy had never stayed there, and she had often wondered what luxury was like; now she would know. She tried to look cool as she stepped from the car beneath the ornate archway of the hotel. A parking attendant reached for her keys and disappeared with her car, without so much as a fare-thee-well. While Tracy puzzled over the disappearing Thunderbird, Ruth rushed ahead to make sure their luggage did not meet the same fate.

Hands unencumbered, Tracy slowed to an elegant model's waltz across the thick plush carpet, pretending she was somebody. Ruth leaned on the counter and watched in disgust as the management rushed to welcome the "star" to Ada. Behind the counter, the flustered clerk dropped his pen, in a hurry to change their accommodation to a room with a view—for what that was worth in a hotel surrounded by paved streets, old homes, and businesses.

The room was awesome—two double beds, comfortable chairs, a desk, floor to ceiling windows, and glass doors sliding open onto a balcony. The bellboy placed their luggage on racks, opened the draperies, and asked if he could be of further service. Tracy fumbled in her purse for a tip, and he left with a smile. On his way out, he picked up the newspaper lying outside the door and handed it to Ruth, his eyes never leaving Tracy. As he left, Tracy bent over laughing. "Isn't this great? I feel like royalty."

"When you get the bill, you may not think it's so funny." Ruth opened the glass door and peeked over the balcony railing to the street below. "Look at that," she said, pointing to a police cruiser rolling down the alleyway. The driver looked up, searching windows of the hotel. He slowed as his eyes caught sight of Ruth. When Tracy walked out, he stopped.

"What do you suppose he's looking for?"

"Beats me. Maybe there's been a hold-up."

Knowing the area was being watched by an officer brought no sense of safety to Tracy. From experience, she knew that policemen did not waste their time looking for innocent people.

"Maybe they're looking for Nora."

Ruth plopped into a chair and unfolded the newspaper. "Oh, my God. Look at this." She pushed the front-page headline toward Tracy.

"DOCTOR'S BODY FOUND." Tracy grabbed the paper, shaking her head and moaning, "No, no, no." She mumbled through the story, announcing that Dr. Nora Smeltzer's body had been found in a cistern in Arkansas. The story gave little background on the case, stating that the doctor did not show up at her clinic the prior Monday, yet police had seen no reason to suspect foul play. A reporter's insistent questioning brought an admission from the FBI that Dr. Smeltzer had contacted them twice, but they were not able to respond to her concerns because they had no jurisdiction. The transportation of her body across state lines had eliminated that problem. Hers was now a federal case.

Sobbing, Tracy dropped her head to her lap. Why had she not taken

Nora's problems more seriously? "I can't believe this," she cried. "I just can't believe it. Why wasn't I listening? How could I have been so stupid?" Her face burned with anger. How could things have changed so much in Ada since she left? She handed the paper back to Ruth and went to the bathroom to splash cold water on her face. "I need some fresh air. Let's go running. We'll come back and eat an early supper. Maybe drive out to see the old house where you and Emily lived when the doctor came by to see you. We can go to the farm tomorrow. I told Dr. Jordon I'd call him in the morning." She opened her suitcase. A sweat suit and running shoes lay on top.

"Do I look like someone who runs?"

Tracy glanced in her direction. "No. You look like someone who should. Put on your tennis shoes. We'll walk."

"No. I'm on vacation. I'm going down to the coffee shop. I smelled cinnamon rolls in the lobby. That will hold me over until you get back. Maybe I can find a newspaper from Tulsa or Oklahoma City with more information about Nora's murder than this one has."

"That's a good idea. I won't be long. Do you feel like more driving today or shall we put that off?"

"Let's put it off until we've talked to the doctor. I want to hear what he remembers about those visits."

Saturday morning, Paul glanced at the clock and decided he could no longer put off the call to Tracy. He must meet this woman, whether he wanted to or not. His mind was torn between fear and anticipation. What if she proved to be his daughter? What would happen to his marriage if Kit found out? How would his children react to the knowledge that their hero father was guilty of violating the sanctity of someone else's marriage? On the other hand, his heart quickened at the thought of seeing Sarah's child. He needed an answer to his greatest fears. He picked up the telephone and called the Palace Hotel.

The phone was ringing as Tracy and Ruth returned to their room from breakfast. Tracy answered with a quick, out-of-breath "Hello."

"This is Paul Jordan. Have I called at a bad time?"

"No, no. We just walked in the door. Can we all get together today?" she asked.

Paul hesitated at the word "all."

"Yes," he said. "Maybe we could have lunch."

"That sounds good, if we can make it late. We just finished breakfast. Oh, I didn't tell you. My sister, Ruth, came with me. She remembers you."

Paul almost dropped the telephone. He found it impossible to respond. His intrigue, the secret he thought he would take to the grave, was in danger of being revealed, depending upon what Ruth, the eldest child, might remember. The birth certificate debacle was a minor blip compared to the possible discovery of his affair with Sarah. He closed his eyes and cleared his throat. "It's been a long time," he said.

"Yes, but Ruth's memory is phenomenal." Paul stood for some time before he realized he had stopped breathing.

What could he say? Memories lie. Memories are influenced by whether the subject is a hero or a villain in the eyes of the beholder. Ruth may have seen him as a villain the day of her sister's birth, plus, she was a kid at the time, so things could be distorted in her mind. He could see her now, hands on hips, reprimanding him: *Emily said you dropped the baby in the snow!*

He shook his head to clear it. "Why don't we drive out to Louie's Roadhouse? It will give you a view of the beautiful fall leaves, and his menu pleases everyone."

"Oh, I love that idea. We high-school kids used to drive out to Louie's every Saturday night after the movies. What time shall we meet you?"

"Make it around one thirty. The lunch crowd will be leaving, and we'll have the place to ourselves."

"Sounds great. One thirty. We'll meet you there."

On the way to the restaurant, Paul worked up an agenda for what he hoped to accomplish at this meeting. First, he could put to rest the troubling possibility that Tracy was his daughter. That should be easy, because he remembered her father well. Tracy should have some semblance of his square jaw, his dark eyes, and the firm, straight line of his lips. A more difficult dilemma was Ruth's recollection of Paul's visits to their home. It might be necessary to convince her that what had happened between him and her mother was limited to an innocent friendship and interest in the children.

As he arrived at the restaurant, Paul wished he had taken some medication to calm his nerves. Once inside, he was pleased to see that his guests were late. He settled into a booth near the back of the restaurant and watched through the front window as a black Thunderbird whipped into a parking place near his Jeep. "Some driver," he mused, then smiled as Tracy and Ruth exited the car and headed for the door of the restaurant.

"I may have met my match," he thought, as the tallest sister strode to the door and swung it open with ease. Tracy, no doubt. The sun glared behind the light blond curls cascading to her shoulders, creating a halo around her face. Paul brushed his own light hair from his forehead, refusing to acknowledge any resemblance.

He stood and waited for the women to locate him at the back of the room. He held out his hand to Ruth as she approached, and then to Tracy. For a moment, still gripping his hand, Tracy stared at his face. "You're not what I expected," she said.

Shaken by his own reaction to the meeting, Paul mumbled, "I'm sorry. Who were you expecting?"

"Umm, Dr. Hodges."

Everyone laughed, but Paul's chuckle was somewhat forced. *Tracy is a picture of her mother at that age—the same smile and voice*, he thought. His own smile disappeared when his eyes targeted traits that had not come from her mother or from Josh Hunter: a single dimple in her right cheek, eyes marbled with dots of brown on green paint, blond hair. Both her mother's and father's hair had been dark. He looked at Ruth's black hair and chocolate-brown eyes, so like her father's, and he understood why Tracy questioned her own lineage. He waited for the women to settle into the booth.

He spoke to Ruth. "It's nice to meet you. Tracy tells me you remember Dr. Hodges. I'm surprised. You were quite young at that time."

She nodded. "Oh, yeah. I do remember him. He was so nice to us, and his nurse always gave us suckers after we got our shots." She pointed to her cheek. "Dr. Hodges had a mole right here. I touched it once, but he said it didn't hurt."

Paul busied himself unwrapping the napkin from the silverware in front of him. Ruth was leaving no doubt in his mind that she had clear childhood memories. If Tracy was planning to sue him for filing a false birth certificate application, Ruth would be a credible witness.

"You must remember walking past our house," Ruth said, "and

bringing candy to me and Emily. You and Momma sat on the porch swing, while we played in the yard." Her eyes searched his face for an inkling that he remembered those days.

Paul looked away as though her pronouncement were unimportant, but in fact, it sent chills through his body. There was little doubt that her recall was keen. His only hope was that she was too young to understand what was happening between the adults at that time.

"Dr. Hodges loved the people here," he said to Tracy. "In fact, his popularity was one reason your mother was so mad at me the day you were born. She expected him to deliver the baby, but she had to settle for a stranger instead."

"You weren't exactly a stranger," Ruth drawled, "and that's not the only reason she was angry." Her tone was dry and blunt, daring him to deny the real reason her mother was upset. "She was angry because you were late—and you had been drinking."

As accusatory as that remark was, Paul relaxed. He could deal with the charge that he had been drinking, and because their father had been driving, it wasn't Paul's fault that they were late. He glanced at Tracy, who seemed puzzled by the tone of Ruth's charges.

"She's right about my drinking," he said. "I apologized to your mother, but I'm sure it would have been difficult for her to forgive me. I agree that it was a miracle nothing bad happened that day. I thought I was sober enough to do the job, but of course, an alcoholic's opinion isn't worth much." He hoped to ignore her charge that he "wasn't a stranger."

"Oh, you weren't accused of doing a bad job," Ruth said. "Grandma told Daddy how you saved Tracy's life. She said she might have died if you hadn't been there." Ruth's voice softened, no longer challenging Paul, but he was concerned that there might be more to come. He felt like a rabbit waiting for a rattlesnake to strike.

"And what did your mother say?" he asked. It was important to know what Sarah had revealed to the family. Had she mentioned their private conversation after the birth, while they were alone in the bedroom?

Ruth glanced sideways at Tracy, briefly at Paul, and then examined her thumb as though the answer lay there. "Momma would never talk about that day. When I insisted you got the babies mixed up and brought a girl, she told me to shut up." She looked at Paul. "Daddy understood why Momma was disappointed that Tracy wasn't a boy. They needed someone to grow up and help out on the farm. But Daddy never let his disappointment show. He just took over raising Tracy, and as soon as she could trail behind him, she was on her way to becoming the boy in the family."

Unexpected tears dampened Paul's eyes and pain tightened his chest. Was Sarah truly upset because the baby was just another mouth to feed instead of a boy who could help on the farm? Or was she angry because of the circumstances that led to the birth?

A waiter appeared, relieving the tension. While Paul busied himself ordering their meal, Tracy pointed to initials the high-school kids had carved into the wooden table. One had the letters "RM loves TH," circled with a four-inch heart. "That's me and Hal," she whispered to Ruth. "When we were in high school, he always had to be biggest and best at everything he did." She looked at Paul as the waiter left. "So, Hal is raising champion Herefords now?"

Paul turned and examined the heart. "Hal Montgomery? Yes. Yes. He's quite the cowboy."

Tracy expected him to smile, but he seemed reluctant to talk about Hal, so she changed the subject. "Tell us what you remember about the day I was born."

Paul dropped his knife, surprised at her question. He moved it back to its place and clasped his hands beneath the table.

"You want to hear about the birth certificate, right?" Perhaps he could limit their conversation to that minor issue. He stared at the table, unable to look at the women. He had memorized his response. "The story starts at the clinic, which closed at noon on the Saturday you were born. I was resting in my room at the back of the clinic, when your dad came to the office looking for Dr. Hodges. I told him the doctor was sick, but he insisted that Dr. Hodges had promised to come out to your house in Oil Center to deliver the baby. He mentioned that his wife suffered from high blood pressure, which scared me, plus it sobered me up a bit. I agreed to go with him, despite the fact, or maybe because, I'd been drinking. It was freezing outside, and I grabbed my open bottle of wine. I'd emptied it by the time we got to your home."

Paul took a deep breath, sipped his tea, then leaned back in the booth. He addressed Tracy. "I've always felt blessed that nothing worse happened that day. In fact, I give credit to your birth and your mother's anger for

spurring the rehabilitation that Dr. Hodges had started with me, after
I was dropped off that train to die." He paused and rubbed at the pain
behind his forehead. "It will be hard to understand all this unless I start
at the beginning."

Tracy and Ruth nodded.

"When I came to Oklahoma, I was running away from a disaster that
had happened in New Orleans. My wife and I were living there, after I
graduated from medical school. We were very happy at the time, because
now Colette could quit working, and we could start a family. If we had
a daughter, we planned to name her Brigitte Cerise." He looked at the
women, not surprised that both were frowning.

"And?" Tracy said.

"My work schedule was hell, and I began drinking every night when
I got home from the hospital." His voice broke. "The night Colette went
into labor, I had come home from the hospital exhausted. I had my usual
drinks and went to sleep on the couch. Colette woke me up about midnight and told me to call a cab. However, I insisted I could drive."

His words became disjointed, as though he was trying to find a way to
change history. He looked up. "To make a long story short, it was raining.
The road was slick. I slid sideways into a bridge. They both died."

He looked downward to hide the tears blurring his vision. "After that
I went a little crazy. I thought I might find some peace in California, but
I became so sick on the train, they thought I was dying, and they dumped
me off in Ada. Someone took me to the Hodges Clinic, and Dr. Hodges
and his nurse saved my life. They tried to rehabilitate me. It wasn't easy. I
kept falling off the wagon when they weren't around. It was the miracle of
your birth that gave me a reason to stop drinking."

He wiped his eyes with the napkin before looking up. "I know that
putting my dead daughter's name on an application for a birth certificate
sounds crazy, but it gave me a sense of peace and put that part of my life
behind me. I never dreamed the certificate would see the light of day, or
cause you all this trouble."

"Why not? Birth certificates are filed with the state aren't they? How
could you be sure no one would find it?" Tracy demanded.

"Because there was no Brigitte Cerise Hunter. I was the only person
who knew about the certificate, so who would ask for it?"

The women nodded at the logic of his reasoning.

The waiter arrived with a sheet of butcher paper, which he used to cover the table. He laid more forks and sharp knives at each place and left a pile of napkins. "Your drinks are coming," he said. Another waiter came with a platter piled with barbecued beef and pork, which he forked onto the papered table. He set bowls of potato salad and pinto beans in front of each person.

"Eat up," he said.

Moments passed while they turned their attention to the food. Ruth was the first to speak. "So you filed the first application for a birth certificate, and you put your daughter's name on it. Who filed the second one?"

"I can only guess that your father brought in Tracy's name the next week, and Dr. Hodges filed another application."

For a few minutes they ate, and Paul was startled when Ruth asked, "Did Mother ever talk to you after that day?"

"No. No. I never saw her again."

Tracy, with wrinkled brows, looked at Ruth and waited for her to follow up on her quest.

"I just thought . . . you acted like such good friends when you stopped at our house. It seems strange that you never met again, or talked about what happened. I think Momma needed friends she could talk to."

"I'm sorry," Paul said. "As I've explained, I was a mental mess at that time. Those afternoon walks had helped me move on from the tragedy I'd suffered in New Orleans. Visits with you and your mother took the place of my own loved ones. Then one day your family just disappeared. I never knew where you went until your father came in looking for Dr. Hodges."

Tracy sighed and looked at Ruth. "I think the move was especially hard on Momma, but it wasn't the only reason she became depressed and unhappy. She was pregnant with me during that time. Bad things add up."

Paul reached out and covered her hand on the table with his own. "Please don't believe that your birth caused her problems. Every case is different, but it's never the child's fault." He hurried to change the subject. "What about now? Is everyone doing well?"

Tracy wiped barbecue sauce from her mouth. "I guess you didn't know that we moved from Oil Center, after I was born, to a farm south of the Lost Creek Ranch. Since Dad had no boys to help him with the farm, I took over that role from the time I was eight or nine. He died of a heart attack when I was fourteen. Emily had graduated from high school and moved to Chicago to live with our Aunt Rose." She nodded toward Ruth. "We were left to take care of Momma. Ruth fell in love with a local boy, and after they graduated from high school, they married and moved to Tulsa." She looked at Ruth. "Your turn, Watson."

Ruth smiled. "Tracy stayed to keep the farm going. Momma had a hard time after Daddy died. She'd never learned to drive while he was alive, and when we insisted that she learn, the process scared her to death. One day she drove the pickup out in front of a big truck on the highway, where she was killed. Neither of us has gotten over that."

"I should have driven her," Tracy said, "but my excuse was that we were haying that day."

Ruth nodded. "After Momma's death, Tracy followed Emily to Chicago. She went to college and wound up becoming a policewoman."

"All in all, we're doing fine," Tracy said. "What about you? Do you have a family here?"

"Yes. My life turned around after you were born."

"Really?" Tracy eyes searched Paul's face for traces of serenity and happiness—emotions she'd never seen on her mother's face.

"I give full credit to my wife, Kit. After Dr. Hodges died, Tillie took it upon herself to save me. As part of her plan, she introduced me to Kit, who was her roommate in school. They are both native Chickasaw Indians. Kit is beautiful. She's caring, and she's a great wife and mother."

"How many children do you have?" Ruth asked.

"Two, Jonathan and Becky. Jonathan went into the Air Force after college. He's flying bombers now, stationed in England. Becky is a picture of her mother. She wears an Indian head band and likes being taken for a hippie. She's at Berkeley, working on a PhD in sociology, with plans to rebuild the world after Jonathan bombs it to pieces." They laughed.

"Why didn't you name your new daughter Brigitte Cerise?" Tracy's voice was challenging, her eyes accusing. It was not a question Paul expected. How could he tell them he'd never told Kit the full story of his past, or how much he wanted to keep it secret?

"It brought up too many painful memories," he said. "I wanted to forget that part of my life." Again he tried to change the subject. "What happened to the farm after you moved?"

"It became part of the Lost Creek Ranch. Mr. Crosier tried to buy it from Daddy for years, but he wouldn't sell. When Momma died, I went off to college, and there was no reason to keep it."

Tracy set aside her empty beer glass, still not willing to close the subject of her birth. "Did you really quit drinking because of what happened that day?"

Paul frowned. "Yes. When I got back to the office, I realized that you could have died because of my carelessness. Your mother's anger was justified. I was drunk, and I had to admit to myself, for the first time, that I was an alcoholic." He paused, and without looking up, he added, "I did stop drinking that night, but I've never lost my longing for it. Some people don't." The women had ceased eating, and Paul, looking at his watch, became aware that the other tables in the café were empty. The two-hour conversation had left him exhausted, and he dreaded delving into other topics where Ruth's memory might reveal more problems. He had already learned too much.

"Maybe we should go," he said, and no one objected. "How long will you be in town?" he asked, as they reached their car.

"Longer than we planned," Tracy said. "It shouldn't take me long to get the records from school to amend my certificate, but I saw in the paper today that Nora Smeltzer's body was found in Arkansas. I can't get it out of my mind." She looked at Ruth. "I may have to take you home and come back, but I can't leave until we know more about what happened."

"The whole thing is hard to believe," Paul said. "It's a sad day, both because we lost her, and because of what it says about our town. Nora had been here ten years without any problems. Her services are needed because of the poverty, and many women won't allow a male doctor to examine them. This organized effort to ban abortions caught fire from the wide publicity about Thalidomide babies. We've had no cases here, but that hasn't kept certain groups from jumping on the bandwagon to change laws. Where that's too slow for their purposes, they try to shut down clinics like Nora's." His voice softened. "They say the FBI has been called in. Maybe they can stop this madness."

"Maybe," Tracy said.

"I would encourage you to stay away from the clinic. Nora's nurses and an intern are volunteering their time to keep the doors open, but it's still a dangerous situation," Paul said.

"What are the chances the killers will be brought to justice?" Tracy asked.

"Don't expect too much from the police here."

"Why not?" Ruth asked.

"This town houses a large pocket of religious conservatives who believe that women should submit to their husbands, and in this community, that means the men make all the decisions. For instance, men don't want doctors telling their wives how to avoid pregnancy, and these sects elect police chiefs from their own congregations."

"But Nora wasn't doing abortions!"

"No, but she made the mistake of advising someone who works in the police department to use birth control, and to leave her husband if he continued to beat on her. The wife left her husband a week later. The police chief took that as a personal affront to his right to manage the lives of his staff and their families. That's when the demonstrations started."

Tracy and Ruth shook their heads in disbelief.

"Drop by my office Monday," Paul said to Tracy. "Tillie can help you find the health records you'll need to amend your birth certificate."

"Thanks so much. That will give us time to look up some of our old friends."

They moved to enter their car when Paul called to them. "I just thought of something. You mentioned wanting to see Hal Montgomery. How would you like to go out to the Lost Creek Ranch tomorrow for their annual cattle auction? It's a big affair. Lots of people will be there, maybe some of your high-school friends. It would be a sure way to meet Hal."

Tracy's lips puckered, and her eyebrows lifted as she considered the proposal. "What do you say, Ruth? Shall we check this out?" She paused, leaning on the open car door. "I suppose Hal's mother and wife will be there," she said to Paul. "Does he have children too?"

"He's married to Muffy Fortenberry, but they have no children, and they've been separated several years. She lives in Oklahoma City with her dad, who pretty much runs the Oklahoma Senate. However, she'll be down for the auction. And you should remember Hal's younger brother, Brandon. He'll be there."

Tracy nodded. "He was a kid when Hal and I dated."

"He stayed on the ranch with Hal and Muffy when his parents divorced, and then Muffy left, so Hal has been like a single parent to him."

"Why did Hal and Muffy split?" Ruth asked over Tracy's shoulder.

"Hal never talks about it. But they didn't get a divorce. I don't know what their connection is."

"No doubt the family fortune," Tracy said. "Dividing the ranch, plus oil and gas assets, wouldn't be easy. Not to mention his mother's influence. I'm sure she still controls the purse strings."

"Sounds like you know this family pretty well," Paul said. "And do I note some disapproval of Beatrice? I find that woman charming."

Tracy wrinkled her nose. "Everybody to his own taste."

"Humm. Are you sure you want to go out there?" Paul asked. "I'm not pushing it."

"Oh, yes, we want to go. And I assure you, we will dress so that no one suspects we're from across the tracks."

Ruth nodded. "You should have seen Tracy putting on airs at the hotel. You'd have thought she was from Hollywood."

"Well, I don't want to start a class warfare at the social event of the year." Paul smiled, to show he was teasing.

"Don't worry, Doctor. We promise not to embarrass you. We can pretend we don't even know Hal or his family. I'll be surprised if his mother remembers me."

"Don't expect to hide from Hal. He's looking forward to seeing you. I'll pick you up in the morning, around eleven."

"We'll be ready," Tracy said. The women got in the car as Paul drove away, shaking his head. He worried about what might happen between Tracy and Beatrice at the auction. Hal would be less of a problem. He would be so busy, they might not even see him face to face.

Of more concern to Paul were the unanswered questions that surrounded the meeting with Ruth and Tracy. During the ten-minute drive to the wooded suburb, where his spacious home sprawled amid scrub oak near the city lake, he reviewed what had been left unsaid. It was obvious that Ruth remembered his visits to their family home outside of Ada, and from her questions, it seemed possible that she was at least suspicious that something was going on between him and her mother. He suspected a latent hostility and disbelief in her direct questioning. Could she be hiding secrets even from Tracy? He shuddered to think some bomb might fall from her lips if she put two and two together. Such revelations could ruin the life he had built on lies.

On the other hand, having met Tracy, he felt an unexpected need to claim his right to parenthood. Where had it come from, this visceral urge to connect to the child—his child—whom he had helped to survive? While he had refused all these years to allow himself to think about the probability that he had fathered Sarah's child, he now questioned whether he could continue to live with that deception. Did Tracy deserve to know the truth, even if that revelation might put an end to his happy marriage to Kit? Or did he owe a greater duty to his wife and their children than to this presumed offspring? Was it fair to his wife, his son, and daughter to open up this painful episode of his past life to ease his own guilt, if in turn, it caused his family irreparable damage?

He arrived home, parked the Jeep, and let his head fall forward onto his crossed arms on the steering wheel. Sobs wracked his body. He saw no clear solution to the mistakes he had made in his life, no way to resolve these issues without hurting someone he loved. Perhaps the lifelong punishment for his indiscretions would be never to hear his love child call him "Father." That would be the cruelest punishment. The decision was his to make.

Minutes passed before he slid from the Jeep, and Charley ran to greet him. He stooped to allow the dog's wet tongue to massage his face. He needed to be comforted, and it was safer to trust his heartache to Charley than to his wife. She knew him too well.

At 11:15 p.m. that night, Beatrice Montgomery lifted the receiver of her telephone, and with a tired voice asked, "What now, Brandon?"

"I need your help, Mother."

"Of course you do. You only call me late at night when you're in trouble. What's the problem this time?"

Her body stiffened as her son described the evening's happenings at the fraternity house. "Did you get rid of all the evidence?" she asked.

"Yes. I put the stuff that came out in one of my pillowcases and gave it to Tommy—the guy she came with—and told him to get rid of it."

"That's not exactly getting rid of it, Brandon. Did you give him one of the embroidered pillowcases I sent with you when you went to live at the fraternity house? They had your initials on them so you wouldn't lose them in the laundry."

"They're the only ones I have."

"Well, who knows what he'll do with it? Has he started home?"

"About fifteen minutes ago."

"Was the girl with him?"

"Yes."

"We have to get that pillowcase back and destroy it. There may be lawsuits over this. Do you know what vehicle he drives?"

"It's an old fifties blue Ford."

"Let me take care of things. Stay in your room and don't speak about this to anybody. Demand that the initiates not discuss the matter either. You could all get thrown out of the university because of this stupid act."

"What can we do?" Brandon was crying.

"You don't do anything. I'll take care of it."

She disconnected the call from Brandon and dialed Jerry Falco. He answered on the first ring.

"Jerry, we have to do something quickly. Some of the boys at Brandon's fraternity party got one of the girls in trouble. She's bleeding and her boyfriend, a boy named Tommy Bucco, is bringing her back to Ada. He may take her to the hospital. He has some evidence wrapped up in one of Brandon's embroidered pillowcases. We need to get that back. He's driving an old fifties blue Ford. Can you go outside of town and wait for him? He left the university about twenty minutes ago, so you'll have plenty of time to get there. Follow him into town and see what he does with the pillowcase. If he goes to the hospital, he may leave it in the car, and while he's out of the car, find it and get rid of it. Do something. Do you understand?"

"Yes, ma'am. I know that car, and I know Tommy Bucco. It's just the same as done."

SEVEN

Early Sunday morning, Tracy left Ruth sleeping as she set out to find Wintersmith Lake Park where, the bell boy assured her, there was a great trail for walking. She located the lake without difficulty, parked her car near a pier at the trailhead, and as the sun rose over the low scrub oaks and plowed a broad, orange swath across the mirrored surface of the water, she began stretching what felt like atrophied muscles in her legs. Bending over to tighten her shoelace, she was unprepared for a rear-end assault by a large Shepherd-Heeler mix dog. She tumbled to the ground and rolled over to avoid the wet laps of his tongue on her face.

"Charley!" A voice called from the pathway behind her. The dog bounded away as Paul ran to her rescue, pulling Tracy to her feet. "I'm so sorry. Charley has no manners whatsoever. Are you hurt?"

Tracy addressed the dog as she brushed dirt from her sweat suit. "I've been known to karate chop grown men for less offensive pats on the rear than that, doggie. You'd better watch it."

Charley moved behind Paul's leg and looked away, feigning innocence.

Paul laughed. "You'd better apologize, boy. It won't be safe to hike on the same trail with an angry ex-policewoman. She may pawcuff you and take you to the pound."

Tracy smiled and stooped to make friends with Charley.

"I'd forgotten you were a runner. Where's Ruth?" Paul asked.

"She doesn't run. She was still snoozing when I left the hotel."

"How did you find this trail?"

"They told me at the hotel." She pointed to the enormous home at the top of a sloping pathway. Redwood walls surrounded dramatic windows reflecting the woods and water. "Is that your home?" she asked.

Paul nodded.

"Not exactly a log cabin."

"What's that supposed to mean?"

"For a bum who was dumped off a passing train, I'd say you've done all right for yourself.

"What you mean is that in the midst of poverty and hunger, my lifestyle is gross and unbecoming."

She grinned. "Sounds like you've heard those words before."

"I don't apologize for enjoying my view of the lake. I didn't grow up on a farm like you did. I was born with a silver spoon in my mouth, and I work hard to keep it there. My guess is that when you become a famous investigator, you will build your own monstrosity."

"You could be right." She removed a light sweater and tied it around her waist. Her faded blue sweat suit, with the University of Chicago logo on the front, showed wear and tear. She poked her ponytail through the hole in the back of her Cubs baseball cap and drank from a water faucet near the trailhead. She pulled her camera from the pack tied around her waist, pushed her sunglasses to the edge of her nose, and peered at the dog. "Lead the way, Charley. I came here for exercise, not to discuss politics."

Charley wagged his tail and looked at Paul.

"This peasant plans to join us, boy." The dog barked. Paul turned to Tracy. "I should warn you that I never run twice with a woman who beats me to the finish line."

"Don't worry. I don't go for speed, and I won't go around the entire trail. I brought my camera to take pictures of these gorgeous fall colors. They told me at the hotel that this trail is easy to follow, so I shouldn't get lost if you leave me behind. I'm sure Charley can find his way home."

As they set off, Paul increased his speed and left Tracy, who kept the same steady pace she began. Charley trotted beside her, making detours into the brush each time she stopped to take a picture.

Tracy glanced at the red, yellow, green, and orange leaves on the underbrush. The water in the lake shimmered green, and along the bank ducks paddled, half flying, looking for food. It was a perfect Oklahoma autumn. The squawking ducks rattled Charley, and he sprinted past Tracy to explore the next turn in the trail.

Tracy felt her bladder complaining, and she veered off the trail where Charley stood near a dirt path that led through the bushes. She followed him into a huge open space hidden among the trees. In the center of the circle, ashes from campfires and scattered cigarette butts suggested teenagers gathered here on weekend nights. Tracy grinned, remembering her own high-school days. She pushed aside underbrush near the edge of the meeting place and lowered her sweats.

As Tracy stood, Charley began whining and digging at a pile of leaves nearby. She called to the dog. "Come on, Charley Leave the rabbit alone."

Charley growled and stood stubbornly over his prey. Pushing him aside, Tracy gave a sweeping kick into the pile of debris. The corner of a faded Indian blanket flipped up with her foot. Shocked, she stared at a woman's leg protruding from the leaves.

Tracy gasped and jumped back. "My God. It's a body!" she whispered. She looked around the open space where shafts of light shot through the tall trees. As she watched, the sun passed behind a cloud, and the light in the large alcove dimmed. She grabbed Charley's collar and searched the surrounding bushes and trees for a possible killer. The deathly quiet seemed to hide something ominous. Even Charley lowered his whine to a soft moan. Tracy's police training clicked in, and she reached for the blanket, drawing it further off the body. Caked blood soaked the woman's dress, and stains ran down her legs. It was a scene similar to many Tracy had witnessed in Chicago. She took a deep breath. She knew what to do in a case like this. She replaced the blanket. Thank God, she had brought her camera. But first, she had to get rid of this dog. She wondered if he lacked all training.

"Sit," she ordered, and Charley plopped down on his belly, a disgusted look on his face. Tracy wondered how long that pose would last. She pulled out her camera, edged closer to the corpse, and snapped shots from all angles. She stooped and pulled the blanket further aside. Ragged blond hair covered the woman's face, but Tracy could see that she was a young girl, maybe one of the teenagers who partied here. A heavy sweater with a rolled collar and sleeves that hung to her knuckles had kept her warm.

Charley stood and started toward her. "Sit, Charley," she ordered and this time he sat, his nose pointing toward the bushes surrounding the back of the enclosure. She finished taking pictures of the body and surveyed the scene for footprints. She snapped overlapping pictures of bloody leaves, broken twigs, and footprints of cowboy boots, sneakers, holes she felt sure were made by high heels, and others quite flat, made by moccasins or huaraches. Except for her own footprints and the dog's paw prints, not much was left to record. She must get this dog out of here before the two of them compromised the site. She replaced the blanket over the corpse and pulled her notebook from her backpack, ignoring Charley's impatient whines. When she had finished recording the scene, she whispered, "Come on, Charley," and the dog almost tripped her as he darted to the open trail. Police training aside, she found her heart pounding from a rush of adrenalin.

Running toward the trailhead, Tracy relaxed as she heard Paul calling for Charley. She slowed as he rounded the bend, stopped, and waved both arms. He paused, then began running toward her.

"There's a woman's body back there," she called, pointing down the trail.

"A body? You mean someone's dead?" Paul stopped and looked toward the opening.

Tracy nodded. "I was taking a pit stop. Charley followed me and started barking at this pile of debris. I went over and kicked through the leaves and . . . it's the body of a young woman."

"Show me. I'll check her vitals."

"Paul, she's dead. Whoever killed her may still be there. Do you have a gun?"

"Of course not. If the killer was still around, he'd have attacked you." Paul began running down the trail toward the body, ordering Charley to heel.

Traccy's list of dos and don'ts for investigating a crime scene flashed before her eyes as she rushed to catch up with Paul and Charley. She had forgotten to note the time of day. She followed Paul as he entered the open space and bent over the body. He pulled the blanket off the girl's head. Long blond hair fell across her face, and Tracy reached for her camera again.

"My God," Paul said. "It's Carolyn."

"Carolyn who?" Tracy asked, as she snapped a picture and walked past him to the foot of the corpse. She snapped another shot.

Paul touched the girl's arm and moved the blanket from her lower body. "Oh, God, no." He fell to his knees. "How could she have done this?"

"Done what?"

He shuddered, looked at the girl's face again, and tucked the blanket over her body. He rose, pale and shaking.

"You know her?"

Paul stared at Tracy. "She came into my office this week. She was pregnant. From the looks of things, she either miscarried or got an abortion. No doubt she bled to death."

"Where would she get an abortion?"

Paul shook his head. "A good question. Let's go. We have to call the police." He hooked Charley's leash and headed for the house, not waiting for an answer.

In the kitchen, he spent a few minutes on the telephone while Tracy sat at the table, scribbling the facts as she recalled them.

"The operator will send the fire department emergency crew out. Shouldn't take more than ten or fifteen minutes," Paul said, as he hung up. "It's the police chief's day off, and he goes deer hunting this time of year. She'll try to send the county coroner to pick up the body, but the firemen may have to take it in."

"They're not going to move the body before the police have a chance to search for evidence, are they?"

Paul grimaced. "Don't expect a big-time investigation, my dear. This isn't Chicago." He looked at Tracy as she pushed the pencil and pad into her camera bag, pulled on her sweater, and buttoned it.

"You should stay in the house, or better, go back to the hotel," Paul said. "There's no reason for you to be involved. I've got to change clothes before they get here. There's hot coffee from breakfast. Take a cup with you." He pointed to the cabinet and hurried up the stairs.

Charley watched, his head to one side, as Tracy poured the coffee. There was no way she was going back to the hotel until this matter was concluded. First, Nora Smeltzer had disappeared. Now a young girl is dead from what may have been an abortion. But could it be murder? Suppose the deaths were connected? She took her coffee to the kitchen table overlooking the lake, pulled out her pencil and pad, and made more notes, adding the time of day, what she had seen, and what Paul had said. She described the scene, filling in items she had overlooked.

Paul came running down the stairs buttoning his shirt, deep worry lines creasing his face. "Find everything?" he asked.

"I poured you some coffee and left the cream out."

"Thanks." Paul looked at the clock. "The rescue unit should be here any minute." As he spoke, a siren announced the arrival of a fire department emergency truck, and they watched it roll to a stop on the gravel road leading to the lake. Medical aides jumped out. Paul gulped his coffee. "I'll be back soon." He headed for the door.

Tracy rose. "I'm coming, too. This is my specialty."

Paul shrugged, his mind on other things. They left the house as an ambulance pulled up beside the fire truck. Behind it, a police vehicle glided to a stop, and an officer in a neat blue uniform jumped out. A loaded gun hung from his holster, and he expertly flipped an automatic shotgun from one hand to the other. Sure of himself, he headed for the coroner's vehicle, and Paul hurried to join them, ignoring neighbors who were beginning to gather yards away.

"Where's the body?" a fireman asked.

"Down the trail." Paul tipped his head in that direction.

"Bring your gurney," a fireman directed the ambulance driver.

Paul led the way, and Tracy followed, her long legs keeping pace with the men carrying a body bag and a stretcher. Footsteps crunched on the gravel as neighbors trailed behind.

"How long will it take the chief to get here?" Paul asked the officer.

"He's out deer hunting. No telling when he'll be back."

Paul slowed and turned off the gravel trail into the trees. The darkness and soft padding of footsteps created an eerie atmosphere broken only by heavy breathing. As the coroner bent down and drew the blanket from the body, onlookers gasped. Some uttered shocked curses under their breath. Scratches lay like red pencil marks across the body's bare, tan legs. One shoe was missing. The scarlet toenails looked like drops of blood. Her skin was mottled with dark splotches. As the coroner motioned for the firemen to remove the body, Paul sucked air and turned away from the scene. Tracy reached forward and pulled Paul's sleeve.

"They shouldn't move the body until the police have time to collect evidence," she said. Paul seemed to be in shock, staring at the body. When he didn't respond, Tracy held out her hand to keep the neighbors from approaching the body. She spoke to the man who seemed to be in charge.

"Sir, it's standard procedure to leave a body where it is and to keep people away from the scene until the crime division does a sweep for evidence." She wished she were wearing her police uniform. Who would listen to a woman in sweats?

The coroner scratched his head as everyone stared at Tracy. She searched for support from the policeman she had seen exit the Jeep. She saw him standing at the clearing's entrance, in earnest discussion with a group of onlookers, paying no attention to what was going on inside.

"Who says?" the coroner responded, showing no intention of following an outsider's dictation.

"I've been a crime investigator for ten years with the Chicago Police Department," Tracy responded. "I say."

All action stopped as people stared from the coroner to Tracy. The coroner's chin dropped, and he stared over his glasses, letting his eyes shift from Tracy toward muffled snickers from the back of the crowd.

"What kind of investigatin' did you do, honey?" he asked.

Tracy's teeth clenched. So, it's too pushy, too sexy, and talking when she should be listening all over again, she thought. She'd been there, done that. She knew the routine and stood her ground.

"Murders. I suspect the policeman will agree with what I said."

"Well," the man spoke above the impressed whispers of the crowd, "We can't just leave a body laying out here like this. Matt may not git home before dark."

"We don't have all day, neither," another man said. "This is my day off."

"There's a police officer present. Let him take charge," Tracy said.

The crowd stared at her through squinted eyelids and frowns, some nodding in agreement.

"She's right," Paul said. "This could be a murder scene. Let's leave the body as it is until the police chief gets here." He looked around. "Unless the sergeant can take over."

Everyone turned to watch Sergeant Falco, who seemed reluctant to come forward to view the body. "Maybe we ought to wait for Matt," he said. Low grumbles of disapproval followed his statement, and he shuffled toward the body, as if he would rather be somewhere else.

The mumbled impatience from the county employees spread to the crowd, and a few onlookers moved toward the trail. Two men nearest the body turned toward the opening, shaking their heads. "Damn good look-ing broad, wouldn't you say?" one muttered.

Tracy exploded. "Get out!" She covered Carolyn's face with the blan-ket. Shocked, the stragglers moved farther away, backing into each other, peering up from beneath lowered eyebrows at Tracy.

Tracy's yell seemed to motivate the sergeant, and he pushed his way through the crowd. "Okay. Everybody out," he directed. "No telling when Matt will show up, so I'm in charge. Give me room and some time to go over this place, and then we'll let the coroner do his job. Won't take too long." He nodded to Tracy, who slipped around the coroner to get a clear view of the officer's actions. He never looked at the body, but began kicking through the leaves. When he approached Paul and Tracy, Char-ley stood, lifted one foot and sniffed softly in his direction. The sergeant made a quick circuit of the area, picked up the lost shoe, then waved the coroner back in. The body was wrapped in a tarp and placed on a gurney, but before they could move it, a siren announced the police chief's arrival. Someone outside shouted, "Matt's here."

Unsettled by the sergeant's lack of interest in the corpse, Tracy zoomed in for a picture of his face. He was young, with a Lincoln-like nose bronzed by the sun, full lips, and puffy eyes, as if he'd had no sleep the night before. A cowboy hat rested low on his head, touching his ears. He could have been handsome, Tracy thought, except for an allover effect of weakness, disguised beneath the police uniform. Why hadn't he promptly taken charge of this criminal matter?

The crowd separated to allow the chief to approach the body. Paul pulled Tracy aside, hoping to avoid another firestorm.

"What's going on?" the chief wheezed.

"We got a problem," the sergeant said, pointing. "Dr. Jordan and this lady found a dead girl while they were out walking." He pointed with the arm holding the shotgun.

Chief Mayfield barged forward and pulled the blanket from Carolyn's face. The crowd's eyes shifted to watch Tracy's response as he leaned over the body. "Huh. Been dead several hours. Anybody know this girl?" He looked at Tracy who motioned to Paul.

"You recognize her, Doc?"

Paul cleared his throat and nodded. "She came into my office this week."

"What for?"

"Matt, you know that's confidential information between a doctor and his patient."

"You can tell me who she is, I guess."

"She said her name was Carolyn Pittman. No one from her family had been to see me before. I think they're new in town. That's all I know."

"You're gonna have to do better than that, Doc. It's mighty strange she comes into your office one day, and then dies a few days later from what looks like an abortion, only a couple hundred yards from your house."

The sergeant came alive, nodding, his eyes wide with agreement.

Shocked at the implication, Paul stifled the urge to slam his fist into the police chief's face. Tracy placed a hand on his arm and moved between them. Mayfield stared at the corpse and shook his head. "She was a mighty purty girl," he said, flipping the blanket over the girl's face and pointing to the men holding the gurney. "Git her out of here." He shooed people back with his hands and spoke to the gawking crowd behind him. "Anybody know the family? What did you say her name was?" He looked at Paul.

"Carolyn Pittman."

"Anybody here know the Pittmans? We'll have to notify her folks."

The officer holding the shoe lifted his hand. "They live in them temporary trailers out on the Lost Creek Ranch. We got a call to go out there last week. Old man got drunk and beat up his woman." The officer smiled at Tracy now, as if they were in this investigation together, Ada and Chicago.

Mayfield nodded. "I saw your report about that incident. Don't guess he was stupid enough to do this was he, Jerry?" He pointed to the body.

Falco shrugged. "Somebody was."

"You better get out there and bring the folks down to the mortuary to identify the body. If it's their girl, bring 'em on over to the office. I'll have some questions." He pointed at Tracy and Paul with a sweep of his hand. "Let's go up to the house and talk. I need your statements." He looked at the remaining gawkers shuffling away from the scene. "Anybody else got firsthand knowledge of what happened here?" All heads ducked and most of the crowd hurried back to the trailhead.

"Get me a report on how she died as soon as you can," he said to the coroner, who nodded.

Paul turned to Tracy. "Why don't you take Charley up to the house? I'll bring the chief."

When he and Mayfield arrived, Tracy was sitting on the floor with Charley's head in her lap. The dog's eyes rolled up and his tail wagged to acknowledge Paul, then he looked away and nuzzled a little closer to Tracy.

Sergeant Falco followed Paul and Chief Mayfield into the kitchen, where the chief sat down at the kitchen table and pulled out a well-worn tablet and short pencil. Falco leaned against the back door as though he were guarding the chief's back but hoping to remain aloof from the investigation.

"Ma'am, I'm Chief Matt Mayfield. I'm sorry to take up your time, but I gotta ask you some questions." Tracy rose from the floor and sat across from him at the table, pleased that some evidence was being recorded.

"What's your name and spell it for me. Gimme your address too."

Tracy enunciated each syllable as if she were responding to a child learning to read and write.

"What're you doing down here?" The chief looked up, his eyes squinting.

"In Oklahoma or at the lake?"

"Both."

"I came to Tulsa on vacation. I came to Ada on business. I'm waiting for the Clerk and Recorder's Office to open Monday so that I can look up some records."

The corners of Chief Mayfield's lips dipped almost to his jaw line, pushing his lower lip outward as he nodded. "What wuz you doing here at the lake?" His eyes shifted between her and Paul. Falco's eyes widened and focused on Tracy.

"I was looking for a trail where I could get some exercise, maybe take pictures. They told me about this park at the hotel."

The chief looked uncomfortable. "We don't have a lot of female runners in these parts. You may want to stay away from the park until we get to the bottom of this mess." He looked at Paul for confirmation. Paul nodded.

"How did you find the body?"

Tracy related the story of her discovery.

"You down here visiting the doctor?"

"No," Tracy said. Falco relaxed, agreeing with her answer.

Paul felt his face warming, angry at the chief's second insinuation. He turned to the sink to get a drink. "She's one of the Hunter girls," Paul said over his shoulder. "You remember Josh and Sarah, don't you?"

"Oh, sure. Nice family. Too bad about Josh. Died of a heart attack when he was still purty young, didn't he?"

At the reminder of her father's death, Tracy reached out to pet Charley.

The chief chatted with Paul, covering the same questions he'd asked Tracy. He finished with, "I believe I've got all I need here. You goin' to be in town for a while, ma'am?"

"A few days."

"Where you staying?"

"At the Palace."

His eyebrows lifted and he nodded. "I'll be in touch then. Let me know before you leave town." He turned to Paul.

"You got any more to say about this girl?"

"No."

"You haven't seen her outside the office?"

"I told you she was a patient. I think that answers your question." Paul's voice could have sliced ice.

The police chief backed off. "Didn't mean to offend you. Just doing my job. I guess you'll be around if I need you to sign a statement later?"

"I'm going nowhere."

Mayfield folded his tablet, nodded to Tracy, and left through the back door, waving the sergeant to follow.

"Looks like you've found a friend," Paul said, nodding at Charley.

"Yes. He's a nice dog when he isn't nosing around where he shouldn't." She stood up and patted the dog's head. "I'd better get going."

Paul looked at the clock above the refrigerator. "What about the auction?"

"Oh. I'd forgotten about it." Tracy looked toward the lake. "I don't feel very sociable, but Ruth will be disappointed if we don't go. Is there anything we should do first to follow up on this case?"

"You're the investigator. What would you suggest?"

"I don't know. I was just so disgusted with how the matter was handled. How do they expect to find who did this when they didn't collect any evidence, and the sergeant went stomping around the area as if his intent was to destroy evidence? He didn't look for footprints or anything. Maybe we could go look for a weapon."

"I don't think you'll find a weapon. Carolyn told me she would get an abortion across the tracks or do it herself." He sat shaking his head. "I should have taken her seriously."

"What could you have done?"

Paul looked up. "I could have found a way to help her."

I guess there s no point in looking for weapons then. Maybe a . . . a coat hanger?"

Paul frowned. "Maybe, but I doubt that she'd do it in the park. Probably at home. What I can't figure out is why she was in the park in the first place. There must be a reason."

"I'll bet you're right. The abortion happened somewhere else. She may have come here to meet someone; he found her dead, panicked, and covered her body. We need to find out who."

Paul shook his head. "It isn't our place to get involved. You can see how suspicious the police are already." He looked at the clock again. "I have to make an appearance at the auction, and it may be the only chance you'll have to see Hal before you leave. If Ruth wants to go, let's do it."

Tracy nodded and pulled her car keys from her pocket. Deep creases formed between her eyes. "Okay, but tomorrow we should start pushing the police to find the cause of Carolyn's death. I didn't like the way he kept insinuating that you may be involved in her murder." She left Paul standing in the kitchen, patted Charley goodbye, and hurried to her car.

Paul dragged himself to the ringing telephone.

"Paul," Kit yelled. "Where have you been? I've been calling all morning. I got hold of Tillie, and she said you left the office late on Friday, and she hadn't heard from you since. You didn't call last night. What's going on?"

"You want the good news or the bad?"

"All of it. I couldn't get much out of Tillie, which makes me wonder what in heck is happening. I've been frantic."

Paul described the morning's tragedy, leaving out as much as he could.

"My God," Kit said. "That's right by our house. Is it someone we know?"

"Strange as it may seem, the girl came into the clinic on Thursday and again on Friday with her mother. That's the first time I'd seen her."

"What was her problem?"

"I can't go into it now, Kit. She and Tommy were dating, and Tillie wanted me to talk to them. She was worried they were having sex. We'll talk about it when you get home."

"Is Tracy alright?"

"She seems to be. Charley's taken a shine to her. He misses you."

"Well, that settles it. Andy has offered to take Mom to Muskogee with him, so I'm coming home today. The police will need prodding on this one. We can't sit by and let Matt sweep two murders under the rug to satisfy the kooks who elected him. I should be there by late afternoon."

"Kit, we agreed that you'd stay out of local politics."

"We agreed I wouldn't do anything to hurt your business. If I could help it. But this sounds like someone needs to get on the chief's back and do a little bronc riding." She paused and added, "I may have to run for office one of these days to clean up this place."

"This is not to be taken lightly, Kit. First Nora's death and now this one. People are getting nervous."

"All the more reason to find the bad guys."

After a long pause, Paul changed the subject. "Hal's auction is today, you know. I plan to run out there for lunch. Tracy went to school with Hal, so she and Ruth want to go. Can you be home in time to join us? We'll wait for you."

"No. I won't get home until suppertime. Tell Hal's mother I'm sorry I missed the party."

"I will. You drive carefully."

"Honey, if you want to throw steaks on the grill and bake potatoes, we could invite the girls for supper. If they're leaving in a day or two, I may not get to see them."

"I'll think about it." Spending the evening with three power-packed women after a day like this might be more than he could take.

"Love you," Kit said and the telephone went dead.

"Love you, too," Paul said to nobody, as he laid down the telephone and sighed. He admitted to himself that the police chief's insinuations about a connection between him and his patient were troublesome. Perhaps the chief would need some prodding to find the real killer.

Beatrice had spent a sleepless night worrying about the pillowcase. Even after she received a report from Falco that he had followed the blue

Ford past the hospital and then to the park, and despite his assurance that he saw Tommy bury the pillowcase in the park where no one would find it, she had a premonition that something might go wrong. "The pillowcase and what was in it must be recovered and destroyed. Do you understand?"

"Yes, ma'am," he said. "I'll go back and get it." At sunrise, he hurried back to the park where he found Carolyn's body, already cold. Falco panicked and decided to cover her body in case someone came by while he was looking for the buried pillowcase. As luck would have it, a dog came sniffing into the open circle as Falco finished piling leaves and fallen branches on the body. He heard a woman's voice calling the dog. Terrified, he rushed through the woods, forgetting the pillowcase

EIGHT

I'm almost ready," Tillie shouted into the telephone. Her voice was stressed, not revealing her usual bubbly self.

"What are you almost ready for, Tillie?"

"Oh, heavens, Paul. I thought you were Beulah. I'm late picking her up for church. Why are you calling me on Sunday morning? Don't I ever get a break from you and that clinic?"

"This is a personal call, Tillie. I need you to fill me in on what Tommy was doing last night."

"Tommy?" Tillie's voice softened and became cautious. "He and two of his friends drove over to the university last night to a party at Brandon's frat house. Can you believe he's hobnobbing with Hal's brother?" Her voice was high, stressed.

Paul considered her question. No, he couldn't see Tommy and Brandon socializing, but he wouldn't say that to Tillie. "Being a candidate for quarterback will get you everywhere, I guess," he said.

Tillie paused. "Why are you asking about Tommy?"

"It has to do with Carolyn Pittman."

"What does?" Tillie was almost whispering.

"She died last night. Someone hid her body out here by the lake. I wondered if Tommy was with her last night."

"No. I told you he went over to Brandon's party at the university." There was a long silence on the phone. "This is so sad. How did it happen?"

"We don't know for sure. There were lots of bruises on her body, but I couldn't tell whether they were from trauma or just postmortem lividity. I'm guessing she bled to death from an abortion. The coroner's report should be back in a few days. I wondered if Tommy knew she was pregnant."

"If he did, he didn't tell me."

"I'm glad he was out of town. The police will be interrogating the school kids. Let Tommy know he'll have to answer questions."

"I will. Thanks for calling, Paul." Tillie's voice trailed off. Her response to the news seemed strange to Paul, as if she weren't surprised at the abortion but was shocked at the death. Had Carolyn asked Tillie where to get an abortion? Would Tillie have encouraged it to protect Tommy's college career? He should have asked her if she saw Carolyn last night, but he couldn't worry about that now. It was ten minutes until eleven. He'd have to rush to be at the hotel on time.

He made it, his hair still wet, as Tracy and Ruth came down the steps of the hotel. Tracy was in blue jeans, cowboy boots, and a white shirt. Her curly hair was pulled back and pinned with a leather clip. Ruth wore khaki pants with a boldly printed shirt hanging low to cover her hips. Her black hair hung in a straight Dutch bob that reminded Paul of her father's native coloring.

"Feeling better?" he asked Tracy, as they piled into the Jeep and headed for the ranch.

Distracted, Tracy hesitated. Across the parking lot, a Jeep with a police department insignia was pulling out at the same time they did. It seemed to be following them. She shrugged and spoke to Paul. "Yes, I'm recovering. How about you?"

"Me too," Paul said. "I talked to Kit. She's coming home today. She asked me to invite you ladies over for supper tonight."

"Umm. That sounds great," Ruth said, "Hotel food is getting boring."

"Good. I also talked to Tillie to see if she knew whether Carolyn was with Tommy last night."

"Who's Tommy?" Ruth asked.

Too late, Paul realized he had revealed information that he should have kept secret. He looked from one woman to the other. "Tillie's son."

"Why should he be warned about Carolyn's death?"

"You're both much too curious for your own good. Let's pretend I didn't mention Tommy. Okay?"

"No, it's not okay," Tracy said. "Quit treating us like children or morons. I have a degree saying I'm qualified to be a crime investigator. Being curious is part of my business. Ruth has three sons very close to Carolyn's age. She understands kids."

"And we know how to keep secrets," Ruth said.

"What if the police ask you whether you are aware that Tommy and Carolyn Pittman were a hot item? Are you going to lie?"

"They dated?" Tracy asked. The Jeep following them no longer held her attention.

"Yes," Paul said. "Carolyn was fifteen going on twenty-five. Tommy's seventeen, a star football player who thinks he's a Greek god right now."

"I know kids like that," Ruth said. "Where was Tommy last night?"

"Tillie says he went over to the university to Brandon Montgomery's fraternity party. I hope she's right."

"Unless Carolyn went with him," Tracy said.

Ruth nodded. "Yeah. Lots of wild things happen at those parties. Believe me, I know. Dickie belongs to a fraternity at A&M, and those kids are saints compared to most."

Paul stopped breathing. Had Tommy taken Carolyn out of town, without his mother's knowledge? In his heart, he knew teenage boys did lots of things they didn't reveal to their parents.

"Jesus," Paul said. "I'm sorry I told you."

"We're just guessing that Tommy was involved. Give us more facts. We'll try again," Tracy said.

"I can tell you about boyfriends," Ruth said. "Boyfriends are less likely to kill a girlfriend than is someone in her family. You should have learned that in medical school."

"We didn't spend our time in medical school talking about how to kill people. We concentrated on keeping them alive."

"Huh," Ruth said.

Tracy wanted to keep them on track. "Maybe there were problems in her family. The police officer said they had been called out there last week because the father was battering his wife. I suppose he could have beaten Carolyn if he found out she was sleeping around."

"It's possible," Ruth said. "But the usual scenario in abusive families is the husband beats the wife and makes out with the daughter."

"She's right," Paul said.

"If that happened, maybe the mother got jealous and killed her."

Ruth shook her head. "Probably not. When the mother gets tired of her wifely duties, she accepts the dad's sleeping with the daughter, because it keeps him away from her."

Tracy and Paul looked at Ruth.

"You're right, of course, but where did you learn all that?" Tracy asked. "Reading trashy magazines?"

"I volunteer at the domestic violence hotline. We go through training."

"Talk about sick. What you described ranks right up there with the worst disease," Paul said.

"Of course it's sick, but there are a lot of sick people in this world."

"What if the daughter refuses to cooperate and squeals on him?"

"That's not very likely either. In most instances the father threatens to kill his daughter unless she keeps it a secret. Or he tells her he will go to jail if she tells. So, she keeps it a secret. Sometimes, if it gets too bad, she kills herself."

"Maybe Carolyn did that. She told me she had a good reason for wanting an abortion. Incest would be a good reason."

Tracy was busy jotting a summary of their conversation into her notebook. The names of Tommy, Brandon, frat boys, Carolyn's father, and her mother were listed as possible suspects. Reviewing the summary, she wondered if the police chief would have added Dr. Paul Jordan's name. He knew the girl was pregnant, that she wanted an abortion, and he lived very near where her body was found.

With the ranch in view, Paul turned off the highway onto an unpaved road and slowed down when they reached cars that were parked along the fencerow. Behind them, out of sight, the police department Jeep eased into a parking space, and the driver sat watching them head for the house.

"This is fine. Let's walk past the corral. I want to pet the horses." Paul and Ruth followed and stood aside watching, as Tracy patted each horse and murmured loving words.

"Shall we leave you here while we go eat and mingle with people?" Ruth asked.

Tracy laughed. "No. Let's go find Hal. I want to see the look on his face when he discovers who I am." Mischievous glints sparkled in her eyes.

They walked across the gravel path and moved onto the broad lawn behind the ranch house. Brightly colored tents shaded tables covered with checkered cloths. In the food tent, Louie was directing his restaurant crew to fill the long barbecue pits and tables with steaks, hamburgers, and hot-dogs. A shorter table was manned by white-coated bartenders sporting red neckerchiefs, busy handing out drinks and passing plates of hors d'oeuvres.

Bob Wills and the Texas Playboys had set up their instruments and mikes on a platform overlooking a smooth wooden dance floor constructed for this event. Young people and grandparents were square dancing to music played by the most popular cowboy band in the state. Women, dressed in long skirts with several petticoats showing, kicked to the music. The men wore blue jeans with big belt buckles and bright shirts with scarves. The women's handmade skirts matched their partner's shirts made from the same material. Everyone laughed at his or her mistakes in attempting to follow the steps of the caller.

"Boy, Hal's gone all out for this shindig, hasn't he?" Ruth asked, as she recognized the hoe-down music from Tulsa.

"He does every year," Paul said. "Let's check in with our hostess." He guided them to an arbor on the side of the house where Hal's mother was surrounded by friends.

"Paul." Beatrice stood and offered her cheek for a kiss, at the same time surveying the two women who had come with him. "How nice that you could come," she said, without smiling. "Where's Kit?"

"She's in Tulsa, caring for her sick mother. She said to tell you she's sorry she missed the best party of the year."

"And who are your guests?" She turned to Tracy and Ruth, showing no sign of recognition.

"This is Tracy Hunter and her sister Ruth. Tracy's visiting from Chicago, where she's been working as a top-notch criminal investigator. A regular Sherlock Holmes." He grinned at Tracy's glare. "Ruth is visiting from Tulsa."

Beatrice frowned and failed to hide her alarm at the introduction. Recognizing Tracy's name, her eyes wavered toward the barn then back to Paul. "Please get drinks and have some food. Muffy has done a wonderful job of planning this year. Hal is so busy with buyers that I doubt he'll have time to see you." She turned away toward other guests, and Paul led the way to the bar.

"That's Muffy at the bandstand," Paul whispered. "She's a lobbyist at the state capitol. Powerful people attend this event. They know she's Senator Fortenberry's daughter, and she makes sure they also see and remember her as the wife of Hal Montgomery. He represents a different power base."

They settled at a table, and Tracy scanned the crowd, wondering if she would recognize Hal if she saw him. Her question was answered when she discovered a young man who resembled the Hal Montgomery she knew as a teenager. This boy was older, college age. His manners were impeccable. He hugged Beatrice, showing warm affection. They were whispering confidences until Muffy appeared and took the boy's arm, pulling him to a group of mothers, whose daughters giggled and blushed as they were introduced.

Tracy's eyes moistened, and she tried to swallow the tightness forming in her chest. This must be Hal's younger brother Brandon. He was five or six when she and Hal dated, but he had developed into a duplicate of his brother as a teenager. His eyes were framed with the same beautiful lashes. He tilted his head in the same way, not committing himself but teasing the young girls into believing he cared for each one as he was introduced. His pressed chinos, white shirt, and the small red scarf around his neck showed impeccable taste. The polish on his boots reflected the sun like a mirror.

Tracy was swept into the past, lost in the odor of Old Spice shaving lotion, shy touches, and the warmth of innocent kisses. A voice that made her shiver pulled her back into the noise and excitement of the party.

"Paul, what the heck? I thought you were coming alone. I hope you told these pretty ladies that you're married to a wildcat." Hal walked up and shook hands with Paul, pulled off his hat and nodded toward the women, his mind on business affairs.

Tracy looked at him, surprised, her lips parted. She was still breathless from the shock of seeing Brandon, unprepared to face this man, instead of a teenager. Hal was no longer a sweet child. He was the charming man his father had been. He still had the beautiful eyes, set off by thick, curly lashes that should have belonged to a woman. He squinted and waved away the smoke from his cigarette. His skin was tanned and weathered.

Laugh wrinkles spread from his eyes and lips. His teenage acne scars now added character to his face, although the smile had not changed. He stood a good four inches taller than when he was in high school.

"Wildcats are our specialty," Tracy said and winked at Ruth.

Hal hesitated at the unexpected rejoinder and held out his hand to Ruth. "I'm Hal Montgomery. Have we met?"

"Hal, you remember the Hunter girls. This is Ruth. And Tracy."

Hal froze. He stared for a moment before throwing his cigarette to the ground and destroying it with the heel of his boot. When he looked up, he was composed.

"Tracy!" He nodded, backed off, and replaced his hat as if to hide his embarrassment. "I'll be damned," he said. "It's been a long time. You've changed." He nodded to Ruth. "Nice to see you again. What brings you ladies to Ada?" His eyes wavered toward Tracy and did not leave.

"Oh, Tracy talked me into coming down with her while she gets her birth certificate fixed. I'm just running away from home."

"Where've you been hiding all these years?" He was looking at Tracy.

"Chicago."

"That's a long way from here. I get up there every year for the stock show, though. Didn't know you were there."

Tracy looked away. Big deal. He had not searched very hard. "I saw Brandon a few minutes ago," she said. "He's a picture of what you looked like in high school."

Hal's eyelids tightened as he scanned the crowd. "Yeah. He lives with me, or he did before he went off to college. I rarely see him since he moved into a fraternity house. Most of the time he makes me glad I didn't have children." He and Paul exchanged quick glances. "I saw Kit last night," he said. "I flew up to Tulsa on business, and she and her mother were having dinner at my hotel."

Paul frowned. When he talked to Kit a few hours ago, she had not mentioned seeing Hal

Hal pushed his hat off his forehead and spoke to Tracy. "Let's get together before you leave. Where are you staying?"

"The Palace."

"Good place. Mother lives in the penthouse." He looked toward the barns, where someone was calling him, and then back to Tracy. "I gotta go. I'll call you as soon as this shindig is over." He addressed Paul as he was leaving. "Come out to the barn before you leave. I'm selling the state's grand champion bull this year."

Paul's gaze followed Hal to the barns. "That's strange. I just talked to Kit, and she didn't mention seeing Hal last night, which is unusual. She always tells me when they run into each other out of town."

"Maybe she just forgot to mention it," Tracy said.

"Yeah. Make excuses for him." Ruth's eyebrows lifted.

Tracy could have bitten her tongue. Why was she defending this guy? Let Paul be mad at him too.

Paul looked at her with a frown. "We've been friends for years, but you may know him better than I do." He set his glass aside. "Let's eat and head back to town. I've taken all the socializing I can for one day."

Tracy pouted. "I want to see the cattle auctioned. Don't you, Ruth? Or shall I go by myself while you people eat?"

"Go by yourself," Ruth said. "The smell of barbecue beats the odor of cow manure any day. But stay away from Hal," she cautioned. "I detected smoldering coals between the two of you. We don't want the barns catching on fire."

"Good idea," Paul said. "Meet us here when the smell of manure overcomes you."

With Tracy gone, the other two loaded their plates with spicy barbecued burgers, salads, and desserts and sat down. Brandon came with his plate and sat across from them.

"Hi, Dr. Jordan," he said. "Who's your friend?"

"This is Ruth Gordon. She's visiting from Tulsa." He turned to Ruth. "This is Hal's brother, Brandon. You people may have met in an earlier life."

Brandon ignored the introduction. "Where's the sexy doll I saw with you?"

Paul's irritation at the slight to Ruth was palpable. "Brandon, does your mind ever extend to subjects beyond hitting on women?"

"Not often, Doc. So many opportunities. It's hard to keep up."

"Well, you would have more luck if you stuck to girls your own age. Tracy's quite a bit older than you are."

"You never know till you try, man. Did you say 'Tracy'?"

Paul nodded.

"That must be Hal's old girlfriend. She's not that much older than I am."

"Take my word for it. She's mature." He looked toward the house where several giggling girls in summer dresses or blue jeans glanced their way. "Those young ladies seem interested." He regretted his suggestion.

Brandon followed Paul's gaze. "High-school girls are nothing but trouble," he said. He picked up his sandwich and nibbled from the edge before wiping his lips. "Did Tracy go to the barns?"

Paul changed the subject. "How was the party last night?"

Brandon's face reddened. "What party?"

"The fraternity party that you and Tommy went to."

Brandon forced a smile. "It was a drag."

"Did Carolyn Pittman show up?" Ruth believed in getting right to the point.

Brandon looked at her with narrowed eyes. "I don't recall a Carolyn. There was a big crowd." He stood up, nodding to Paul as he wiped his hands together. He turned and walked to the house, stopping to whisper in the ear of one of the girls he had flirted with earlier. Paul and Ruth watched as he led her to a side door of the home. He turned and waved toward their bench.

"What do you make of that guy?" Ruth asked. "I'll bet my next meal that he's hiding something. Maybe he takes after his brother."

"He's spoiled and rude. I can't believe Hal would allow him to get away with that kind of crap."

Ruth laid her hand on his arm. "Thanks for putting him in his place. I know I can't compete with Tracy's good looks, but I'm not used to having it pointed out so clearly." She picked up their plates and dumped them in the trash can. "I wish ladies could say words like crap," she said.

Paul laughed. "You just did."

"Yeah, and I liked it. Come on. Let's go find Tracy and see what kind of crap Hal is selling at the auction."

They walked toward the noise of the loudspeakers inside the barn, and Sergeant Falco appeared, leading the way to the bleachers where Tracy was sitting, elbows on her knees, eyes scanning the benches. Falco made himself at home beside her, thighs touching.

Surprised, Tracy scooted to the right. "Have you learned anything new about what happened in the park?" she asked, to hide her embarrassment.

He frowned and shook his head, his eyes searching the auction barn as if he had business there. Tracy shrugged and turned to Paul and Ruth.

Buyers were lounging in box seats with padded chairs on the same level where the cattle were being led in circles past the bidders. "That's him," Tracy whispered. She pointed to a hefty man in a white hat, his shirt decorated with blue inserts and cording, shining beads, and pearl buttons.

"Him who?"

"Someone we're supposed to know?" Paul asked.

"Yes," Tracy said. "It's Gene Autry, the famous singing cowboy in the movies. How could you live in Oklahoma and not know who Gene Autry is? They named a town after him. I think he owns a baseball team out in California now."

Of course. This was the man who sang "The Red River Valley" over the radio the night of Tracy's birth. Paul had tried to forget it. "Baseball I know," he said, "but cowboy songs don't move me. Plus, I'm afraid of cows and horses."

Tracy looked at him with her mouth agape. "Tell me it ain't so."

Falco smothered a chuckle.

"There's Hal," Ruth said. They watched as he walked from the stalls and headed for the boxes to sit with Autry. At the same time, an enormous red bull with white, curly hair on most of his face, and matching belly and leg markings was led into the show pen. Autry sat back and crossed his arms over his stomach. He might be a professional actor, but he was not good at pretending to be a disinterested bystander at the auction. He was tense as he watched signals bouncing around the arena.

"I wonder who's bidding for Autry," Tracy said, as the price advanced to $80,000.

"The man in the brown vest," Falco said, pointing to a business man leaning on the corral fence. The auctioneer banged his gavel and announced the animal sold. Hal leaned over and shook Autry's hand. A broad smile indicated the singing cowboy was happy with his purchase.

"We can go now," Tracy said.

"Sure you don't want to buy something?" Paul asked.

"Don't make fun. I'll pet the horses on the way to the car. That's all the animal flesh I can afford."

They rose, shook hands with Falco, and Tracy hurried ahead of them to the corral for one last pat on the horses' muzzles. She climbed into the Jeep, apologizing for the delay. "I've missed my horse every day since I moved to Chicago."

"If you stay long enough, you can ride with Kit. She goes out every day."

"She does? I would love that. I think I'm going to like Kit."

"I'm afraid you will," Paul said, not bothering to explain his fear that they would feed on each other's activism.

"Liking isn't good?"

"It's good," he said not wanting to explain himself. Paul pulled out of the parking space and headed for town, but soon pulled over to the side of the road as they came to a settlement of mobile homes off to the right on ranch property. They watched as a driver jumped out of a pickup near the first home and slammed the door. He walked to the back of the vehicle, then hesitating, stared at Paul's Jeep. He pulled a faded Indian blanket from the pickup bed, rolled it into a tight ball under his arm, and hurried to the door of the trailer.

"That must be Carolyn's father. He's carrying the blanket her body was wrapped in," Paul said.

It should have been kept for evidence, Tracy thought, and scribbled the fact down in her notebook. She wished she could take a picture.

A woman was slower to climb down from the pickup, almost as if hoping the Jeep would pass while she waited. A long, full skirt fell short of her worn moccasins. She pulled a wool shawl from her shoulders to cover her head, lifting a handkerchief to hide her face as she ducked from the pickup and ran toward the mobile home.

"That's her mother," Paul said. Tracy sighed.

"Is our ghoulish curiosity satisfied?" Ruth asked.

"Not really," Tracy said. "I'd love to see inside their house. Go through Carolyn's room. There may be evidence that would lead us to the reason she died. I wonder if Chief Mayfield has been out searching."

"Maybe. He's not totally incompetent," Paul said. "We'd better get back to town. Maybe we can drive around before you leave town. If you stay long enough, I'm sure Hal will give you a private tour."

"I bet he will." Tracy was quiet for a moment and then added, "It's been a long time since he and I spent Sunday afternoons at the lake house. I doubt if those feelings of magic can return."

"You don't have to tell us about those days," Paul said. "We have good imaginations."

"No? I thought you'd be interested."

"In hearing about your love life with Hal? No, I don't think so."

"Speak for yourself, Paul," Ruth said. "Tracy's always been very close-mouthed when it came to talking about Hal. I wouldn't mind hearing what she has to say." Ruth leaned her arms on the back of the front seat and rested her chin on top.

"It was a childhood infatuation," Tracy said. "Girls tend to idealize those things. Boys don't. From the way he acted today, he hasn't thought of me since I left."

"You underestimate the amount of time men spend dreaming of and idolizing the opposite sex. When you called, Hal was in my office, and he said he did remember you, and he seemed very interested in meeting you again. What makes you think he didn't?"

"I don't know. I guess I wanted him to turn cartwheels when he saw me. He used to do that when we were kids. This time he seemed distracted. But that's okay. I wanted closure, and this is it. I can forget him now."

"I'm no expert on men," Ruth chimed in, "but that was not my impression at all. Maybe your new admirer is influencing your opinion."

Tracy looked at her in wonder. "What new admirer? You're pulling my leg, right?"

"The policeman—what's his name? He definitely seems interested. He keeps showing up everywhere we go."

"Really, Ruth. That's because we're both interested in the same case."

Paul interrupted. "I agree with Ruth that Hal was trying to hide his real feelings. He doesn't want to be hurt again, and he doesn't want to hurt you again. That can be accomplished if you say goodbye."

"Done," Tracy said.

Ruth tried to stifle her giggle from the back seat.

Unwilling to be challenged on her new position, Tracy changed the subject. "I've been thinking about that poor girl we found in the park. Her parents deserve an answer to what happened to her. If the police fail to do a proper investigation, I think we should get organized and show them how it's done. I'm worried it's connected to Nora's death."

"What makes you think that?" Paul asked.

"Their relevance to the broad issue of abortions. Nora is accused of offering abortions—Carolyn died from a butchered one. It doesn't take a person with a PhD to see that connection. Even Falco might do it." She looked over her shoulder.

"Have you discussed this possible connection with Falco?" Ruth asked.

"No. I asked him if they'd gotten any new information about the case, but he didn't answer. If they're protecting someone and looking for other suspects, they may add me to the list of suspicious characters. Besides, I'm itching to do a little more research on this case myself."

"Right on, girl," Ruth said. "I've always thought I'd be a good private eye, and with your special training, we'd make good partners. I tend to barge right in and get things done. You go slow, mull things over, take pictures. Having swept Hal out of the picture, we'll need something to keep us busy while you're waiting for the clerk's office to finish your birth certificate." She leaned over Paul's shoulder. "How about your wife? She must know a lot of people in this town. Could she give us the lowdown on who was threatening the lady doctor?"

A muscle jumped on Paul's right jaw. He was already dreading Kit's return, because he was sure she would be stirring up trouble in the police department the day after she got home. Her leadership skills kept her busy on the Indian Council, but she had always felt free to get involved in local politics every time a woman's issue came before the public. The deaths of the two women would serve to fire her off like a rocket. If she met Tracy and Ruth, anything could happen.

Dark clouds were rolling in from the north, and the temperature was dropping rapidly. Paul ignored the question and turned on the heater. "Are you warm enough?" he asked.

"The heat feels good, thanks. I expected it to be hot in Oklahoma. I'm afraid I didn't come dressed very warmly. Do you think we'll have an early snow?"

"Looks like we could. Kit will lend you coats. You may have to buy snow boots if we get several inches."

"I have my cowboy boots. Ruth, maybe we should go get you some boots and wool pants."

"I never object to shopping." They fell silent again and were lost in their own thoughts, wondering why Paul refused to inject his wife into their plans. No one spoke until they pulled up to the hotel.

"Thanks, Paul. We had a wonderful time. Being on the ranch put to rest lots of old memories. I can go home in peace." Tracy slid out of the Jeep and opened Ruth's door. "Call us if Kit is too tired for company tonight."

Paul watched as they hurried up the steps and disappeared into the hotel. He was surprised and pleased that the meeting between Hal and Tracy was so low key. He could envision complications rising in his own family if the two became a pair and joined his social world. Tracy, at least, pretended to be washing Hal out of her life. Maybe she would leave before fireworks exploded.

When he reached home, the police chief's Jeep was parked beside Kit's Cadillac. He was surprised that Mayfield was working on Sunday. He was also worried that Kit would be upset about the death that happened so close to their home. He parked his Jeep and watched Kit and Chief Mayfield in animated conversation, walking up from the lake front.

Kit was dressed in a leather skirt that hung to her high-topped shoes and a loose sweater that slipped to the edge of her shoulder. She wore a traditional Indian headband across her forehead. Her long black hair swung across her shoulders as she walked beside the police chief. Paul watched the fluid movement of her body and hoped the chief would not be staying.

Kit hurried into Paul's arms. Mayfield looked away, calling to Charley, as the couple kissed. Paul released her and shook hands with Mayfield. "How's the investigation coming?"

"Oh, haven't learned anything new. Talked to the parents this morning. They're pretty close-mouthed. They say they don't know where she was last night or who she was with." Mayfield spit tobacco across the driveway, validating his disgust.

Paul forgot to breathe as his mind flashed to Tommy. He would have to call Tillie to find out whether Tommy's alibi was holding up, or whether the police had even uncovered that lead.

"Won't you come in?" Paul asked.

"No. I just came over to take another look at where you found the body." Mayfield frowned and was almost talking to himself. "It seems weird that she would be dumped at the lake. Lots of kids use the park for necking after the movies on Saturday nights, so it wouldn't be where one would go to hide. You'd think someone would have seen what happened."

He squinted at Paul and spit again. "I'll git out to the school tomorrow and see what I can find out from the kids."

They arrived at the chief's Jeep, and Mayfield climbed in, grunting as he boosted his heavy body behind the wheel. He waved goodbye, as Paul and Kit stood with their arms around each other.

Inside, Paul smelled freshly brewed coffee. Kit knew what he needed was a drink, and she'd prepared an alternative. For the second time, he scolded himself for longing for the smell and taste of good wine. This whole birth certificate issue was creating vistas of his past. He swallowed the saliva slipping across his tongue and hurried to pour coffee into the cup Becky made for him when she was eight years old. Kit walked behind him and put her arms around his waist, rubbing her forehead between his shoulder blades. She never mentioned his drinking, but he was sure she could read his mind like a journal.

"I'm so glad to be back," she said.

Paul set the coffee mug on the cabinet and put his arms around her. "I'm not very good at being a bachelor. I hope you won't have to go back again."

"Momma isn't her old self yet, but Andy has agreed to help, and she loves to visit him and Celeste. So I'm home for a while."

"Maybe she can come down here when the doctor releases her."

Kit smiled and sat down at the table. "That would be perfect. Now tell me what you know about this murder victim. Chief Mayfield seems pretty muddle-minded about it."

"Okay. But first let's talk about supper. I invited Tracy and Ruth. They're eager to meet you." He looked at Kit and smiled. "Maybe I should call and put our invitation off until tomorrow night. I'll tell them you're too tired."

Kit rose from the table and moved into his arms. She pulled his head down and their kiss was long and exciting. "I'm not too tired for anything," she said. She looked at the clock. "Call her and tell her to make it seven instead of six. You can use the telephone in the bedroom."

"By the way," Kit said, stripping off her sweater on the way upstairs. "Did Tracy remember me?"

"I forgot to ask her."

"Now the truth is out. You didn't spend as much time thinking about me while I was gone as you've pretended, did you?"

She was nude except for the high-topped shoes that she wore with her long skirts. She sat down on the bed and bent over to untie them.

"Let me do that," Paul said and dropped to his knees in front of her. Her breasts hung like lightly filled balloons in front of him. He fumbled with her shoelaces while he nuzzled her breasts.

"I like your ulterior motives," she said. "Come to bed."

NINE

The potatoes were baked, and Paul removed the steaks that were soaking in their Texas marinade and placed them on the grill when he heard Tracy's car arrive. He walked to the front yard, as Kit came off the porch to greet the sisters. They hugged, the way women do, so easily. It would be a night of reminiscing, and he doubted that it would be possible to set boundaries for their discussions. He prepared reasons to escape to his upstairs office in case they began reliving moments with Sarah or Tracy's birth, or brought up Carolyn's death.

After dinner, the three women settled like old friends in the living room. Kit looked at Tracy. "Paul promised to tell me about the body you found. Is it too gruesome to discuss after eating?"

"No. In fact, it would be nice to get a fresh opinion on the subject," Tracy said. She looked at Paul, but he did not seem inclined to talk, so she began the story, ending with, "To make a long story short, a woman's leg was sticking out of the leaves. I took some pictures, looked for items of crime evidence, then Charley and I hightailed it back to the trail and ran for help. Paul was waiting near the pier. We went back together to get a better look at the body." Tracy looked at Paul again, but he chose not to add to the explanation.

"How did you identify the body?" Kit asked.

"I did that," Paul said. "Carolyn and her mother came to my office the day before she died."

"One of the policemen knew the family," Tracy added, and explained the domestic violence report.

"I think everybody's suspecting the father," Paul said. He stood up. "While you private eyes solve this murder, I'm going to run up to my office to work." Before he left, he pulled the draperies against the evening chill. He looked at Tracy. "Don't leave without saying good night."

Kit poured more wine and continued the conversation. "If she died because of an abortion, why is her father considered suspicious?"

"Good question," Ruth said. "I don't think he should be."

"Unless Carolyn or the mother performed the abortion at the trailer on the ranch," Tracy said, "and he didn't want the body found at home. He could have been trying to divert attention from the ranch, which had its own rumors of covert criminal activity going on. Finding her body in the park puts the suspicion on the high-school kids who gather at the lake on weekends." The room became quiet as each person rolled the ideas around in their minds.

Kit began pacing behind the couch. "Let me think. Nora told me she heard rumors that Hal is running poker tables where lobbyists come to launder money by losing to Senator Fortenberry's campaign workers. I didn't give a lot of credence to it. Hal has been our friend for years, and he says he leaves the politics to his wife and mother. We haven't broached the subject of using poker parties to launder money with him. It's just not something you ask a friend. Nora says she told the FBI, and they seemed interested, but I haven't heard of any follow-up."

"If there's truth to that rumor," Tracy said, "it could also be true that the body was moved from the ranch to the park."

"You're right. But why the park? I doubt that the father even knew where the kids hang out. They've lived here just a few months. That policeman said they moved to the ranch in June to help with Hal's auction and the roundup."

"Carolyn could have talked him into taking her there," Tracy said.

Kit set down her empty wine glass. "I think you're right—we need to help the police solve this mystery. Tracy, you have pictures of the scene. Why don't we start by reviewing them?"

"I left them to be developed and should be getting them back by Tuesday. Let's get together then."

"The job is bigger than it looks," Ruth said. "If these two deaths are connected, we could be dealing with big-time gamblers or gangs. Are we prepared to play games with the big boys?"

"You can't play with gangs any bigger than I tangled with in Chicago."

"That's true. So where do we start?"

"We know that Nora was murdered, but we're just guessing that the anti-abortion people did it. The cause of Carolyn's death is to be determined, but it looks like a botched abortion. And it happened after Nora was killed, so she couldn't have been involved." Kit looked at Tracy for confirmation.

"Right. The demonstrators were accusing Nora of doing abortions in her clinic. Maybe someone wanted Carolyn's death to look like evidence of that."

Tracy spoke to Kit. "Do women get a fair shake from the police and the courts down here? Do you know the judges?"

Kit nodded. "I know both of them. They're part of the 'good old boy' world. We have no women on the bench, nor in the D.A.'s office. And there are no women deputies to nudge that department. I've been a lone voice in this county arguing for women's rights. Paul clamps down on me when I get too loud. He'll have more trouble squelching all three of us."

"It's too bad we won't be here long enough to see this to the finish, but we can help get it started," Tracy said. "We may be handicapped by being outsiders. People will be suspicious and may not cooperate." She looked at Kit. "Your good name will help to make us legit."

"Paul will love this," Kit said. "He's already told me not to get involved." Charley yawned as if bored with the conversation. He rose and whined to be let out.

Kit called up the stairs. "Paul, did you want to go walking with Charley?"

Paul came running down the stairs and followed Charley to the door. As he opened it, snow blew into the room.

"Hey, those were snow clouds we saw. It's coming down hard. There's half an inch out there already," he said and turned back into the room. "You two will need something warmer than sweaters." He looked to Kit.

"I can fix that," she said and opened the nearby closet.

The phone was ringing as they entered their hotel room.

"Tracy. I hope I'm not calling too late." It was Hal's low, intimate voice. Tracy felt her resolve to forget him melting away.

"No. We just got back from the Jordans." She searched inside for the brave words she had spoken on the way home from the ranch, the ones stating that she was over Hal. The tingling of blood beneath the hairs on her arm suggested that those words were not true.

"It was great seeing you today, honey. You've grown even more beautiful than I remember—and my memories are pretty good."

"And you are still prince charming. However, you're ruling a much larger kingdom than when I knew you."

Hal laughed. "That somehow doesn't sound like a compliment."

"It is. I'm quite impressed."

"When we were kids, we said we'd build a place together. It would have been a lot more fun if you'd been here to help."

"Don't blame me for disappearing. You're the one who left."

"I know. I accept the blame. My only excuse is that I was a kid. I've changed."

"I noticed," Tracy said. In fact, she was shocked at how hormones had changed his teen-age body. He was taller, muscled from hard work, and there was a maturity in his demeanor that was lacking in high school. Her hope to meet him and wipe his memory from her mind was backfiring. She felt as though she were playing with fireworks set to explode at her first false move. More than ever, she needed to put an end to that episode in her life, so that she could look ahead to other relationships. The question was how to do it.

"I call with a proposition," Hal said.

"Do I dare ask what it is?"

"The snow is getting deep out here. Tomorrow will be a good day to lie back and do nothing. But it would be more fun to do nothing with you. Remember when we used to double date with Ruth and Howard out at the lake house on Sunday afternoons? What would you say to having dinner out there in front of a log fire? I could pick you up, say, about two in the afternoon?"

Tracy cleared her throat. This was the opportunity she had hoped for over the years, but one which she thought she had put to rest at the ranch auction. Now the urge to be with him returned, although something told her to slow down.

"It sounds like fun," she said. "I'm a little confused, though. Paul says you're still married."

There was a long pause. "Muffy lives in Oklahoma City. I assume Paul told you we're separated and have been for years. She stays in the city with her friends. I run the ranch and socialize with mine. She came out today for the auction, which was strictly business. She's a lobbyist at the legislature, and she came here to meet cattlemen. She went home as soon as the auction was over." His voice was matter-of-fact. He paused, and his intimate voice returned. "I was hoping you and I could get together and pick up where we left off. I wasn't satisfied with the way we said goodbye."

"I don't recall getting to say goodbye." Tracy knew her voice was biting. "However," she continued, "your marriage puts a few constraints on what we can do to remedy that, don't you think?"

"If you're worried about Muffy, you don't have to be. We have an understanding. She does her thing and I do mine."

"A marriage of convenience?"

"It was from the beginning. Our mothers thought combining my wealth with her family's political power would make a perfect marriage. It looks good on paper, but it was doomed from the start." He repeated, "Will you come?"

Tracy turned off the nagging voice that told her what she was planning to do violated her moral code. She was sure her parents would be horrified. But she was tired of having Hal pop up in her daydreams every time a love song interrupted her day. Closure was what she wanted, and he was offering it on a silver platter, or on the couch in front of the fireplace, to be exact. In her mind, she clicked off the things she had to do to help Ruth and Kit lay out the investigative agenda in the Smeltzer/Pittman cases. Two o'clock at the ranch sounded doable. "Yes," she said. "I'd like to see the lake house again. I'll be ready."

"Great. See you at two." Tracy thought she noted a touch of triumph in his voice, and the pain that had developed in her chest earlier in their conversation sharpened. Was she being played for a sucker again? Was Hal the one who would come out of this meeting happy that he had gotten what he missed out on in high school, and would she come out feeling unsatisfied and used? She laid down the receiver and looked across the room at Ruth, who was grinning.

"Momma always told us to be careful what we asked for, because we might get it," she said. "Like the measles. We hoped we'd get them so that we could stay out of school. Boy, was I ever ready to go back after a week of scratching."

"You don't sound encouraging," Tracy said. "If meeting with Hal is as bad as the measles were, maybe I should go on yearning instead of asking to be immunized."

"Look at it this way," Ruth said flinging her arms high and beginning an imitation of Mary Martin singing in South Pacific. "I'm gonna wash that man right out of my hair," she sang, ending with a can-can kick that landed her back in her chair.

Tracy jumped up and pulled Ruth to the floor again. That was the perfect moment. There was no reason both she and Hal couldn't put an end to their yearnings. She was so glad Ruth had come with her.

"Come on," Tracy said. Together they sang and danced the entire song the way they'd performed it in high school. Winded, they laughed and hugged. "That's what I'll do. I'll wash him right out of my hair and leave him heartbroken, so he knows how it feels to be dumped. Let's go hit the boutique downstairs for warm clothes. I can't look sexy with a red nose and frozen fingers."

"You know, while you're out at the lake house, if you can keep your mind off sex for a while, you could check out the gambling facilities. See if they have tables set up, with chips and all that stuff. Look in the wastebaskets for discarded notes or receipts. And check the bathroom to see if the girls leave their perfume and makeup handy for cleanups. Don't forget to ask about Carolyn's parents, who may be around."

"I envisioned this as a romantic interlude, Ruth. What you're suggesting is undercover stuff. I could wind up knocked off instead of knocked up."

Ruth laughed. "Try not to be either. We wouldn't want solving a murder to get in the way of your smooching. But we both know you can handle two jobs at the same time. Work on it. While you're having fun, think of me and Kit. We will be doing the dirty work in town. And from what Kit says, it's possible Paul will be so angry at her for getting involved in this case that she'll never get any more."

"Fat chance. He talks a tough line, but he spoils her to death, the same way Howard treats you." Tracy pouted. "Why can't I find someone to adore me?"

"You will, Tracy. Maybe Hal's the one, and you just need to give him the chance."

Tracy went to bed that night wondering whether she had lost her mind, her heart, or both.

TEN

The next morning, Paul cleared snow from his driveway and gave thanks for his Jeep. If he didn't pick up Tillie on the way to the clinic, she would never make it to the office. She'd had a wreck last winter and informed him that if he needed her at the office on days like this, he could come and get her. He did not mind, because days like this kept most patients from coming in, and it gave Tillie time to work on the files. When he arrived, she stood by the curb holding a large sack.

"Something smells good. Am I invited to lunch?"

She nodded. "Fried chicken. It's compensation for picking me up. My Bug would never make it in this snow, and I don't want to stay home all day, worrying by myself."

"What are you worrying about?"

"Tommy wouldn't come out of his room all day Sunday. I've been taking food to him and begging him to talk to me, but he won't. I don't know what to think. I guess he was crazy about that girl."

"Did you find out for sure whether he spent Saturday night at Brandon's fraternity house?"

"That's unclear. He went, but he won't say how long he stayed or what happened. I figure the police will be arresting someone any minute. I told Tommy to call me if he heard anything at school. I guess he will."

The telephone was ringing when they entered the clinic. Paul went to his office and Tillie soon followed.

"It's Tracy," she said and closed the office door.

Paul picked up the telephone. "Hello, Tracy. What are you up to?"

"Must I always be up to something?"

"Kit told me what the three of you plan to do. That's something in my estimation. I thought I made it clear what I thought of your interfering with police work."

"I'm not injecting myself into this case. The police chief did. I got a message from him 'inviting' me to come in and talk."

"That's strange. You're not a suspect, and finding the corpse doesn't give you any special knowledge about this case."

"On the contrary, I think I have more intimate knowledge of this matter than anyone else on the scene. I was there first and last, all the time collecting evidence. And I have pictures galore."

"All of which amounts to nothing."

"You underestimate the importance of my position as finder of the body. After the morning paper announced my involvement, everyone at the hotel began treating me like a celebrity. I suggested to the policeman who called that he come to the hotel to interview me so that he can take my picture in the lobby beside the Will Rogers statue. I can send it to my friends in Chicago."

"That would be real cute, I'm sure. However, the best part is that if you sit in the lobby all morning, you won't have time to get into more trouble. Too bad the clerk's office is closed because of the snow. You could have finished your work today and gone home."

"Sounds like you're trying to get rid of me, Paul. I also called to let you know that Hal is taking the day off, and he asked me out to the ranch. He's having the cook pack a picnic basket from the party leftovers, and he ordered logs laid in the fireplace over at the lake house. Sounds romantic doesn't it?"

"I thought we talked about this, Tracy. I can see no good coming from your getting involved with Hal. I told you he's married."

"Who said I was going to get involved? Seeing Hal is only one reason I'm going to the ranch. It's the perfect opportunity to investigate the murder. I want to find out more about the poker parties, how chummy Hal and Brandon were with Carolyn, and maybe meet her father and mother. I haven't ruled out either of them as suspects. And I think Hal knows more about this girl than he's revealing."

"Why do you say that?"

"She was beautiful, wasn't she? He's attracted to beautiful women. Please don't deny that. Carolyn lived on his ranch, and he can smell estrus a mile off. Kit and I agree that he's a prime suspect. In fact, it was her idea."

"Tracy!"

Tracy continued talking as if she had not noticed his reprimand. "We girls were discussing this case last night, and we decided the police department is bush league when it comes to understanding why women become murder victims. What this case needs is a force of inquiring female minds, persons not afraid to snoop, and who have the unique ability to make people talk. I'm a professional snooper, and Kit and Ruth are fast learners. We're going to call ourselves the Kit and Caboodle Investigation Agency. KCIA. What do you think?"

Paul sat at his desk, shaking his head. Tracy's sense of humor had been evident from the beginning, but for some reason this did not sound as funny as she meant it to be. And Kit was encouraging her to butt in where none of them had any business.

"Kit will let you know how the investigation goes," Tracy said and hung up. Grinning, she felt pleased at this little payback for all the trouble Paul had caused her over the birth certificate. She looked out the window at the deep snowfall. It was possible the roads would be closed, and her ill-conceived trip to the lake house might have to be canceled. However, Hal was not one to let bad weather interfere with his dating plans. One very rainy night after a movie, they had been stranded when the creek rose, and he was unable to take her home. She spent the night at his home, in his sister's room. It was after that episode that his mother enrolled him in Ada High.

Tracy wondered what would happen tonight if they were snowed in at the lake house. Would he take her to his home, or would they spend the night at the lake house? She smiled at the thought of his possible dilemma. It seemed like the perfect setting for the one-time event Tracy had fantasized.

She jumped out of bed and showered. Ruth was out getting bagels, coffee, and a newspaper. She returned just as Tracy was slipping into the soft, brown corduroy pants she had purchased last evening. The telephone rang as she pulled on her boots, and she hopped on one foot to answer it.

Kit was on the line gasping. "Oh, God, Tracy, I'm glad you're there. Charley found something else in the park." Her voice cracked.

"What else? Not another body!"

"No. But almost." Kit sounded panicky.

"Calm down and tell me what happened."

"Charley was following me when I went horseback riding. He ran ahead and started barking wildly farther down the trail. I called, but he wouldn't come, so I got off my horse and followed him. I kicked around in the snow until he pushed me aside and started digging like crazy. When he reached what looked like a piece of cloth, I pushed him away and pulled out a bloody pillowcase. Oh, Tracy, I'm afraid it's ..." Kit was sniffling.

"What? What does it look like, Kit?"

The line was quiet except for Kit's soft sobs, and it dawned on Tracy that this might be an important piece of evidence.

"Kit, calm down. Ruth and I will be there in ten minutes. Let us look at it before you call the police."

"Please hurry. I've got to unsaddle the horse. Go in the back door if I'm still at the barn," Kit said.

Tracy hung up the telephone, feeling her adrenalin pumping. Solving this mystery might prove easier than she had imagined.

"What happened?" Ruth asked.

"Get your coat. Charley dug up some evidence."

"What kind?"

"I don't know, but it's in a pillowcase. I hope it's what I think."

"Where did he find it?" Ruth asked.

"Kit didn't say exactly. It was in the park somewhere."

The phone rang again. Tracy looked at it, wondering if she should answer. Her voice was quiet and secretive.

"Miz Hunter? Is that you?" She recognized the police chief's voice.

"Yes, it is."

"Sorry to bother you again, but I wonder if you could come down to the office today? We've got your statement typed up, and we need you to sign it. I got a few more questions too."

"How long will it take?" Tracy was no longer confident. Her day was full, and she did not want the police department to know what she was doing.

"Oh, a half hour, I'd think."

"Can we do it tomorrow, sir? My day is full."

"The clerk's office is closed today because of the snow. Did you have other business in town?"

"I've made other plans, sir. Is there a particular rush to sign the papers?"

"Miz Hunter, when I crack the whip, people are in the habit of jumping. I guess under the circumstances, I could crack it tomorrow. You be in my office at eight o'clock in the morning, you hear?"

He hung up the phone and Tracy stared at it. Asking for a delay might have been a tactical error. Now that she had pissed off the police chief, he would be a lot less inclined to listen to theories the women hoped to propose. On second thought, they had nothing to propose at this time, so maybe his anger would not affect them.

"Who was that?" Ruth asked.

"The police chief. Come on. I'll tell you on the way to Kit's."

When they arrived at the Jordan home, Kit was running from the barn to the house, dodging Charley, who wanted to play. When he saw Tracy, he bounded toward her, leaving Kit behind. Tracy brushed the snow off the dog's coat and waited for Kit to open the door to the back porch.

"Charley, you stay out," Kit ordered, and he dropped his head and plopped down on the bottom step.

"This scares me to death," Kit said as she led them inside. "Are you sure you want to look at it?"

"No, but I think we'd better," Ruth said.

Kit had laid a grocery sack on newspapers spread on a work table on the back porch. The cloth bag protruding from the sack looked like a pillowcase. A monogram decorated the opening. "BRM."

"Somebody left a calling card," Tracy said as she memorized the initials. Snow and ice were melting in areas of the pillowcase, leaving it soggy and softening the scattered blood stains and dirt. Tracy opened it and moved back. The smell was nauseating. She took a deep breath and flipped the top further back. A lump of flesh the size of her fist lay curled in the folds of the cloth.

"Oh, God," Tracy said and closed the bag.

"Is it a fetus?" Kit asked.

"It looks like it. Yeah—a fetus."

"That's what I was afraid of."

"Where did you find it?" Ruth asked.

"Just down the path from where Carolyn's body was," Kit said. "I'm sure we'll be in trouble when Paul finds out we've interfered in this. How am I going to break it to him?"

"You couldn't very well leave it out there, with the dog digging around. Paul already knows we planned to snoop. I told him over the phone. I was trying to be funny, but when he warned me not to get you involved, I told him it was your idea." Tracy ducked her head, imitating Charley when he was scolded.

Ruth took charge. "Let's not apologize for what we're doing. Paul needs to get on board. Go ahead and call him."

Kit dialed the clinic, and they could hear Tillie's voice on the other end. Tracy poured three cups of coffee and searched in the refrigerator for cream. Fresh muffins on the countertop reminded her that she had forgotten to eat breakfast, and she looked at Kit for permission to take one. However, Kit was involved with Tillie, so Tracy took an extra to share with Ruth. They sat down at the table.

Tracy watched Kit at the telephone, as she waited with her mouth open over the muffin. She could hear Paul's voice, but his words were not clear.

Kit's voice rose as she tried to sound natural. "Nothing much, honey, but . . . I . . . I think you ought to come home. Right now. Right away, okay?" She hung up the telephone and dropped into the chair beside Ruth at the table.

Tracy choked on her muffin. "Kit, you've scared him to death. What's his number? I'll call him back." But she didn't have to. The phone rang, and Tracy picked it up.

"Kit?" Paul shouted.

"It's Tracy. Kit's right here, Paul. She's okay. She just had a bad experience this morning, but she's okay."

"What kind of bad experience?"

"While she was out riding, Charley found something that may be relevant to Carolyn's case. We were going to call the police, but Kit wanted you to see it first." Tracy was pleased that her professional demeanor had returned. Dealing with men did that to her.

"Don't touch anything until I get there." The phone slammed down, and Tracy replaced the receiver. To her dismay, Paul now seemed to be in charge.

"He's on his way. He wants us to wait to call the police until he gets here." Tracy sat down at the table and held a muffin toward Kit. "Did you have breakfast?" she asked.

"How can you eat at a time like this?" Kit, wringing her hands, began circling the table.

"I've never seen her when she couldn't eat," Ruth said. "And she never gets fat. There should be a law against people like her."

Kit shook her head and doctored her coffee. "She never gets out of control, does she? Me, I fall to pieces all the time. Paul helps to calm me down."

They heard the Jeep drive into the backyard, and the door slammed the moment the motor died. Kit ran to the back door, into Paul's arms. He hugged her before moving to the worktable where the pillowcase lay. Without speaking, he pulled it open and stared. "Where'd this come from?"

"Charley found it while Kit was riding around the lake this morning."

The muscle in Paul's jaw was twitching as he spoke to Kit. "And you called them instead of me or the police. I knew the three of you together were trouble." He glared around the circle.

"We called you before the police," Tracy said.

Paul sighed and opened the sack again. He backed off. "It's hard to say what it is. I'll call Matt."

"We're betting this is the fetus Carolyn wanted to get rid of," Tracy said, as he hung up the phone. She was not willing to have him think they were completely stupid.

"It could be," he said.

Tracy paced the floor. "It seems obvious that she couldn't have buried it. Someone else was involved."

Paul looked at her over his glasses. "That sounds like a brilliant deduction. Do you suppose you're the only one who will come to that conclusion?"

"No. But we may be the only ones curious enough to find out who that other person is."

"And how do you propose to start your investigation?"

Neither Kit nor Ruth answered.

"We should start with Mrs. Pittman," Tracy said. "It seems very likely that she knew Carolyn was pregnant and even that she had been bleeding. But why would she have taken her to the park under those conditions? And if she didn't take her, what does she know about who did?"

Paul looked at Kit. "This is much too serious a matter for the police to ignore, and they don't need the help of three rattlebrained junior leaguers who have nothing better to do than play games."

Kit's face flushed. "I don't belong to the junior league, thank you, and not one of us is rattlebrained. I know you well enough, Paul, to recognize your tactics. You always attack me when you can't argue with what I'm doing." Kit's voice was rising, and Tracy nodded her head in agreement. Ruth, who realized that husband-wife arguments can become volatile, backed off and reached down to pat Charley.

Kit was blinking away tears when Paul reached for her hand. "I'm sorry, honey, but people we love may be involved in ways you don't understand. I'm just asking you to back off and let the police do their job."

Kit nodded her head and wiped her tears. Tracy was not giving up so easily.

"People you love? Are you talking about Hal? Tommy? Maybe Tillie?"

The police department's Jeep came sliding to a halt in the front yard, and Paul hurried to the door without responding. He turned around. "You leave Tillie out of this. Do you understand?" Kit nodded, but Tracy and Ruth were noncommittal.

The chief gave a curt nod to the women, as Paul led him to the back porch, where he inspected the sack, muttered a loud "Humph," and placed it in a plastic bag, marked "Evidence."

"Let's go see where you found this," he said to Kit, and they all trailed along to the park. The chief carried his camera with him, which Tracy thought was an improvement over his past investigation.

While Paul and the police chief talked about how far apart the sites were, the women looked for a tool that could have been used to dig the grave. Charley and the snowfall had destroyed any evidence of footprints.

"Well, I guess this solves our case," the chief said. "I'll take this here fetus to the coroner as proof that the girl died from a self-inflicted abortion." His stare slid from Tracy's stony glare to Kit and Ruth. "Case closed," he announced and headed up the path with Paul.

Tracy held out her arms to delay the departure of her cohorts. "I beg to differ with that conclusion," she said. "How about you ladies? Do you think this case is solved?"

"No way," Ruth said. "Why would she have buried the fetus down the trail from where she performed the abortion?"

"And where did she get the pillowcase to put the fetus in? Those weren't her initials on it. Somebody else had to have been involved in this mystery," Kit said.

Tracy nodded, and they headed for the trailhead. "We will have to work fast to keep the coroner from rubber stamping the chief's analysis of how this death occurred." She spoke to Ruth. "Why don't you stay here with Kit while I'm at the ranch? You two make a list of suspects with motives and opportunities. That way we can decide what investigation needs to be done and divide the tasks among us. We'll start in the morning."

"Good idea," Kit said. "You look for evidence at the ranch. Ruth and I will outline what needs to be done first."

Tracy made a dash for the car. She didn't want to be late for her rendezvous with Hal.

ELEVEN

Tracy arrived at the hotel in time to take a quick shower. She slipped into the shirt and vest she had purchased from the local boutique. A knock on the door surprised her. Her expectation was that Hal would call from the desk, but here he was, holding an armload of yellow roses.

"Is milady ready?" he asked.

Tracy took the flowers and breathed deeply. She smiled at Hal. Even as a teenager, he had been the romantic, bringing candy on Valentine's Day and flowers for her birthday. He'd remembered that yellow roses were her favorites.

"Let me find a vase for these," she said, running around in her wool socks. She pulled dried flowers from a container on the bureau, filled it with water, and arranged each rose with care.

Hal leaned against the door and grinned. "I didn't intend for the roses to get all your attention. I should have brought something less appealing."

"Not on your life." Tracy placed the vase on the table beside her bed and came over to kiss him lightly on the cheek. "They're beautiful," she said. "Like old days."

He pulled her into his arms, and she breathed in the odor of Old Spice. Would she never forget? The essence was the same, but the warmth of his mouth against hers was like nothing they had known before. She trembled and wondered if she were making a big mistake. Where were her piranha instincts? Pulling away, she resorted to joking about the situation.

"Wow. Roses and kisses. This is my lucky day." She moved to the chair where her boots lay and put one foot in, pushing the heavy wool stocking against the leather.

"Let me help you," Hal said, and he bent on one knee in front of her. He placed her boot against his thigh and she pushed her foot into it. He picked up her other foot and massaged it for a moment before placing it inside the boot. The job completed, Hal pulled her face to his and kissed her again. "All done," he said. "Let's go."

Tracy adjusted her scarf in the mirror by the door and drew the coat she had borrowed from Kit over her shoulders. *You're right*, she thought. *It's too late to turn back now. It's already done.*

They hurried down the back stairs to his blue Dodge pickup, which was parked in the alley. He looked both ways, as if checking to see whether they were being observed, a reminder to Tracy that he was not a free man. Truth was, she thought, he was bent on committing adultery, and he had done it often enough to know how to cover his tracks.

Tracy felt a surge of anger at herself. Her intentions had been clear until now. She had planned to use him to put an end to the nagging wish to relive part of her past, no strings attached, no one hurt—just put an end to the dreaming. Ruth's warning that she would be interfering with his marriage had not daunted her. But if he had a mutual understanding with Muffy about other women, why was he sneaking out the back door of the hotel? Tracy saw her plan being lost in the shuffle. Hal was the one in control. She was being manipulated, and he seemed quite happy with himself. Was it too late to change her strategy? She gritted her teeth and followed.

They arrived at the lake house, where Hal turned off the motor and let the vehicle roll closer to the entrance. A small deer tiptoed out of the woods and moved to the edge of the lake. The doe looked at the pickup, and unconcerned, began drinking.

"Let's wait. There'll be others following her," Hal said, and he pulled Tracy close while they watched. Hal's eyes left the scene at the lake as he pushed Tracy's hair behind an ear. He kissed the soft indentation near her eye and his tongue moved over the skin to find her pulse. It was a signature touch he had made many times when they were teenagers, but now he was distracted when the doe lifted her head and shook it at an eight-prong stag moving out of the trees. The doe danced out of the water and ran into the woods. Snorting, the buck followed her.

"Show's over," Hal said and jumped out to open Tracy's door. The path to the house had been cleared, and he went ahead to open the cabin door. Inside, Tracy gazed at the beautifully set table, with a bottle of champagne cooling on the side.

"Hey, the table's set and the fire's going. Hershel's a good man."

Where was the picnic she had expected? Her eyes shifted to the man who had arranged this dinner. Handsome and suave, he moved to the kitchen and inspected the refrigerator to see that all of his directions for the meal had been executed. He opened the oven and the pungent smell of barbeque filled the room. Satisfied, he returned to the living room and threw another log on the fire. Tracy pulled her coat closer around the emptiness she felt. He must have done this many times, and she was just another notch on his six-shooter. That conclusion irritated her immensely. But why did she care?

She turned to the fire and frowned. Hershel, he had said, set the table and prepared the fire. A chill raced through her as she looked at the flames. Her first mission on this trip had been to seduce Hal. No problem. He was miles ahead of her. Her second assignment was to look for evidence of poker parties, or proof that Carolyn had met here with the man who impregnated her. Her father was on the list of possible villains. So was Hal, for that matter.

He interrupted her racing thoughts. "Are you up for a hike? I'd like to show you some of the ranch before we eat."

"Sure. I'd like that," she said, but first she needed to follow up on her suspicions. "Is this Hershel the one who lives in the trailer house?"

Hal looked surprised. "That's right. How did you know?"

"I found his daughter's body in the park. A policeman told us where she lived, and we saw her parents in the trailer park on Sunday, after we left the auction."

Hal knelt before the fireplace and stoked the logs he had thrown into the fire before. He spoke without looking at Tracy. "I heard what happened. Have they found out who did it?"

"No." Tracy tried to sound conversational, rather than like a police investigator digging for the truth. "Did you know Carolyn?"

"I don't remember the name. Brandon brings lots of girls around, but I don't pay much attention."

"You would remember this girl—a beautiful blond." Tracy leaned toward Hal to see his response.

He turned his back and walked to the kitchen.

"Sorry. My memory isn't that good."

Tracy shrugged her shoulders. Maybe the owner of such an empire as the Lost Creek Ranch, with oil wells on the side and influence in high places, did not associate with the families of his hired help. His mother had not. Tracy wavered, walking a tight rope, a little embarrassed that she had thought the worst of Hal, who was being the perfect host at a rendez-vous she had dreamed of for years and even encouraged when he called. Who was she to judge him? She decided to forget the investigation and pursue the dream.

Tracy patted the couch beside her as Hal returned from the kitchen. He pretended not to see her gesture. "Shall we go? It will get dark out there pretty soon," he said.

Tracy let her hand move off the couch. Hal had ignored her invitation. Where were the wolf instincts she had expected? Maybe this would be a quiet evening after all.

They walked in the heavy snow for half an hour, slogging to a forest of trees at the top of a hill, Hal holding her gloved hand as though he were afraid he would lose her. At the top of the hill, surrounded by fragrant cedar and pine trees, he pointed to the boundaries of the Lost Creek hold-ings on the south. Far away in the valley, ranch hands were throwing hay from trucks to a large herd of Herefords. The breadth of his holdings was awesome, and his wish to impress her was understandable.

"The cattle have to be pastured closer to the barns over the winter. The roundup should happen before the first snow, but this year, it came while we were busy with the auction. There's a thousand head over that ridge that we'll have to feed by tomorrow."

"When we were kids, did you think this is what you'd be doing for a living?" Tracy asked.

"No. I hated the ranch. I blamed Dad's job for what it did to my parents' marriage. He was always gone to meetings around the state, or to auctions. I didn't want to be like him. But I love raising cattle, and I'm good at breeding. We have a champion bull at the state fair almost every year. When Dad retired and moved to Mexico, I took over as manager. Then I made money in oil and decided to buy the ranch in order to be free to do things my way." He looked at Tracy. "The funny thing is, I'm more like my dad than I like to admit."

"Why did your father go to Mexico?"

Hal turned away, reluctant to discuss his parents' divorce. "He spent a lot of time with a woman he met down there. Finally got a divorce and went to live with her."

Somehow it didn't surprise Tracy to learn that Mr. Montgomery had spent his spare time with another woman. That accounted for all the lonely evenings Beatrice had filled by driving her son and his girlfriends to the movies before Hal had a driver's license. And now Hal admits he is like his father. Does that mean he has a mistress?

"Is that what happened to your marriage?"

"What do you mean?"

"Do you have a lady friend on the side?"

"No. Marriages can fail for other reasons." Hal turned to face Tracy. "As I told you, my marriage was arranged. Our mothers decided we would be the perfect couple because I had money and Muffy had political ties to the highest offices in the state. We allowed them to talk us into marriage while we were still in college. It was one of those cases where we were comfortable with each other, and assumed love would follow. I thought it might make me forget you. It seemed like a sensible thing to do at the time, but neither of us was happy. She finally left and went to work for her father."

He ran a finger along Tracy's cheek. "The only thing I knew about love was what I felt for you when we were in high school. Mother insisted that it was a childish infatuation, and that I would get over it. Maybe if my marriage had been better, I would have." He bent down and kissed Tracy lightly on the lips. "But I've never forgotten you." He pulled her coat tighter against the cold. "We'd better start back. It's getting dark."

The flames in the fireplace now glowed as embers. Hal threw on more apple wood, which crackled and sent heat across the room. While he tended the fire, Tracy threw her coat and scarf on a chair in the bedroom and returned to survey the enormous living room. She counted four round poker tables folded against the far wall. A number of folding chairs were stacked beside them, and a small side table held a number of boxes filled with chips and cards. Ruth had told her to look through waste baskets, and she saw them, empty, stacked inside each other. She would be able to report that there were poker tables at the lake house, but she could not determine whether they were for professional or family use. She sat down to remove her boots, and Hal came over to help.

"My toes got cold," she said. Hal clasped her left foot behind the heel, pulled off the boot and pushed her foot into the warmth of his crotch.

"That better?"

"Much better."

"How hungry are you?" he asked.

"It depends upon which appetite you're talking about." She would get him on the couch if it took all night.

Hal chuckled. "You always did know the right answers. Guess that's why you made A's in school."

Tracy smiled and lay back on the couch, her eyes closed. Hal pulled off his jacket and knelt before her, maneuvering both her feet to share the warmth of his body. She felt a swelling beneath her toes. She held her breath and felt her own body responding with an embarrassing dampness. No one had ever used her feet in an act of foreplay. What other pleasures were in store?

Hal continued to massage her feet until they warmed, then his hands moved higher, removing the corduroy pants and her undies in one smooth effort. She heard him undressing and, her eyes closed, she relaxed as her legs parted and she waited for his thrust. Instead he touched her wetness, pulled aside her shield of pubic hair, and gently massaged until juices flowed, as fragrant as honey. She gasped as he moved above her, filling her longing with his passion.

Her body shuddered in response to the slow and gentle thrusting. Marriage had not been like this. She tried to remember the disappointing experiences with her former husband, hoping it would slow down her response, but her body would not cooperate. "I have to go," she whispered, and an orgasm she couldn't control flooded her being like none she had ever had before. As it tapered, she became aware of Hal's own burst of energy, a long, explosive ending to her dream. Fulfilled, they lay satiated, not speaking for minutes. Tears came to Tracy's eyes as she realized how hard it would be to say, "This is it. It's over."

Hal moved to lie beside her. "Was that okay?"

"Better than okay."

"I wish we could have done this when we were dating. Our lives would have turned out much differently."

"Maybe. Who can tell? I don't think either of us was ready for this kind of grownup stuff, do you?"

"I must admit I thought about seducing you more than once, and I did a lot of dreaming about it. Guys didn't mess with nice girls."

"Because they expected to marry a virgin, which meant they had to leave some of us available for the wedding bells, right?"

"Something like that. You sound angry."

Her voice was tight. "Were you a virgin when you married?"

The room was deadly quiet. "No," Hal said.

"If I'm angry, that's the reason. I was being 'nice' while you were out tomcatting around."

"Not so. Not while I was dating you. It happened in college. The world had changed by then. Nice girls did do it. As I recall, my first time was instigated by the lady."

They lay without moving. Tracy felt her jaws clenching as she reviewed the mess she had made of her life. Where had she gotten the idea that consummating their teenage love was all she needed to be content with her past? Taking care of that problem had created another. She was afraid she would never forget tonight. The unknown was being replaced by the known. From now on, she would follow Ruth's advice and be more careful about what she wished for. In the meantime, she had to convince herself and Hal that it was over, finished, the end. The sooner she did, the easier it would be.

Tracy turned in his arms. "This not-so-nice girl thanks you for a lovely time. I came to put an end to painful memories from the past. We've done that, and now I say, let's drink a toast to their burial." She turned to rise, but Hal pulled her back.

"Wait," he said. "I don't buy that. This can't be the ending. I'm angry at myself for letting Mother ruin my life, but it's not too late to go my own way."

"Hal, I don't know what happened between you and your mother. For me, being rejected at that stage of my life was devastating. I've never been good at forgetting and forgiving, which I guess is why I've clung to our memories, wanting a chance to replay those times . . . not to change the ending, but I wanted to prove to both of us . . . " Tracy poked his chest with a finger. "You missed out on a good thing." She laughed. "How did I do?"

Hal lifted her hair from her face and eased his body over hers again, pushing himself inside before he spoke. "I agree, but just because I flubbed up once doesn't mean I'll do it again. I'm not a quitter. You won't get away this time."

Tracy felt her body go numb. Changing the ending meant staying together, maybe marrying. That had not been her goal. From what she had learned of his possible involvement in Carolyn's death and money laundering for Senator Fortenberry, the idea of marrying him seemed even more far-fetched. However, all argument was lost in their coupling, which was rapid. No time for gentleness. Tracy gasped at the sharp spasms rocking her body as it responded to the forceful thrusts above her. She shuddered, fearful of where this passion might take them. She held on tightly until he collapsed and pulled away. Without waiting to relax in his arms, Tracy rose and moved to stand in front of the fireplace.

Hal followed and put his hands on her shoulders. "I'm sorry," he said. "I got carried away. I didn't hurt you, did I?" He pulled her into his arms, pressing her cheek to his chest. "It's been a long time for me. I'm not as promiscuous as you imagine. I'll be more careful next time."

Tracy shook her head and rubbed her eyes. "No. I was just surprised. I've never experienced anything like this before."

"Why the tears?" Hal asked.

"I don't know. I was just overwhelmed, I guess." She took a deep breath and moved over to the couch, where she began dressing.

"I meant what I said. I'm here to change the ending." He, too, began dressing.

"Sometimes the known is better than the unknown, Hal. I didn't intend for this to make things worse for us. Maybe we should have let well enough alone."

"No way," he said. "I'm glad it happened. And it's just the beginning. Come on, let's eat and do it again. I'll change your mind, or else."

In stocking feet, they gathered food from the refrigerator and removed the barbecue from the warming oven. Hal added more ice to the champagne bucket and opened the bottle.

The fire was reduced to coals by the time they finished their dinner. Hal smiled. "Nothing like having all of our appetites satisfied at once. Let's try the bed this time."

They slipped out of their clothing and touched the chilly bedding.

Tracy straddled his body. "You can warm the sheets," she said, and lowered a nipple to his lips.

"Mumm." He nuzzled the other breast, and she melted into his arms.

An hour later he was breathing in a light sleep, and Tracy rolled off the bed.

He woke. "Don't go," he said. "Let's spend the night."

"No," Tracy said, "I need time to decompress before I get interviewed by the police chief in the morning. I think we now know what might have been. Let's leave it at that."

"You're a hard woman to bargain with," Hal said, as they carried their clothing to the couch by the fireplace

"I'm sorry, but Ruth is expecting me back, and I have to be at the police station at eight in the morning." She walked into the bedroom to recover the items she had left on the night table and to get her coat, all the time listening to Hal banging around in the living room. Her foot extended beneath the edge of the bed as she straightened the covers, and something hard pushed against the sole of her boot. She reached down and picked up what looked like a boy's high school senior ring. It had a thick roll of adhesive tape around the band to reduce its size so that it wouldn't fall off a girlfriend's finger. Tracy had worn one like this when she was a senior in high school. It hadn't been Hal's. She reached over to lay the ring on the night table.

"Why are you going to the police station?" Hal called.

Tracy's mouth opened to respond. She stared at the ring. She was going to the police station to answer questions about Carolyn's death, and this ring might prove to be a key piece of evidence—evidence she had come here to collect. It was unlikely that an older woman would have worn it. She bet it had been on the dead girl's finger at one time, and that she had taken it off while she was in this bed. Why? Because she was in bed with someone other than the high-school boy who had given her the ring! That boy could be Tommy Bucco, Tillie's son. Tracy pulled at the tape, but it would not tear away. She would need a knife or scissors to get it off so that she could look for the owner's initials. Without hesitating, Tracy dropped the ring into her coat pocket. She looked around the room for other evidence but found nothing, so she walked back into the living room.

"The chief wants me to sign a statement about how I found Carolyn's body. Nothing serious." She looked with wide eyes at Hal's back. He acted so normal that it seemed impossible that he could be involved in Carolyn's death.

They were silent throughout the ride to town, giving Tracy time to run various scenarios through her mind concerning the ring. First, she had to find out if it were Tommy's. Perhaps the two had used this hideout for their necking parties. Or could Carolyn have tried to hide it from Hal while they were in bed together? If so, had he lied about not knowing the girl? How about Brandon? He could not be eliminated as a suspect. It would be the perfect place to bring a girl he wanted to seduce. Carolyn's family had moved here during the summer while Brandon was home from college. The workers' campground was just down the road.

It was dark when they pulled into the alley behind the hotel. They walked up the three flights of stairs, and Hal put her key in the door, looking both ways down the hall.

"Ruth will be asleep," Tracy said, reaching for the door knob. She stood on tiptoes to kiss him goodnight. His arms penned her between his chest and the door.

"When will I see you again?"

"I don't know, Hal. I have a little more work to do here in town, and then I have to go home. It's been great seeing you again. Thanks for everything." Truthfully, "everything" had left her feeling empty, afraid she was learning to lie as easily as Hal.

"This isn't over. We'll work something out." His eyes were dark and troubled, the same way she felt. Her impulse was to say, "Yes," to comfort him, but she shook her head and inserted the key in the door without responding. As the door closed, his rapid footsteps echoed down the stairway.

Inside, Tracy threw her coat on a chair and collapsed on the bed, exhausted from the emotions of the evening. She longed for Ruth's calming counsel, but her sister was snoring, deep in sleep. Tracy curled into a fetal position and went to sleep on top of the covers, still dressed.

TWELVE

The strident ring of the telephone woke Tracy the next morning. She heard the noise of water spraying in the shower and Ruth's latest rendition of "Gonna wash that man right out of my hair." She looked at the clock. It was eight thirty. *Oh, my God. I was supposed to be at the police station at eight o'clock.* She reached for the telephone.

"Miz Hunter, is that you?"

"Yes, it is," she said. "I'm so sorry, Chief. I was sick last night, and I overslept. I'll be there in half an hour."

"I think that would be in your best interest, ma'am." The telephone clicked dead.

Tracy stripped off her clothing. Her mind was numb, and she wondered how she would be able to answer the police chief's questions. *Oh, God*, she thought. *I hope he doesn't ask where I was last night, or whether I know anything about a lost high-school ring.*

Ruth hurried out of the shower with a towel covering her damp body. She backed against the wall as Tracy rushed past her. "Well, pardon me," she said.

"Sorry," Tracy yelled. "That was the police chief calling, and I'm late for my appointment."

Ruth set about dressing, mumbling "You're always late for your appointments."

Tracy ran out of the shower wondering if her mane of unwashed hair still carried the scent of Hal's shaving lotion. Late or not late, she did not have time to shampoo and dry her hair. She pulled on a turtleneck sweater and rolled it high to her chin, covering the scratches Hal's beard had left on her throat.

"What are you mumbling about?" she asked.

"I said being late to an appointment is nothing new with you." Ruth grinned. "Maybe your excuses are, though. How did it go last night?"

Tracy stopped and stared at Ruth. "You won't believe this. Under the bed, I found a high-school ring that some high-school girl must have lost while she was romping around. It could have been Carolyn. We've got to figure out who. As soon as I'm through with the police chief, I'll come back here. Call Kit and see when we can meet to go over the possibilities." She dashed out the door, leaving Ruth standing with her mouth open.

"What were you doing under the bed?" she called.

Still worrying about being late, Tracy hurried into the police station and was told to have a seat. The chief was busy. She wished she had not hurried. She picked up *Women Out West Magazine* from the coffee table. Seated next to her was a woman who looked familiar, and Tracy kept sneaking looks at her from behind the magazine. It dawned on her that this was Carolyn's mother, the woman they had seen at the ranch. Maybe they could talk. She glanced at the receptionist's counter. It was far across the room, and the receptionist was hidden behind a Plexiglas window. Tracy moved to a chair beside the woman.

"Mrs. Pittman?"

The woman's head jerked toward her, eyes wide and frightened.

Tracy held out her hand. "I'm a friend of Dr. Jordan's. Visiting here from Chicago. The police are asking me questions about your daughter, because I'm the one who found her in the park." Mrs. Pittman frowned as Tracy made her introduction. Her brows drew together, and Tracy was tempted to stop talking when she saw the tears, but looking at the police chief's office, she felt stronger.

"I wonder if we could meet and talk sometime. I'm a police detective from Chicago, and I'm concerned that the police here may drop this case and never find out why Carolyn died." She stopped talking and looked at the mother for a response.

"Carolyn was a good girl. I don't know who could have done this to her, unless it was that Indian boy." The woman's voice was deep, like a man's, and Tracy worried that it might carry to the receptionist office, but there was no movement there. She leaned closer and whispered, "Do you know where Louie's Roadhouse is, out on the highway?"

The woman nodded.

"Can you meet me there as soon as we're through here, so we can talk?"

Mrs. Pittman shook her head. "I ain't got a way to git there."

"Then wait for me outside. I'll pick you up as soon as I've talked to the chief."

"I work at the school. I just got enough time off to come down here."

"They won't know how long this appointment will take. I'll drop you off at the school as soon as we're through." The woman nodded as the door from the chief's office opened. Tracy hid behind her magazine.

Mr. Pittman walked out of the office, looked at his wife, and jerked his thumb over his shoulder.

"He's ready to see you," he said. "I'm going back to the ranch. You can catch the bus back to work." The man was angry and in a hurry.

Mrs. Pittman walked into the office, leaving the door open. Tracy sighed as she watched the receptionist pull a pack of cigarettes from her blouse pocket and head toward the back of the building. She heard her speak to someone, and there was laughing and a rattling of cups. It would take at least ten minutes for her to smoke a cigarette and drink coffee. Tracy moved to the chair closest to the office door and pulled out her notebook and pen. The front door squeaked open. Letting her hair fall forward to cover her face, Tracy doodled on the pad. The footsteps stopped, and she glanced over her lap to see a pair of cowboy boots and the legs of a blue uniform in front of her. Her eyes swept upward to the face of Sergeant Falco. She remembered seeing his vehicle at Louie's Barbecue when she and Ruth met with Paul and her surprise when he showed up with Paul and Ruth at the auction on Sunday. He smiled down at her as though they were the best of friends. "Good morning, ma'am."

Tracy nodded.

"We keep running into each other," he said. "You remember Sunday, out at the park. And again at the cattle auction. Didn't know you came down from Chicago to buy cattle." His voice was casual as he walked over to the receptionist's window and leaned one hand on the counter, giving Tracy room to admire him, head to boot. Pleats down his shirt front stretched over a muscled physique. He was slim, with boots and a cowboy hat that Tracy suspected were standard police uniforms in Oklahoma, attire intended to make the public feel safe in his presence. Tracy felt like bait set for the pounce of a mountain lion.

She nodded. "I remember you."

Falco flushed with pleasure, and Tracy regretted having massaged his ego.

"How long will you be in town?" he asked.

Tracy started to answer, thinking it was a business question, but Falco's nose was actually twitching as he waited for an answer.

"I'm leaving right away," she said, pleased to see air leaving his chest like a deflating balloon.

"Anything I can do to help you while you're here, just let me know," he said, and he walked past her into the police chief's office.

"Damn," Tracy said under her breath as the door closed. She'd hoped to hear the conversation with Mrs. Pitman. She looked through the opening in the Plexiglas window and saw that she could reach the telephone if she stretched on tiptoes. She pulled it out and dialed Kit's number, relieved when she answered.

"Kit, this is Tracy. I can't talk long. Can you and Ruth meet me at Louie's Roadhouse in about thirty minutes? Mrs. Pittman will be with me."

"I think so. How did you manage that?"

"She's here at the police station, and I talked to her for a minute." Tracy heard the receptionist walking down the hall. "Oops. Gotta go." She replaced the telephone and smiled at the sour-faced woman, who glared back at her, not sure why she should be suspicious.

"Had to call home," Tracy explained, and then realized she didn't have a home, or if she did, it would have required a long distance call. She sat down and hid behind her magazine again.

She was surprised when Mrs. Pittman came out of the interview after ten minutes. Tracy looked the other way hoping no one would guess that the two women were acquainted.

Sergeant Falco's smile revealed beautiful teeth as he beckoned Tracy into the office.

"Found any more bodies in the last few hours?" The chief's voice was mocking as he pushed a typed document with a carbon copy across his desk.

"No, sir." She read the brief description of what she had told the police on Sunday. It was correct, and she signed it.

"Good." He looked at her over his glasses. "The coroner says the pillowcase had a fetus in it. Guess you knew that when you found it."

"I didn't find it."

"That's right. You were just visiting with the Jordans, who turned it in. Guess the doctor knew what it was."

"I think he did, but I'm not a specialist in that area. Why would you expect me to know what it was?"

"I don't know what your area of expertise is, ma'am. Every time I turn around, you're snooping into places where you got no business. I hear you're a private investigator. For your information, my department does the investigatin' in this town, and we don't need any outside agitators butting into our affairs."

Tracy felt like a naughty student, sent to the principal's office.

Falco stood leaning against the window sill, out of his boss's view, and he gave her a supporting smile that disappeared when the chief added, "You could get yourself into a lot of trouble if you're one of them women's rights people, come here to inform the local lady folks on how to get abortions."

He frowned, waiting for her to refute those charges. Tracy stood up and leaned with both palms on the chief's desk. "I beg your pardon. I didn't come to this office to be insulted or accused. I graduated from the University of Illinois with a major in criminal justice, plus I attended a number of classes on this subject at the police academy, before I decided to become a private investigator. You can be assured that I know what is legal and what is illegal. Abortions are illegal in this state unless it's to save the mother's life, and if I were involved in such an action, I could be denied a license to work in my field. I'm not an outside agitator, and if you're going to keep up this line of accusations, I want an attorney present."

Falco strolled across the room and stood near the door. He checked the chief's demeanor to see what he should be thinking.

Tracy's face was red, and the chief rolled his chair away from the desk to avoid her hot breath. He walked to the window. "Sorry, Miz Hunter, but this case has me befuddled. I talked to a few of the high-school kids yesterday, and they pretended they didn't know this Pittman girl. Swore they hadn't seen her Saturday night. I'm not making any progress with

the parents either. They didn't keep very close tabs on her whereabouts."
Tracy straightened, and the chief turned back to his desk and sat down,
his good-old-boy tactics exuding friendliness. *Playing the good cop*, Tracy
thought.

She backed away from the desk but remained standing, cautious of
what was coming.

"You seem like a smart woman, Miz Hunter. Maybe you're looking
to do some government work while you're here?"

"What do you mean 'government work'?"

"FBI, maybe?"

"No."

"They're swarming all over the place, buttin' into the doctor's case.
Makes it hard for us to do our business. I wouldn't want 'em trying to
make this local case into a federal fiasco."

"I assure you, I'm not working with the FBI."

"What's your special interest in Carolyn Pittman, you being from
Chicago and all?"

"Carolyn Pittman was an innocent young girl who should not have
died. She should not be buried and forgotten about, so the murderer can
go free to prey on other women. I've been a police officer for ten years, so
my interest in such cases comes naturally." Tracy's voice had risen, and
the chief placed his arms across his chest as though to protect himself.

"Maybe you've got some ideas on how to follow up on this evidence we got then. Maybe they taught you that at the academy." He
paused, reluctant to concede further ground. "Where would you go
from here?"

Tracy was taken aback. Was he asking her for advice? Or perhaps he
was trying to find out how much she knew. It was much too early to show
her cards. On the other hand, she might learn more by playing his game
than by folding. "Have you gotten the coroner's report?" she asked.

"Naw. Won't have it 'fore Wednesday. Coroner's been tied up over in
Waters County. Comin' back tonight, I think."

"Maybe that will help," Tracy said. "Once we know how she died,
we can eliminate those people who couldn't have had a hand in it." Tracy
was shocked that she was aligning herself with this unimpressive police
department, but that was better than being a suspect. And it was possible
this man wanted to find the killer.

"I guess you're right. We'll have to wait. Thanks for your time." He rose and nodded for Falco to see her to the door. "Keep in touch," he called as she hurried out the door, not quite sure what had happened.

Mrs. Pittman sat on a bench in front of the building, appearing as though she were waiting for the bus. Tracy stopped the car, and the woman scrambled in. Tracy turned her head to check the traffic and caught a glimpse of Falco walking away from the window in the police chief's office.

Kit and Ruth were sitting in the car at Louie's when Tracy and Mrs. Pittman arrived. They all walked inside and were seated near a window. Tracy was disgruntled at the sight of Sergeant Falco pulling into a parking place. Her suspicions were correct; Falco was following her. The question was, why? Perhaps the police were not incompetent, but it seemed a waste of time and effort to have her followed. She couldn't be a suspect unless they thought she had something to do with the abortion. The waiter appeared and they ordered. As he left, Kit leaned toward Mrs. Pittman.

"We need to know who picked Carolyn up from your house Saturday night, and what time they left."

"That's what the policeman asked, and I'm sorry, but I shore don't know. I went to town Saturday night with friends who live next door. We played bingo in the church basement in town.

"What time did you get home?"

"Between eleven-thirty and twelve."

"And your husband was home already?"

"Yes, ma'am, he was asleep. They've been working awfully hard with the auction, and he was plumb wore out."

"Was Carolyn home when you arrived?" Tracy asked.

"Yes, ma'am. She was asleep too." The woman's eyes shifted away from Kit, and she concentrated on her food.

"A police officer said he was called out to your house this month because your husband had been beating on you. Is that true?" Ruth asked.

Mrs. Pittman swallowed and laid aside her fork. It rattled against the plate. "Yes, ma'am. When he gits drunk, he gits mean."

"Did he ever beat up on Carolyn?"

The woman's lips disappeared in a straight line. "Hershel didn't beat on Carolyn. He was too loving to her, if anything."

"What do you mean he was too loving?"

"He spoiled her. Carolyn could do no wrong as far as her daddy was concerned. He gave her everything she asked for."

"Did he know she was pregnant?" Kit asked.

"No, he didn't, and he says if he finds out who did it, he'll kill him. I hope he don't go to prison."

The three inquisitors sympathized with her—feeling her pain—but were stunned that she was more concerned with her own needs than she had been with Carolyn's. Tracy got back to the purpose of their visit. "What else did the police chief ask?"

"He asked a lot of questions about where we came from, whether either of us had a jail record. He wanted to know who could have gotten Carolyn pregnant, which makes me mad. How did he know she was pregnant?"

Tracy was reluctant to reveal the discovery of the fetus. "There was a lot of blood on her dress and legs. It looked like an abortion or miscarriage had taken place. The autopsy will tell for sure, but the coroner is out of town and won't be back until Wednesday. I gather you didn't know she was pregnant?"

Mrs. Pittman lowered her chin to her chest. "I went with her to see Dr. Jordan last week. He didn't tell me, but I guessed it. I can tell you I was suspicious. When we first moved here, last spring—it was June, after school was out—that Brandon kept driving over to the house and begging her to go riding with him. She did, a few times. I don't know where they went or what they did. Me and Carolyn had words about him, but then she started dating that Indian boy when school started. I figured Brandon was a better match. At least he has money and could have taken care of her."

All three women sighed.

Mrs. Pittman continued. "Lately, she'd been going with her dad to the lake house on poker nights. She fixed their coffee and served snacks. She liked to get out of the house, and it seemed safe enough with her dad there."

"Do you know of anyone else she could have had sex with?" Tracy was writing and asking questions at the same time.

"No, ma'am."

"Did you talk to the police about the poker games?"

"No. I don't know nothing about them. That's Hershel's business." Mrs. Pittman looked at her plate and frowned. "Hershel got into trouble in Texas and spent time in jail for assaulting a sheriff's deputy. It was silly. He was drunk. He's not a bad man. He wouldn't hurt Carolyn."

Tracy was not impressed. Mrs. Pittman's defense of her husband was both a good sign and a worrisome one. Wives often turn their heads when a father abuses their daughters. How could they find out whether Mrs. Pittman was lying, or perhaps was ignorant of his actions?

"One last question," Tracy said. "Was Carolyn wearing Tommy's high-school ring?"

Mrs. Pittman nodded. "She wore it on a chain around her neck most of the time. She didn't wear it on her finger around home. Her daddy was pretty strict with her."

"Did you know she lost it?"

Mrs. Pittman frowned. "I wondered why it wasn't in her things that the coroner gave us."

They finished eating, and the waiter cleared the table and left his bill.

"We have to hurry," Tracy said. "I need to get Mrs. Pittman back to her job." She nodded to Kit. "Maybe you could drop her off. That policeman keeps following me." She glanced toward Falco. "He'll no doubt tell Mayfield we met with Mrs. Pittman, and the chief could call one, or all of us, in by tomorrow to ask what we've been talking about. Let's get together again as soon as we can. I'll be busy at the clerk's office, but it won't take all day."

"Why don't I take Ruth home with me, and we'll go over the evidence we have. I can bring her back if we finish before you do." Kit turned to Mrs. Pittman. "Thank you so much for coming. Please try to remember the names of everyone Carolyn talked about, especially the school kids she knew. And listen at school for any rumors about where she was Saturday night, okay?"

Kit left money for the waiter, and they headed for the door.

The sergeant turned his back to them, but Tracy watched as he entered his vehicle and pulled out behind Kit. She was pleased to see that he was focused on Mrs. Pittman rather than herself.

Tracy wanted Paul to confirm Mrs. Pittman' story about Carolyn's physical examination, but first she had to get to the clerk's office to get the paper work started on her birth certificate.

THIRTEEN

Tracy drove to the county clerk's office, a stark, brick building on Main Street. The mistake on her birth certificate must have started here on its way to the State Bureau of Vital Statistics, so it seemed the appropriate place to seek the amendment. She ran up the concrete steps and opened the heavy door. A long line of people stood in front of the information window. Tracy took her place at the back of a line of women dressed either in heavy wool sweaters or long coats over cotton dresses. Wool scarves covered their heads and wound around their necks, falling to their waists. Most had rubber galoshes to protect their shoes from the six-inch snowfall, while others wore shoes laced above their ankles. Tracy felt transported to the past, a time when her mother dressed much the same way.

When she arrived at the window, she pushed her birth certificate toward the clerk.

"I got this in the mail. It's not my real one, and it's filled with mistakes. Can you tell me how to get the one with my right name on it?"

The clerk looked at the document and then at Tracy. She stared at the name and said, "Hunter? Are you Tracy?"

"Yes, ma'am. How did you know?"

"I'm Bonnie Heydt. Your sister Ruth and I were best friends in school. I used to spend the night with her. I remember you and Emily as real pests."

"Oh, Bonnie. I remember, too. You know, Ruth's in town with me.

She'll want to see you. I'll tell her where you are as soon as I get back to the hotel."

"Please do. Tell her to come by, and we'll have lunch."

"Can you believe this birth certificate?" Tracy said. "I ordered it last month and discovered that Dr. Jordan put the wrong name on it. I hope you can help me get the right one, or fix this one, whichever is easiest."

"Amending it is easy. You just have to get evidence of the name you used when you were little. You'll find that in church and school records."

"So you've fixed problems like this before?"

"Oh, yes. Birth certificates have lots of mistakes."

"Where do I start?" Tracy asked.

Bonnie explained what evidence Tracy had to collect to make the changes and pushed a form toward her. "Fill this out and bring it back. Are you living in Ada now?"

"No. I live in Chicago. I came down to visit Ruth and to get this matter straightened out. I appreciate your help. I'll tell Ruth I saw you, and I'll get these things back to you as soon as I can." She scribbled her name and hotel room number on a piece of paper and pushed it toward Bonnie.

Downstairs, it proved easy to order her school records. She left the application and walked up the stairs, slowing at the sight of Falco leaning against the wall, surveying the room. His eyes slid over her, then pretended interest in a group gathered near the back door.

The clock on the wall said twelve noon. Tracy hurried out of the building and reached her car, slamming the door as the sergeant ran down the steps, making no effort to hide his presence. Pulling out of the parking lot, she watched as Falco's Jeep eased into the traffic behind her. Angry, she decided to be direct. She would go to the police chief and complain. Maybe to appease her, he would share the latest information from the coroner's report.

Falco beat her to the office. He was entering through the side door as she parked, leaving the impression that he could not have been following her. She approached the grim-faced receptionist and asked to see the chief. The receptionist looked up as Mayfield and Falco came from the kitchen with fresh cups of coffee.

"Hello there, young lady," the chief greeted her. "Come on in. Would you like coffee? I believe there's still some donuts left, if you'd like one."

"No, thanks. I've had my limit today." Tracy regretted lying. There had been no time to stop for coffee, and in her paranoia she wondered if Falco knew that as well as she did. He smiled and touched her arm, guiding her into the office.

"Do you have the coroner's report?" she asked, as she moved away from him to a chair.

The chief shook his head. "No, but I talked to the man over there in the office. He said the girl bled to death like we thought. Looks like a botched abortion. If the fetus is hers, and there's no reason to believe it ain't, she was about four months along. We have loose ends to tie up, but it looks like a closed case." The police chief looked at Tracy as if expecting her to cheer the good news.

"How do you suppose her body got to the city park?" Tracy asked.

The chief paused, not happy with the question. He squirmed in his chair, then stacked some papers in a neat pile on his desk while he spoke. "We figure she aborted the fetus herself or with a friend's help, and they buried it. While she was still there, she hemorrhaged and died. Whoever was with her panicked and covered her up."

Sergeant Falco coughed, and Tracy waited until he had cleared his throat.

"Did you discover who might have buried the fetus so far from where her body was found?" Tracy's voice was ragged with anger. The chief only stared at her, as Falco moved to a table to pour a glass of water. He held it toward Tracy, silently asking if she'd like some. She paid no attention to him, and he drank it himself.

"Was there semen in her body?" Again Tracy knew the answer. She was sure they hadn't looked for that evidence.

"Wouldn't be able to tell after the abortion, but I doubt if sex was on her mind." The chief looked at Tracy over his glasses.

"It may have been on someone else's mind," Tracy said. She allowed her eyes to flicker toward Falco.

"I guess we'll never know," the chief said.

"So, where do you go from here?" Tracy asked.

"I'll do a little asking around, but I don't expect to find out who was with her. Nobody's going to volunteer that kind of information." He smiled at his joke.

"Suppose the abortion wasn't self-inflicted. Suppose she was raped and beaten. In that case, we may have a murderer roaming around the neighborhood." Tracy paused and watched the smile disappear from the man's face before she continued. "Perhaps the coroner's report will clarify things."

"Should be in the mail today," the chief said. "Of course, we don't make those public."

Unless you get a subpoena, Tracy thought. That wouldn't be hard to do, but it would take time and cooperation from the court.

"What have you discovered about Dr. Smeltzer's murder?" she asked.

A dark flush covered the chief's face and Falco turned white.

"And what interest do you have in that case?"

"Nora Smeltzer was a friend of mine. We roomed together in college. I'm very interested in what happened to her."

"I wouldn't advertise that if I wuz you, ma'am. She died under suspicious circumstances, and the killers may still be around."

Falco nodded, his eyes wide.

"Are you threatening me?" Tracy asked.

The chief pushed away from his desk and walked over to the window, slapping his hands together as he turned to face her. "Miz Hunter, you're a very hard person to get through to. What I'm telling you is for your own good. Keep your nose out of police business, particularly the doctor's case. Hers ain't what you call a run-of-the-mill murder. It's got all the signs of a professional hit, and down here they won't hesitate to hit twice."

Tracy stood. "So it is a threat. Thanks for the warning, Chief. I have one more question. Why is this officer following me?" She nodded toward Falco, but stared at Mayfield. The chief cut his eyes toward Falco, who blushed and continued to clear his throat.

Mayfield's voice was patronizing. "Miz Hunter, you ought to understand that your arrival in this town on the same weekend that we found Dr. Smeltzer's body over in Arkansas, and now this young girl dead from an abortion, raises a few questions in our minds. We suspect you are here snooping around for them people supporting abortion rights. You've shown an unusual interest in the death of this high-school girl for no good reason we can determine. You're not a relative. You didn't even know her family, according to your statement, but I noticed you picked up Miz Pittman after you left my office this morning. What was that all about?"

Tracy felt her adrenaline pumping. The chief leaned back in his seat and looked at her. "I thought I made it clear last time you were in here that we don't put up with outside agitators, especially anyone settin' out to stir up the women folk with abortion rights handouts." He leaned over, picked up a pile of stacked papers on his desk, and pitched them toward Tracy. "You left these in a magazine you were reading when you were here this morning."

Tracy leaned over to inspect the leaflets, being careful not to leave fingerprints. She had never seen them before. She felt her heart throbbing, but her voice remained cool. If she were going to be set up as an outside agitator, she might as well act like one.

"I guess that's the answer to the question of why I'm being followed." She stood up. "You know it's laughable to call me an outside agitator. Agitating isn't a crime unless you're inciting a riot. If you think otherwise, you should be out there arresting the demonstrators down at the Women's Health Clinic." She waited to let that charge explode in his brain.

"Second," she said, "every citizen has the right to question a suspicious death anywhere in this country. Carolyn Pittman didn't cover herself with leaves and tree limbs. Whoever did either killed her or is an accessory to the crime. Most officers of the law wouldn't wait around for the perpetrator to walk in and confess."

Tracy watched the chief's face turn purple. Falco's was pale when she turned to him. "You're wasting a lot of gasoline and precious time stalking me, Sergeant. I suggest you leave me alone and go look for the murderers." She walked out of the office, leaving the door open. She heard what sounded like a fist slamming onto a desk, then the chief's voice fuming, "God-damned woman. Don't let her out of your sight. We can't afford to have the FBI nosing around on this case."

Tracy walked out of the building and sat in her car. So it was the FBI he was worried about. That's why he had asked her whether she was working for them. It made sense that federal investigators would be searching for Nora's killers, and that they would be suspicious of the fact that the police department was paying no attention to the demonstrators' efforts to close down her clinic. The question was how Carolyn's death fit into the picture. Tracy suspected the police didn't want the death of a pregnant high-school girl to create attention that would support the involvement of federal agents.

Tracy left the parking lot and pulled into a service station. Falco drove past, no longer bothering to hide his surveillance. She hurried to the pay telephone and called Kit, who answered on the first ring.

"Hi, Kit. I came down to the clerk's office to get started on my birth certificate and discovered that the sergeant is still following me. That makes it impossible for me to meet with you and Mrs. Pittman. Can you call her and set up a time for you and Ruth to visit?"

"Okay, but it would help to have you with us. You know the questions we need to ask."

"Find out everything you can about Carolyn's friends and where she was every minute of her life for the past few weeks. Also, I found out the coroner's report is finished and in the mail."

"Good. What does it say?" Kit asked.

"The police chief says she died from hemorrhaging, caused by an abortion. I'm going over to the coroner's office now to see if I can get a copy of the report. If I have to get a subpoena, we will need a lawyer."

"I'm sure Vera Summers will help us. She has a general practice and does all kinds of law in this town."

Tracy jotted down the lawyer's name for future reference. "Oh, and tell Ruth I met Bonnie Heydt at the county clerk's office. She wants Ruth to call her, so that they can get together for lunch."

"Done," Kit said.

FOURTEEN

Tracy was starving, despite what she had told Chief Mayfield, so she decided to return to the hotel café. She called upstairs, hoping Ruth could join her for supper. There was no answer. She and Kit must have found a lot to discuss. Having skipped lunch and weary from riding the emotional roller coaster she'd been on since arriving in Ada, the mother's meatloaf, as advertised on the menu, sounded much better than she expected it to taste. She ordered two, adding the take-out service for Ruth.

A scattering of people sat in the small café off the main floor of the hotel. Tracy chose a seat near the windows, with her back to the door. Eating alone offered the advantage of avoiding contact with anyone except the waiter. Tracy wanted peace. The falling snow outside the window calmed her. She smiled at a cottontail rabbit huddled under the bush nearest the window.

Surprised at the taste and texture of the meatloaf, Tracy closed her eyes and chewed slowly, thinking of her mother's specialty. As she looked up, Hershel Pittman seated himself at the table next to hers. He faced her, as though wanting her attention. What business could he have at the hotel? Perhaps he was conferring with Hal's mother, who lived upstairs. Could their common interest be Carolyn's death?

Tracy waited until he was served a plate of food similar to hers. She rested her chin on her hand and behind her fingers, spoke his name. "Mr. Pittman."

He looked up, his eyes acknowledging her.

"We need to talk."

Pittman continued chewing, but looked around the room. "Cain't talk here," he said.

Tracy nodded and looked at her plate. "Meet me downstairs in the garage. I'm driving an Avis rental, black Thunderbird. I'll go down there as soon as I've finished eating."

He nodded again. Tracy wished that Ruth had returned to the hotel, or that she could call Kit. Meeting a man who might be involved in Carolyn's murder in the basement parking lot was risky.

Mr. Pittman avoided looking at her, so Tracy took the opportunity to memorize the features she had seen from a distance at the ranch. He was approximately five feet, nine- or ten-inches tall, an inch or two shorter than Tracy. Dirty blond hair, reminiscent of Carolyn's, hung over his collar. Long sideburns and drooping eyelids gave the appearance of an individual who liked being different. Muscles in his arms and shoulders bulged beneath his shirt. She would not want to try matching those in a fight. He kept shifting his eyes around the room, making Tracy nervous.

Banana pudding lost its attraction for her, and anxious to complete this meeting, Tracy set the dessert aside and paid the bill.

She picked up the take-out for Ruth and hurried to the basement parking lot. Inside her car, she struggled to remain calm. The elevator opened and Mr. Pittman rushed out, stopping to search for Tracy's car. She waved as he headed to the driver's side and motioned for her to lower the window.

"I want you to stop talking to the missus," he said.

"Mr. Pittman, I'm the one who found Carolyn's body. From what I've observed, the police have little interest in finding out what happened to her in the park. Someone has to pursue this, or it may happen to some other child."

"That's the police's job, ain't it?"

"Yes, it is, but I've been talking to the chief, and he thinks Carolyn caused her own death. Do you believe that?"

Pittman's eyes narrowed. "No," he said. His voice was harsh and his eyes shifted away from Tracy. "But my wife don't know nothing. Leave her out of it."

"You think it was murder?"

Pittman glanced around the garage. "Most likely."

"Then we need to look for the killer, because the police won't do it. Please tell me what you know."

Pittman moved to the passenger's door and slid in beside her. His eyes were angry. "If I knew who did it, I'd be telling the police."

"Carolyn went with you to the lake house on the nights when Hal's friends played poker, didn't she?"

"Sometimes."

"What did Carolyn do while you played poker?"

"She poured drinks and served snacks." His jaw clenched and his mouth began to twitch on one side of his face.

"Can you tell me the names of the men who played?"

"They only go by first names. They come from out of town. Most of 'em are the senator's friends."

"Could one of them have killed Carolyn?"

"Not likely. They'd be no reason."

"Was Hal there the night she died?"

Mr. Pittman reached for the door handle.

"You must know," she insisted.

Pittman's eyes narrowed. "You're lookin' for trouble, lady. I just got called upstairs to talk to Hal's mother. If I don't keep my mouth shut, I'll lose my job, or I could even be the next body found at the bottom of a cistern."

Tracy stopped breathing. He was tying Carolyn's death in the park to the finding of Nora's body in a cistern in Arkansas! Were the same parties involved in both deaths? More importantly, he was connecting Hal and his mother to both of the murders.

"What did Mrs. Montgomery want to know?"

"Just how much I knew, which ain't much. I do know the police ain't gonna look into no poker playing at the ranch. They git paid off."

The wheels turning in Tracy's head, churning out questions, stopped cold. A quietness settled over her. That was it—the police were covering up Carolyn's death because such an investigation would lead to the poker parties at the ranch. But that didn't make sense. Why was hiding the poker parties so important that the police would cover up a murder?

Tracy had a million other questions to ask. She had to hurry before Pittman quit talking.

"Is Hal's mother the one paying the police to cover up what's going on at the ranch?"

"I told you I ain't gonna talk about that. I been told not to."

Tracy took that as a "yes."

"Was Carolyn at the lake house Saturday night?'

This time he nodded.

"How long did she stay?"

"She left about nine o'clock with Hal. She was going to walk home, but he said he had to leave for Tulsa, and he'd drop her off at home."

"Are you sure it was nine o'clock?"

"Yep. Hal usually don't play the tables. He stakes me because I'm better than he is, and we share the winnings. Saturday night he played, and we kidded him for leaving so early. He was winning."

"Are you sure he took Carolyn home?"

"Where else would he have took her?"

"To the park."

Pittman stared through the windshield, then shook his head. "No way. He was in a hurry to get to Tulsa, and Carolyn had a date."

"Who was her date with?"

"I think it was with that Indian boy, Tommy. Didn't make me too happy, her going with him, but what can you do with kids that age?"

"Do you know where they were going?"

"Gist partyin'."

"Were other women at the lake house that night?"

He nodded again.

"Prostitutes?"

Pittman turned his head and looked out the window.

"What are their names?"

"Julie and Marge. They're regulars."

Tracy felt acid rising in her throat. The meatloaf was not settling so well in her stomach. More links of the story were fitting together. There were political buddies playing poker on the ranch, with girls unconnected to politics invited. She needed a lot more information, but Pittman was opening the car door.

"Did Carolyn sleep with any of the men at the poker parties?"

"No!" Pitman was almost shouting. "I told Hal from the beginning that I wouldn't allow it, and he agreed. Said he'd make sure she was kept safe. He looked after Carolyn like she was his daughter."

"Your wife said Carolyn brought money home from the parties. Where did she get it?"

"Tips. The guys tipped her for the drinks." Mr. Pittman looked at Tracy again. "Hal used to give her a twenty or so when she wanted new clothes or something. Like I told you, he treated her like family."

"What did Hal say when he found out she was dead?"

"He was mad as hell. He cried." Pittman looked out the window of the car. "I've got to go," he said and pushed out of the door.

"Just one more question. Am I wrong in believing that Carolyn's and Dr. Smeltzer's deaths might be connected, that the same people might have done them?"

Pittman was standing beside the car, his hand on the door handle. He paused, and then slammed the door without speaking. He hobbled like an old man to his pickup truck.

Tracy sat for several minutes before telling herself to move. She felt paralyzed. She had not learned a lot that would shed light on how Carolyn died, but she had learned that the police chief was covering up illegal gambling at the ranch and turning his head to protect the "girls" who entertained the players. Pittman's refusal to discuss Dr. Smeltzer's death supported the suspicion that there was a connection between the two. The question of why the police and Beatrice Montgomery wanted to squelch a public investigation of Carolyn's death had been answered. Publicity around it might lead to an investigation of illegal activities at the ranch. But why did small-time poker among friends, even with one or two prostitutes on the side, rate police involvement in covering up these activities?

As she sat there, it dawned on her that the information she had gotten from Pittman could endanger her own life. The man seemed frightened when he mentioned being called to Beatrice's suite at the hotel. She pushed out of the car and ran to the elevator that went only to the first floor, requiring her to use the stairs or change elevators to get to her room.

On the first floor, Hal was standing in front of the elevator, leaning against the wall as though he had known she would appear.

"Hi, beautiful. Have you had dinner?"

Tracy froze, looking at him with her lips parted. What if Hal had passed Pittman in the alley? If he suspected the man had been meeting with Tracy, it was possible she had put Pittman's life in danger—or her own. She gulped and tried to think of some way to escape having dinner with Hal.

He misread her confusion. "If you've eaten, let's go have a drink." Leaving her little room to maneuver, he reached over and pushed her hair behind an ear. Tracy remained speechless. She felt her knees begin to shake. With her mind in turmoil, there was no way she was prepared to have a drink with Hal.

"Sorry, Hal, I've already eaten. The meatloaf is good here. And I can't drink two nights in a row. I've got to get to bed."

"I have no objection to that." He grinned. Tracy felt her stomach muscles contract and push the acid higher. She forced a smile, wishing she could forget everything she had learned from Hershel Pittman.

Keeping things light, she punched him on the arm. "Can I take a rain check?"

"Okay. You're the boss. Just find some time for me before you leave. We have business to resolve." *If he only knew*, she thought. He leaned over and kissed her on the forehead. She closed her eyes and breathed in the essence that had always left her weak with love. This time it scared the heck out of her. Hal turned and sauntered to the alley door, in the same direction Mr. Pittman had gone.

Tracy was numb when she opened the door to her room and dropped her purse on the bed. Ruth's take-out went into the small refrigerator. Seated, she pushed and pulled until her boots fell to the floor. She groaned and reached for her heavy coat, which was still lying on the chair. Hal's guilt or innocence might be tied to the owner of the ring. The tape covering the initials hid that secret. Her hand plunged inside the pocket. It was empty.

Tracy turned the coat upside down, expecting the ring to fall to the floor. It did not happen. She looked on the floor and under the beds. She ran her hand over each of the bedspreads.

Her trouser pockets were flat. The contents of her makeup kit splattered across the table, and she fingered every item. The ring had to be in this room. Exhausted, she picked up the coat again and ran her hand around the hem, but there was no ring.

Tracy began to shiver. Someone had entered her room and taken the ring. The closet door was closed. She looked around the room. The maids had been here. Why had they not hung up her coat? Could they have taken the ring? And how would they have known to look in her pocket? No one knew she had the ring except Ruth. Maybe she took it to show to Kit.

Chills sent sparks to Tracy's nerve ends, and her fingertips tingled as she dialed the phone. There was no answer. They must have gone out to dinner. As the telephone dropped into place, a key turned in the locked door. Too late to hide, Tracy stood with her mouth open, watching as Ruth trudged in, followed by Paul and Kit. They stared at the scattered clothing, the pillows dumped on the floor, the complete upheaval in the room.

"Did a tornado make a direct hit on this room while I was gone?" Ruth asked.

Embarrassed, Tracy began straightening up the mess she had made. "Sorry, I've been looking for something. Ruth, remember I told you I found a ring out at the lake house?"

Ruth nodded.

"Did you take it out of my pocket?"

"Why would I do that? I didn't know it was in your pocket."

"I don't know. Nothing makes sense."

"You think someone came into your room?" Kit asked.

"If Ruth didn't take the ring, I'm sure of it."

"That's scary," Kit said. "How could they do that without a key?"

"The maids have keys. They leave doors open while they're cleaning adjoining rooms. Someone could have come in while the maids were on the floor. My question is how would anyone know I had something worth stealing? I only told Ruth."

She paused. "And listen to this. I have talked to both Hal and Mr. Pittman since I saw you. Hal lied to me about not knowing Carolyn. I know it was a lie because her father told me that Carolyn had been going over to poker games at the lake house for several weeks. Moreover, he said Hal treated Carolyn like a daughter, even buying her school clothes. Pittman told me different people came to the poker games each week, and that two prostitutes came as 'regulars.' He said the police were paid to look the other way. He denied that Carolyn slept with the men."

"He told you all that? When did you talk to him?" Kit asked.

"This evening. After I left the police station, I came back to the hotel to eat supper, and Mr. Pittman sat down next to me in the restaurant. He didn't want to talk in public, so we went down to the parking garage. Foremost, he wanted me to stop talking to his wife, but he answered a lot of my questions about the gambling parties."

"You're saying he accused Hal of running an illegal gambling table and of paying the police to look the other way?" Paul asked. "Why would Hal do that? He doesn't need the money."

Kit threw up her hands, "And bringing in prostitutes?"

"I'm beginning to think the reason the police are trying to bury this murder lies in the fact that Carolyn was at the poker party until nine o'clock the night she died. It's even possible Nora visited the ranch before her death. Maybe Nora was killed because she knew what was going on and threatened to reveal it. In her case, it was convenient to use the anti-abortion demonstrations to divert everyone's attention from the real scoundrels."

Ruth drummed her fingers on the arm of her chair. "The point is," she said, "an investigation of Carolyn's death could lead to scrutiny of several unsavory activities at the ranch. Here's the million dollar question: what could they be doing out there that requires the cover-up of murder? Playing poker and sleeping with prostitutes won't do it."

"And it may not even be murder, which makes the cover-up even stranger," Tracy said.

"If Carolyn's death was caused by a self-induced miscarriage, why go to such lengths to hide the fact?" Kit asked.

"Especially since the ring I found under the bed at the lake is likely Tommy Bucco's," Tracy said. "If it belongs to Tommy, then it had no connection to the activities at the poker parties."

"What were you doing under the bed, for God's sake?" Kit asked.

"Only my foot. Someone dropped the ring beside the bed, and I stepped on it. The scary part is that I put it in my coat pocket, and when I got back here, I threw my coat on that chair." She pointed to where Ruth was sitting. "When I looked for it tonight, the ring had disappeared." She stood and began pacing near the window. "I've been going over what I think Hal knows. Number one, he could have known Carolyn was wearing the ring. He could have remembered asking her to remove it and then wondered what happened to it after her death. Or, when Hal took her home, she could have told him she left it in the bedroom. When he went to look for it, he'd have suspected that I was the only one who could have found it, and he would have come to my room to recover it. Did I tell you he took Carolyn home Saturday night from the poker party?" Tracy asked.

"His alibi for that evening is good," Kit said. "He was in Tulsa. He sent a bottle of wine to my table, although he never showed up to be thanked for it."

Tracy looked at Paul. "So he was telling us the truth when he said he was in Tulsa Saturday night?"

"Yes. I think you can stop looking at him as a suspect in Carolyn's death. What else did you learn from Pittman?"

"He's a little spooky. He was at the hotel because Beatrice called him in. She lives in the penthouse. It seems very coincidental that he wound up sitting near me in the café, and I worried that he was planted there to find out what I'm up to. However, I couldn't think of anyone else who would have known I was going to be there. Also, he was afraid of being fired for talking to me, but he seemed willing to reveal whatever it took to solve the mystery of Carolyn's death—except for the question about Dr. Smeltzer. He ran when I asked him that one. Bottom line is, I don't think he killed Carolyn or knows who did. Now, his wife's involvement is a different matter. He insists that I stop talking to her."

"You think Mrs. Pittman could have killed her daughter?" Kit's voice sounded incredulous.

Tracy grimaced. "She knew Carolyn was coming home from those parties with money. She had to be suspicious of what she was doing there. Secondly, she suspected Carolyn was pregnant. We know Carolyn wanted an abortion. Who would be the most likely person to help her do it?" Both women looked at Paul.

Ruth broke into the explanation. "Also, it could have been her mother or father who took her to the park. They might have been acting at the direction of Hal or his mother, who want to keep the investigation off the ranch."

Paul stood up. "I'm at a loss to understand why you ladies have gotten so involved in this case. You're endangering your lives and may be ruining the reputations of innocent people. Why? This is a police job, and you haven't convinced me that they can't do it without your help. Besides, you don't have a speck of hard evidence. You're spinning webs."

Tracy continued to pace behind her chair. "You may be right," she said. "We may not be able to prove that Carolyn didn't die by her own hand. However, I, for one, will not be satisfied to sit by and let her death, whatever its cause, go unnoticed and unsolved." She looked around the room. "Any of us could be the next victim. As far as reputations are concerned, innocent people should not have to worry if they come forward and are honest."

Paul nodded. "I agree. But you're overestimating the seriousness of Hal's involvement. You're right—gambling is a misdemeanor and, if reported, Hal could have his hands slapped. That's hardly worth getting excited about. The federal government won't waste a lot of time on a small operation. I suspect Senator Fortenberry could squash such an investigation before it even started. Also, inviting girls to a party is not serious, from a legal standpoint. If caught, the girls would go to jail one night and get out the next day. It sounds like the police department is protecting them, so it's doubtful they would be punished at all."

"However, Paul," Kit said, "you wouldn't put the murder of a doctor under the heading of 'minimally criminal acts.'"

"That's all conjecture. You have no evidence that Nora was at the ranch."

"Then I guess we need to get some," Tracy said.

Paul sighed. "I don't know that I can help you except to reveal that Carolyn asked me to abort the fetus, and I wouldn't. Unlike Hal and his friends, I find the thought of breaking the law very scary. The irony is that if Carolyn died from an abortion, I'm the one who could have stopped it."

Paul dropped his head to his hands and moaned. Kit moved over to the arm of his chair.

"Paul, it's not your fault. She had other, better options. She could have had the baby. If it was Tommy's, Tillie would have helped them."

"No. I put the kibosh on that, too. I told Tommy and Carolyn that Tillie didn't have time to rear their babies."

Tracy broke in. "This brings up another possibility. We haven't looked very closely at Tommy. What if he did take Carolyn over to the university to the frat party? If there were drugs and alcohol there, and she was making out with the boys, Tommy could have become jealous and beaten the hell out of her."

"That doesn't account for the abortion," Kit said.

"Sexual activity could have caused a spontaneous abortion, right?" Tracy asked.

Paul chimed in. "I dropped that bit of information in her ear, also. Maybe she planned the whole thing. It's possible. Even likely."

"And if it was Tommy's ring that I found, he may have wondered why it wasn't on her finger or around her neck. More reason to be jealous."

"Someone must have thought that ring was important evidence. We have to find out who, and what its importance is," Ruth said.

"The other person we haven't looked at closely is Brandon. The initials on the pillowcase indicate that he was involved some way," Tracy said. "We know he was on the ranch during the summer when the Pittmans moved here. Mrs. Pittman said Carolyn went riding with him several times. He looks like a prime suspect to me." She stopped pacing and sat down.

Ruth leaned forward. "If he took her to the lake house, she could have taken off Tommy's ring at that time." Everyone nodded. It was the most logical answer they'd heard.

"And if Brandon is part of the puzzle, I can understand why Hal is involved," Kit said. "He feels responsible for Brandon, and he might be trying to cover up for him." She moved out of her chair to stand beside Tracy. "All of these possibilities are scary, especially the fact that someone took the ring from your room. Even before this happened, Paul and I had talked about inviting you to come stay with us until you got your birth certificate finished. We'd love to have you, and now it seems it may not be safe for you to stay in the hotel, where people have access to your room. We want you to move in with us."

Tracy turned to Paul, and he nodded without looking at her.

"That's very nice of you," Tracy said, "but we can't impose on you. I'm sure the worst is over. I won't be going back to the lake house, and there's too much snow for me to hit the streets in town. Ruth and I will stick together when we go out. I'm not worried about our safety."

Paul stood up. "That wasn't intended as an invitation. We insist. It will be best for everybody." He moved toward the door. "Let's go," he said.

Kit looked to Tracy. "Please. It will make our work so much easier if we're together. And it will be fun having the two of you in our home.

We need your support, too." She put her arm through Tracy's. "Get your stuff."

"Okay?" Tracy asked Ruth.

Ruth clapped her hands. "I'm in favor, if you're sure we aren't imposing."

"We're doing this for our peace of mind," Paul said.

The women began dumping their clothing into suitcases and snapping them shut. "We'll have to check out," Tracy said as she took one last look around the room.

FIFTEEN

Tracy awoke the next morning with a wet tongue tasting her lips and cheek. She screamed and sat up in a strange bed. Ruth, snoring peacefully, was the only other person in the room. Behind an overstuffed chair, Charley was peeking out to see if it were safe to take another lick. His head was cocked, and Tracy saw disappointment in his eyes. He trotted out of the room.

"Charley! Come back here. I didn't know it was you." She heard his toenails clicking on the wooden floors, and his nose appeared around the door jamb.

"Come on," she said and patted the covers. He put his two front feet on the edge of the bed and waited for permission to bound onto the middle. He wound up on top of Ruth.

"Get out of here," she yelled. "This was the best night's sleep I've had in ages, and you're ruining it."

"Go," Tracy ordered, and Charley jumped from the bed and ran downstairs. She heard him scratching at the back door.

Oh, it wasn't my company he wanted, she thought. *It was a walk.* The house was quiet, and Tracy guessed that Paul and Kit were gone. She pulled on her warm clothing and boots before hurrying through the kitchen, where she found a note from Kit saying she would return in an hour or two, and that an extra key was hidden outside the back door, under a flower pot. Outside, Charley almost knocked Tracy over as she locked the door, making sure Ruth was safe inside.

Ending their hike a half hour later, Tracy called Charley inside. Before she left for the clerk's office, she scribbled a note for Kit, thanking her for the good night's sleep and warning her that Ruth was still in bed. Again, she made sure all the locks were in place before she left.

Ruth had finished dressing when the doorbell rang. She hurried downstairs, expecting to see a delivery man or a neighbor. She opened the door and was shocked to see a couple whose faces were masked by nylon hose. She tried to slam the door shut, but the man rushed in, knocking her backwards. She screamed and fought until his companion clamped a wet sponge over her face. Gasping for breath, she relaxed, unconscious, and the woman eased a needle into her arm. Charley came bounding in from the kitchen growling, teeth bared. He leaped for the throat of the woman, but the man knocked him unconscious with the butt of his gun.

"Damned dog. We better shoot him," the man said.

"Oh, don't. Let's take him over to the farm."

"We got enough dogs already."

"Not one this nice."

"Okay. But how in the heck are you and me gonna get this woman into the truck? Nobody told me she was the size of a whale, or I'd have brought along one of the guys to help."

"We should have waited to knock her out until we got her on board," the woman said. "Or brought a forklift."

"You suppose we got the wrong house?"

"Nope, but something's wrong. I better call the boss."

"Suppose we got the wrong woman? This ain't the doctor's wife, is it?"

"Nope. He's married to a squaw."

"She must be the right one, then. Why don't you call to make sure?"

He walked to the kitchen, poured himself a cup of coffee, and dialed the phone. After explaining the problem they had encountered, he listened, shrugged, said, "Okay," and hung up the phone. He emptied the coffee cup and returned to the living room. "Boss says we got the right house, just the wrong female. Said we should leave this one here. It'll scare the b'Jesus out of the troublemaker."

"Let's put her in the closet. She'll be knocked out for a few hours. Give us time to get out of town."

It took them ten minutes to bind and hide Ruth's body. They loaded Charley into the truck and headed east.

At the same time, Tracy sat on a wooden bench in the hall outside the Public Education Office, shuffling through the reports, smiling at the teachers' notes. She relaxed. This was the history of the past that she remembered. Only Paul Jordan and Ruth knew for sure where her life began and how it evolved those five years before she started to school.

She took the folder to the information window, disappointed to find that Bonnie was not at work today. Along with the school records, Tracy left a note explaining that the pastor would be mailing her baptismal record to the clerk's office tomorrow. Smiling, she printed her name as it should appear on the new birth certificate. It would be completed soon, and she could get on with her life.

Exhilarated that the aggravating task was complete, Tracy ran out of the building to her car, anxious to proceed with her investigation of Carolyn's death. She placed the address of the coroner's office on her dashboard and drove west. The building was new, and a staff parking lot extended around the building, where she eased into a space hidden from the street. Inside, the coroner's office was empty except for a young man who was reviewing papers stacked on his desk. He looked up without interest until he realized Tracy was not one of the regular legal secretaries wandering by to pick up reports.

"How can I help you?" he called from his desk.

Tracy's heart raced. Her luck was holding out. Billy Sharpton from her eighth-grade homeroom peered over his glasses. "Hey, Billy!" She waved. The clerk ambled over to the counter, a puzzled look on his face.

"Do I know you?"

"Of course you do. I'm Tracy Hunter. We went to school together."

"Tracy Hunter. I'll be danged. What are you doing here? I thought you left the country for good." He looked at her with squinted eyes. "Wow . . . you've changed."

"Yeah," she said. "I've been living in Chicago. I'm back here on business. I didn't expect to meet so many old friends. I saw Bonnie down at the county clerk's office yesterday."

"Oh, yeah. She's been there a long time." Billy nodded and spoke with the same slow, soft diction she remembered. He played with his pen, concentrating on rolling it back and forth in his palms, instead of meeting her eyes. She had always liked his shyness and slow manner, but today she prayed for a way to make him hyper-fast at delivering autopsy reports, or at least fast enough to give her a copy before someone like his boss appeared and thwarted the action.

"Billy," she said. "I need a favor. I'm staying with Dr. Jordan and his wife while I'm here, and he sent me to get a copy of Carolyn Pittman's autopsy report." Her voice and facial expression dripped with sadness.

"We normally don't hand these reports out to the public without an order, but the doc's okay." Billy strolled back to his desk.

Tracy wanted to mention that she was in a hurry. Forcing herself to remain calm, she watched through the window to see if cars were driving into the staff parking lot. Billy found the report and wandered around the office looking for an envelope. A black car drove past the window, and Tracy held out her hand.

"That's okay," she said. "I'll take it this way. Doc wants to see it before closing time."

Billy shrugged and handed her the two page report. She threw him a kiss and he smiled, his eyes squinting, a little puzzled.

"See you later when I have more time," Tracy said and hurried out the front door and around the building. From the parking lot, the driver of the black car disappeared through the back door of the building, and Tracy eased into her rental car, autopsy in hand.

When Tracy arrived at the Jordan home, the back door was still locked, and her knock went unanswered. She found the hidden key and pushed the door inward, expecting Charley to pounce on her. The house was empty. She yelled up the stairs. "Ruth! Charley!" Hearing no answer, she sat down at the kitchen table to read the report. The telephone rang, and she lifted the receiver.

"Tracy, I'm glad you're home," Kit said. "I just talked to Mrs. Pittman, and we need to go over what she told me."

"And I've got the coroner's report."

"Great. I'll be home in fifteen minutes."

"Where's Ruth? Charley's not here either."

"She must have taken him for a walk. They'll be back by the time I get home. See you."

It was strange that Ruth had not left a note. Upstairs, the bed was unmade, and Ruth's night clothes were thrown across a chair. She had left in a hurry. But walking the dog was not a job she took care of in a family of boys. Maybe Charley had charmed her.

Back in the kitchen, Tracy started the coffee and sat down to read the autopsy report. She scanned the definition of autopsy, a postmortem assessment or examination of a body to determine the cause of death. An autopsy is performed by a physician trained in pathology. She mumbled, "I know, I know," and hurried over the sections stating that parental or guardian permission is required before performing an autopsy on minors for medical reasons, unless court ordered. There were no permissions attached to the report. So much for following protocol. It had been written and signed by the Chickasaw County Coroner, Dr. Leonard Humphries.

The report stated that the fifteen-year-old female had died from loss of blood, hemorrhaging from the uterus. The coroner found "no evidence of infection in the uterus, tubes, or ovaries that would have precipitated a miscarriage. Neither was there evidence of peritonitis, which would have been present if death had been caused by an infected abortion site. Nor was there evidence of trauma from the use of sharp instrumentation, which would have been used in a non-medical abortion." So the police chief's theory that Carolyn had gone across the tracks or had performed her own illegal abortion with a coat hanger did not hold water.

Tracy read on: "There is evidence of trauma to the uterus indicative of forced intercourse, usually found in cases of rape." Exactly what she and Kit had thought. Now to find out who did it, she thought. The report concluded that: "The subject died from loss of blood, hemorrhaging related to spontaneous abortion caused by trauma to the uterus. There are tears to the vulva indicative of forceful entry as evidenced in rape cases."

Tracy felt sick. The poor child. She wouldn't allow herself to imagine what happened to cause the abortion. She read the description again: the abortion appeared to be spontaneous, the result of trauma to the uterus caused by rape or forceful intercourse. Her face flushed with anger. Whoever did this was going to suffer for it. She would see to that, even if it were Hal or Tommy.

Tracy was rummaging in the cabinets for coffee cups when Kit arrived home.

"How did your day go?" she asked Kit.

"Not bad. But you gave me the hard job, talking to a mother whose daughter just died." Kit sat down at the table.

"Sorry. Was she able to talk about it?"

"A little, but all the neighbors were bringing in food, and she was so distraught. I didn't stay long," Kit said.

"Did you find out what she meant by the father being too loving to Carolyn?"

"I don't think it was what we suspected. Mrs. Pittman is sure he wasn't sleeping with Carolyn. She was their only child, and Mrs. Pittman described the father as very protective of Carolyn. And it doesn't make a lot of sense that he would take her over to the police station if she were in danger. I don't think he would have let Hal have sex with her, either," Kit said.

"I'd like to think he protected her, but what about the ring I found?"

"Mrs. Pittman said Carolyn had been wearing Tommy's ring since they met."

"Did she say how long Carolyn and Tommy had been dating?"

"I didn't ask her, but the Pittmans moved here in June. Tommy and Carolyn must have met in August, when school started."

"We'll have to ask Tillie."

"I can do that. I should have been calling her, anyway. Things have been so crazy," Kit rose to refill their coffee cups. "What did the autopsy say?"

"Not what the chief said." Tracy picked up the report and summarized it for Kit. "He doesn't have the coroner under his thumb. This report says there is no evidence of injuries related to sharp instruments, but there was trauma to the uterus similar to that left by rape and forced entry."

"She was raped! God, no."

The door opened and Paul entered, carrying his medical bag and several files.

"Why all the homework?" Kit asked.

"I gotta make home calls I didn't have time for today." He laid down the folders and picked up a donut. "Supper will be late, I guess," he said to no one in particular. "Where's Charley?"

"He and Ruth have disappeared. We assume they're walking."

Paul frowned, shrugged, and went upstairs. Kit and Tracy discussed the need to visit with Tillie. When Paul returned wearing cords and a blue sweater, he was met with pleasant smiles from both women.

"Did I hear Tillie's name?"

Kit jumped up and fumbled around with the coffee pot. "What would you like for supper, honey?"

Paul kissed the back of her neck. "I'd like an answer to my question."

Tracy shook her head. "That doesn't sound like a substantial meal to me. Are you sure one answer will suffice?"

"You stay out of this," Paul said, pointing to Tracy. "I have enough trouble keeping one woman in line. I'm not about to contend with two—or three."

"And since when has your role in this family been one of keeping me in line?" Kit asked.

"Sorry. That was a poor choice of words. But it was also an effort on your part to change the subject. Why were you discussing Tillie?"

"Honey, we were saying that it would help to know how long Tommy and Carolyn had been dating. Tracy says the autopsy report shows the fetus was about four months old. That would put conception back in July. She couldn't have been pregnant when she moved here from Texas in June. If she and Tommy didn't meet until August, that leaves a month when she could have been seeing someone else. I offered to talk to Tillie about when Tommy met Carolyn."

"Tillie doesn't know much. I talked to her this afternoon. Tommy is showing signs of serious stress. I'm wondering if it's guilt over having been involved with the girl or whether he knows something about her death. I asked Tillie to get him in for another talk."

"Let me talk to Tillie. She knows more than she's telling you," Kit said.

"What's this about the autopsy report? Where did you get that?"

Tracy found it impossible to prepare a story about how she got the report, leaving out the ruse she used involving Paul's name. She could only hope that he would not probe too deeply.

"Yesterday when I went to complain about being followed by Sergeant Falco, the chief said Carolyn's report would be ready today, so I went over and picked up a copy." She shrugged to show how simple the task had been.

"You just walked off the street and picked up a copy of an autopsy report?"

Tracy squirmed in her chair and shuffled the papers. "It helped when I told them Carolyn was one of your patients, and you needed a copy for your file." Her eyes widened as she waited for Paul to explode, and she held her breath as he reached over and took the report from the table.

"I guess it's mine then. I'll put it in the file."

"I suppose we can have a copy?"

"It depends upon how I'm feeling when you come begging."

Kit looked at Tracy. "Pay no attention to him. I'm personal friends with the office manager, who also runs the copy machine. By the way, we never asked you if the chief explained why you were being followed."

"He spun a wild story about how Carolyn died the day after I arrived, evidently from a botched abortion, and they suspected I had come to town in the wake of Dr. Smeltzer's disappearance to teach women how to do abortions." No one moved. "Come to think of it, the timing makes it sound like I'm being set up as Carolyn's murderer. And the strangest part came after I walked out into the hall. I heard the chief tell Falco I was probably working for the FBI. Are they bringing up the abortion issue to scare me, when what really bothers them is fear of a government investigation into what's going on at the ranch?" Tracy looked toward Paul.

"I don't know, but it sounds to me like you're in way over your head. This could be dangerous territory. People down here, including the police chief, the district attorney, and the judges stick together. If you aren't careful, you could wind up in jail."

Tracy's eyes squinted, and she spoke through tight lips. "They can't charge me with doing something illegal."

"They can manufacture evidence," Paul said. "Think pro-abortion brochures. The big problem here is not the girl's death. It's whatever they're hiding, and they're afraid the abortion has opened a door to the bigger issue. They don't want Carolyn's death investigated." Paul was agreeing with their hypothesis.

"That sounds like what I said to you yesterday," Tracy said.

Paul shrugged.

"The police chief did suggest that I get on the next train out of town."

Kit looked at Paul. "Do you think they would arrest her?"

"They can do anything they want. I suspect they're trying to scare Tracy out of town so that the investigation will die down." Paul looked at

Tracy. "I don't think you should take any chances. Did you get what you need for the amendment?"

"Yes," Tracy said. "Bonnie got my school and church records for me. They prove I was called Tracy, not Brigitte."

"Good. Can you finish the amendment tomorrow? They can mail the new one to you, or Kit can pick it up."

"Paul, I can't leave before Nora's memorial service. The paper said it would be on Sunday."

"Of course, I understand. They called me today and asked if I'd speak," Paul said.

"We must all go," Kit said, and Paul nodded.

"Tracy, I am concerned for your safety. The memorial service may stir things up again, and if these guys aren't afraid to kill a doctor, they certainly won't be afraid to kill a busybody from Chicago."

"You don't know me very well, Paul. I don't quit in the middle of a job."

"But this isn't your job. You've taken on a cause, not a murder. The police chief is right; you're a rabble-rouser. It appears you haven't hit your stride yet. So far, you've only aroused Kit and Ruth. Tomorrow, if you stay, you'll be marching down the street like a pied piper."

"I resent that," Kit said. "It was my idea that we investigate Carolyn's death. Tracy's just going along with me. And you know I'm not a rabble -rouser. Maybe I should go see Matt."

Paul moaned. He looked at Tracy. "I can't believe this. How can you walk into town and turn our lives upside down in less than a week?"

Tracy smiled at Kit. "I think Paul and Chief Mayfield are right. I am an outside agitator." She looked at Paul. "I'm not going to apologize for it. I'll move back to the hotel so that you and Kit aren't contaminated with my presence. But I won't be run out of town. I don't have a birth certificate to prove it, but I was born here, and these are my people." She started for the door. "I wonder where Ruth is." Everyone looked puzzled, and Tracy came back to the table. "I guess we could stay for supper."

"Tracy, you're not going back to the hotel. Paul, tell her so."

"Kit says you can't leave, and she's the boss. You might as well give up." He opened the refrigerator door and surveyed the contents. "Where did you say Ruth is?"

Kit and Tracy looked at him and then at each other. "It's strange she hasn't come back if she went for a walk. It's getting dark. And she's not a walker," Tracy said.

"Why don't I go pick up hamburgers for supper?" Paul asked. "I'll look along the road for them."

SIXTEEN

Around six p.m., Paul returned with hamburgers. Tracy and Kit were riding horses through the park, calling for Ruth and Charley. Unknown to them, Ruth was blinking, returning to consciousness inside the dark closet. When Tracy and Kit returned to the house, they sat looking at the sack of hamburgers and French fries. No one had the heart to begin eating.

"I think we should call the police," Kit said.

"You're right." Paul grabbed the telephone. As he dialed, a strained moan came from the living room, followed by kicking on the closet door. They stumbled over each other toward the sound.

"My God," Paul said as he opened the door. "It's Ruth."

Together they dragged her out and pulled duct tape from her mouth. She sat up, a bit druggy and dazed. She breathed deeply. "Do I smell hamburgers?"

"Ruth, what happened?"

"Call an ambulance. We need a doctor," Tracy yelled, forgetting that Paul was in the room.

"Get out of the way," Paul ordered. "Get my bag." He cut the tape from Ruth's wrists and began monitoring her heart beat. "She's doing okay," he said, looking for bruises and bumps.

"What happened, honey?" Tracy asked.

Ruth sat up, sprawled against the couch. "I don't know. I heard a truck drive up, and someone knocked on the door. I thought it was a delivery or something, but when I opened the door, someone rushed in and knocked me over and put a foul-smelling sponge over my face. I heard Charley attacking them as I passed out. I don't know what happened after that. Thank God, they didn't carry me off. I could be in a cistern in Arkansas by now."

Tracy gulped. "Could they be the same people who killed Nora?"

"Could be. But why?"

"Paul, call the police," Kit said.

Paul laughed. "That, from the lady who doesn't think the police are competent enough to investigate a murder. What makes you think they would get to the bottom of this simple assault?"

"It didn't feel so simple to me," Ruth said.

"I'm sorry. I didn't mean to say it was unimportant. It's very important. We have to find the perpetrators. And we do have to report it to the police, but let's think about it first."

Paul had joined the Kit and Caboodle Investigation team!

Tracy paced in front of the door. "This sounds like what happened to Nora. But why Ruth? And why didn't they take her with them and finish the job?"

"I'd like to see two guys who could carry me out of here and lift me into a pickup. And I think one of them was a woman—a skinny one at that." Ruth struggled to stand. "Did someone mention hamburgers? I haven't eaten since last night."

The other three stood nodding. It would have taken at least two or three strong men to lift Ruth's body off the ground into a vehicle. Paul and Kit stared at Tracy. Her eyes widened in shock. It dawned on them at the same time—it would have been easy for one man to have thrown Tracy into the back of the pickup. They got the wrong sister.

"They may come back," Kit said. "What shall we do?"

"I'll call the police. Maybe they can get some guards out here to watch through the night. And I'll call Keith Henley. His men patrol around the college. How do you feel, Ruth?" Paul checked her eye movements and felt for bumps on her head. She had no broken bones.

"I'm okay. Sort of woozy. Where's Charley?"

"We can't find him. Would they have hidden him somewhere?"

"They may have killed him. He was ferocious, bless his heart."

Kit turned away, weeping. Paul took her in his arms. "We'll find him. But first, let's make sure the doors are locked and the draperies are pulled. I'll call Henley and the police."

The chief and Sergeant Falco arrived within minutes. While they gathered information from Ruth, Keith Henley arrived with two guards, who promised to patrol the grounds around the house.

It was after midnight before the house occupants turned out the lights and made an effort to sleep.

The next morning, the three women gathered around the table in the Jordan kitchen. "Why don't we go over what we know and figure out where the holes are?" Tracy said. "Then we can organize a plan of attack. I'm thinking I should take Ruth home today and come back later, and you and I can finish this up."

"Like heck you will," Ruth said. "I have an important role to play in this case now. I don't plan to go home until we find Charley."

Kit and Tracy smiled. It was like her to be more concerned for the dog than her own safety.

"What's Howard going to say when he finds out about the danger I put you in?"

"Oh, he'll say what a great opportunity he missed to get rid of me."

Tracy punched her sister on the arm. "Don't believe her," she said to Kit. "Howard would die if he knew what happened. He'd be down here tearing up the territory between Ada and Arkansas. Maybe we should call him."

Kit shook her head. "No. We need to use our heads instead of our fists on this one. If we can find out who attacked Ruth, we'll probably find out who killed the women. Let's update our suspects." She opened the notebook.

"Okay," Tracy said. "Let's list all those who might have been with Carolyn on Saturday night and decide which ones might have had sex with her."

"That should limit our list. Mrs. Pittman left for the bingo game while Carolyn was still at the poker party."

"Can we rule out the mother, then?"

"I think so. The autopsy ruled out a wire hanger abortion, and that's the thing the mother might have done."

"Did you find out if Carolyn was home when the mother got back from playing bingo? If so, the mother could have driven her to the park."

"I asked her, remember?" Tracy said. "She told me Carolyn was home, asleep. Maybe she wasn't asleep. Maybe they did go to the park."

"That's a real possibility. Let's follow up on it. Who's next?"

"The father. We know he took her to the lake house. He says she left with Hal because she had a date with Tommy, and Hal was on his way to Tulsa. The father looks clean."

"And when I talked to him, I didn't get the impression he was involved. He may be hiding information about who was involved."

"Okay. Take him off the list. Number three."

"Hal?"

"That seems farfetched," Kit said, "but I guess you have to turn over every rock when you're looking for worms. He had the opportunity, since he took her home from the poker party. He covered his tracks by making up the story about being in Tulsa the rest of the night."

"He what?" Tracy asked.

Kit pushed her hair behind her ears, hiding her face behind her hand. "I'm sorry I didn't tell you sooner, but this is very personal, and I didn't want you to make a big deal of it." She stared at Tracy. "I didn't think you'd understand, but Hal and I are just good friends. He treats me like a mother. He can discuss things with me that he can't say to Beatrice."

No one moved or breathed aloud.

"Hal called while I was at Mom's and said he'd like to come up—he needed to talk. I told him my brother would be in town that night, so he decided not to come . . . but he did have a bottle of wine sent to our table. It's the kind of thing he does." Kit rose from the table and walked to the cabinet counter where she lifted a Kleenex from the box and began wiping tears from her eyes.

Ruth looked at Tracy, who stared at Kit, who came back to the table and bent over the list she was preparing, her hand shaking.

Ruth was the first to recover. "Put him on the list. If he's behind the assault on me, I'll tell Howard to come take him out." If she was trying to bring lightness back to the meeting, she failed. No one laughed.

"Yes, put him on the list," Tracy said. "We can assume he was up to no good, evidenced by the fact that he was hiding his whereabouts. While it may have nothing to do with Carolyn's death, it may point to why the police are trying to cover up what's going on at the ranch."

"How do we get to him?" Ruth asked.

"Leave that to me," Tracy said.

Ruth objected. "Absolutely not. You're not getting out of my sight. You're not going back out to that lake house with him."

"Perhaps a cozy little dinner in town, then . . . with a bottle of good wine." Tracy looked at Kit, her eyes smoking.

"You know, Tracy, going after Hal is playing with fire. Paul will be livid," Kit said.

The idea that Hal and Kit had met alone in Tulsa—and who knew where else—was astonishing. Would Paul be livid to learn about that?

"Who's next on our list?" Ruth asked.

"I suppose we have to look at Tommy. I feel so sorry for Tillie. I wish we could rule him out," Kit said.

"I'm afraid there's no way. It may have been his baby, and he may have taken Carolyn to the fraternity party on Saturday night."

"I need to talk to Tillie. I'll call her for lunch tomorrow," Kit said. "Why don't you two come?"

"Sure," Tracy said, "Unless I get a better offer." She lifted her eyebrows.

Kit ignored her. "What's the bottom line on Tommy? What do we need to know?"

"Whether he took Carolyn to the fraternity party, what happened there, whether he took her home, and at what time," Ruth said.

"Maybe we can get that from Tillie."

"Maybe," Tracy said, "but I don't like to rely on secondhand information. I'd like to talk to Tommy. Who's the next suspect?"

"I suppose Tillie's a wild card for hiding the body," Ruth said. "She didn't like Carolyn, and she would do anything to protect Tommy's future."

"Also, here are the pictures I took of footprints near the body. Look at this one," Tracy said. "Someone was wearing heels. It wasn't Carolyn. Why don't we check out Tillie's shoes?"

"Really, gals. I've known Tillie too long. Murder isn't a possibility for her. She doesn't even approve of abortion. Let's leave her off the list."

"We don't leave people off the list just because they're our friends, Kit," Tracy said, unable to get past her disappointment at Kit's revelation of her out-of-town meetings with Hal. "How about Brandon? How well do you know him?"

"We were around him when he was younger," Kit said. "He clung pretty closely to Hal until he got into high school. He's a very good-looking boy and polite. Girls go for him."

"Polite doesn't count," Tracy said. "Nor good looks."

"Let's leave him on the list. If Carolyn was at the fraternity party, there's always the chance he was involved. He may not have gotten her pregnant earlier, but he definitely was after her for sex."

"He's in. Who else?" Kit asked

"We need to find out if the police have names of suspects for who killed Nora. They must have been the guys who came in the white pickup."

"Right. I guess that's all, unless we want to investigate each other." Kit looked over her glasses at Tracy and smiled in an effort to clear the air. "Let's get started. I'll call Tillie and set up lunch."

"I'll call Hal and arrange something with him," Tracy said.

"Something?" Ruth's voice was husky.

"Good investigators have to make sacrifices to uncover the truth. Trust me. I can handle this man."

"The men who attacked me were scum bags, and there is no way you can handle them any better than I did, which was not at all."

"You're right. We now know we're dealing with hired thugs, not just some sick person playing a game. I'll be careful."

By ten o'clock, Paul was in the examination room at the clinic, waiting for Tillie to finish a smallpox vaccination she was giving to a frightened little boy. The child was screaming bloody murder, but stopped crying on a high note as Tillie handed him a cherry-colored sucker. With her thumb, she wiped away the tears flooding down his cheeks.

"I thought Tommy was coming in today," Paul said.

"He better be here in five minutes or I'll take a board to that boy," Tillie said. "By the way, Hal called today and said his tonsils were doing fine. No more fever. He wanted to know why Tracy's not at the hotel and asked if she'd gone home. I told him I didn't know." Tillie looked over her glasses, waiting for an answer.

The front door opened, and Tommy walked in, pulling his ball cap low over his eyes.

"See if you can move my morning appointments to the afternoon," Paul said, as he led the way to his office.

He looked across his desk at the tall, imposing teenager teetering somewhere between a momma's boy and a man. Paul was betting that manhood would win as soon as Tommy got to college. He remembered when his own son went through the same stage.

"Your momma says you're not sleeping."

"Momma worries too much." Tommy waited for Paul to respond, but the doctor sat looking at him. The room was quiet, and Tommy avoided Paul eyes, focusing instead on the fireplace. Paul remembered the cold Saturday afternoons they had spent together, chopping and hauling wood, stacking it into a rick behind the clinic. The two had always been comfortable talking and working together, much like Paul and his own son, until Tommy entered high school.

"Okay," Tommy continued. "I can't sleep. It'll pass."

"Maybe I can help."

"How? Momma brought home some sleeping pills, and they didn't help."

Paul groaned. "Your problem started with Carolyn's death. Right?"

Tommy screwed his face into a scowl. "Do we have to talk about that?" He pushed his chair further from Paul's desk.

"Is there a reason you don't want to talk about it, Tommy?"

"It won't bring her back." He looked at Paul, daring him to deny the truth.

"Talking about how one feels helps to take some of the weight off. It's worth a try."

Tommy looked at the flames again. "I'm scared."

"What are you afraid of?"

"Momma said sleeping with a fifteen-year-old girl is a crime. I could go to prison."

"Your momma's not a lawyer. Statutory rape is sex between an adult and a minor. You're not an adult."

Tommy's eyes widened. "So you don't think I'll get into trouble?"

"I didn't say that. It depends on what you did Saturday night." Paul tapped his pen on his knuckles, and Tommy watched, hypnotized by the rhythm. "Did you have sex with Carolyn Saturday night?"

"No."

"Do you know who did?"

Tommy snorted air through his nose. "No, I was downstairs." He stood and began walking around the room, his boots scuffing on the hard-wood floors.

"Do you think she was having sex with someone upstairs?"

Tommy nodded.

"Maybe more than one?"

Tommy looked at Paul through narrowed eyes. "Maybe. Why?"

"It's important, Tommy. I can't help you unless you're willing to get this off your chest." Paul leaned forward. "Did you know Carolyn was pregnant when you brought her to my office?"

"No. We went over that! I told you she wasn't pregnant." Tommy fell into a nearby chair and braced his elbows on his knees, pushing his fists against his brows. His head moved back and forth to emphasize his denial.

"You also told me you'd only had sex one time! When did you find out she was pregnant?"

Tommy sank deeper into his chair. "I didn't know about it until that night, and I was too dumb to know what was happening even then. She didn't tell me why she was bleeding. And she wouldn't go to the hospital." He began to cry. "It's all my fault. I should have worn condoms like you told me to. I killed her." A low howl escaped his throat, much like a whipped dog. Paul let him cry until the worst was over.

"You're being too hard on yourself, Tommy. She was pregnant before you even met her. It happened in June or July, and you didn't date until August, did you?"

Tommy pulled tissues out of the box and blew his nose. He looked at Paul. "We didn't start going together until the middle of August. And we didn't have sex right away."

"So it couldn't have been your baby. If she'd been honest with you, we could have helped her. Tell me about the fraternity party. How did she get invited?"

"We ran into Brandon at the movies one weekend, and he mentioned the party. Asked me to come and to bring Mike and Howie. He looked at Carolyn and said to bring her along, too. I didn't want to, but she was excited about it." He wiped tears from his eyes again. "She'd be alive today if I'd just said 'No.' That was my fault, for sure."

"Did you know Brandon and Carolyn had dated before you met her?"

"She said she went riding in his car a time or two before she met me. She didn't like him that much."

"But it could be his baby. Let's get back to the party. Was there a lot of drinking?"

Tommy nodded.

"Drugs?"

"Marijuana; some pills, I think. I didn't do any."

"Do you know whether Carolyn did?"

"Not while she was with me."

"She wasn't with you all the time?"

Tommy glared at Paul. "Has somebody already told you what happened?"

"No, but I can guess. I know a little about frat parties."

Tommy sprawled in his chair, resigned to spilling his guts. "Brandon took the new members of the fraternity upstairs. They told us high-school kids that we couldn't go with them—they were gonna have an initiation rite. Carolyn went off with the girls to fix her makeup, and us guys went to the basement to play pool. After an hour or so, I got tired waiting for Brandon to come downstairs and decided to go home. But I couldn't find Carolyn." Tommy pulled air in short gasps through his nose, and it escaped through his mouth in noisy sobs. His shoulders convulsed with each constricted breath.

Paul walked to the window and stared at the dirty snow that was piled against the fence. The crying continued, and he sat in the chair beside Tommy, his hand on his shoulder.

"I'm sorry, Tommy. But get it out. What happened next?"

Tommy blew his nose. "I went upstairs to look for Carolyn and to tell Brandon we were leaving. I got to the door of his bedroom and all these guys were standing around whispering. When they saw me, they started pushing to get out of the room. I went inside and saw Brandon coming out of the bathroom. He handed me a wadded up pillowcase and told me to get rid of it. I could see Carolyn in the bathroom, and there was blood all over the floor. When she saw me, she shut the door. I knocked and asked her what happened. She came out, and she was crying and said, 'Let's go.' She wouldn't talk, and I figured her period had started or something. I don't know what I thought. I got Mike and Howie, and we came home."

Tommy began pacing the floor, caged, looking for an exit. "I'm such a dumb idiot. I should have known what was going on," he said. He sat down again. "It's a good thing I didn't. I'd have killed those guys. I still may do it if I find out they killed her."

"What happened on the way home?"

"Nothing. Carolyn slept all the way. I dropped the guys off, and she told me what was in the pillowcase. It scared me, and I drove over to the hospital, but she wouldn't go in. Said she just needed to go home and go to bed." Tommy looked at Paul. "I should have made her go in. I didn't know what to do. I drove by your house, but you weren't home. We were parked in your yard by the lake, so I walked over there and buried the stuff off the trail. Carolyn didn't want me to, but I told her we had to. I didn't know what else to do with it, and she was afraid to take it. I drove her home, and that's all I know." He sighed and slumped low in the chair.

"Were her folks at home when you got there?"

"I don't know. Their truck was. The lights were out."

"What time was it?"

"I got home about twelve thirty."

"You don't know how she got back to the lake?"

"No." Tommy began hiccupping, and Paul poured him a glass of water.

"Tommy, I'm not a lawyer, so I can't tell you for sure what your legal problems are. What you've told me is between us. But I suggest you talk to a lawyer."

"What about my scholarship? This will kill Momma."

"It'll be hard on her, but she'll stick by you. I suspect the university will find a reason to keep your scholarship active. They take football more seriously than life or death."

"Do I have to tell the police?"

"Not unless there's an investigation and you're subpoenaed to testify. But you need to talk to an attorney now. They have client confidentiality, unless you admit to killing someone, which you're not going to do. Why don't I call Vera Summers and have her come over and listen to what you have to say? Your mom needs to hear it, too. Mrs. Summers can advise you on what to do."

Tommy began to cry again. "I know this will kill Momma," he said again.

"Shall I call the lawyer?"

Tommy nodded. Paul picked up the telephone.

When Vera Summers arrived, she insisted that Tillie sit in on his statement. Afterward, Tillie excused herself and left the clinic without speaking.

It was almost noon when the women finished their list of suspects, and Kit called the clinic to reach Tillie. There was no answer; concerned, she called Tillie at home. She nodded as Tillie explained what Tommy had just told Paul and Vera Simmons about what happened Saturday night.

Kit hung up the phone, shaking her head at Tracy and Ruth. "We can revise our suspects chart. Tommy just told Paul and Tillie and an attorney what happened to Carolyn Saturday night. I need to go comfort Tillie. You two come with me, and maybe she'll fill us in on the whole thing. When Paul gets home, we'll pressure him into telling us what he knows about Brandon's involvement."

At Tillie's home, they found her door open, and she was lying on the couch, shoes kicked off, a blanket covering her body and face. She pulled the blanket away, and they listened to the same story Tommy had confessed to Paul. She said Vera Summers had assured Tommy that he was, at most, an accessory to the crime, since he had not participated in the initiation rite.

"His life is over, though," Tillie said. "He'll lose his scholarship, and I can't afford to send him to college."

"Tillie, you're jumping to conclusions," Kit said. "Wait until we know the whole story. Some school will want Tommy to play football, and I'll bet it's our own university."

"I don't want him going to a school where this kind of thing happens." Tillie closed her eyes and pulled the blanket over her face again. As the women prepared to leave, Tracy knelt near the couch and examined the sole of Tillie's pump. Dried mud clung to the two inch heels. Could the heel prints in the park belong to her?

As they crept out of the house, it was difficult for Tracy to worry about Tommy's scholarship. She was afraid that he and his mother had a much more severe problem concerning his immediate future.

When the women arrived back at the Jordan home, they pulled out their chart to delete more names. "When Tommy took Carolyn home, she was still alive. Someone brought her back to the park, either dead or alive. Hal is one of the persons who could have dumped her in the park," Tracy said.

"That's crazy," Kit said. "Why would he do that?"

Tracy pointed to the chart under "motives." "His motive could have been to cover up the poker parties or his involvement with both Carolyn and Dr. Smeltzer, who have been murdered, or because of some criminal actions that he and the police department are trying to hide from the FBI. We also have to look at Tillie. Did you notice that her pumps had dried mud on them?"

Kit stopped, her mouth open. "You're kidding," she said.

"No, I mean it. My pictures show links made by heels like those on her pumps. The dried mud might have come from the park. We have to find out what she was up to."

"Who else is on the suspect list?" Ruth asked, concerned for Kit's best friend.

"Brandon, of course," Tracy said.

"Let's eliminate those we can and go after the ones who are left, including Brandon," Kit said.

"Starting with Hal?" Tracy asked, hoping she sounded objective.

"Yes, starting with Hal," Ruth said. "It seems as if he had nothing to do with Carolyn's death unless, after the rapes, he helped get her body to the park. Did your pictures show any cowboy boot prints near the body, Tracy?"

"Yes, but Falco and half a dozen others stomped around there when we first arrived. I do think you're right that Hal would not have taken her to the park, but he may know who did."

"Why don't I invite him to come over for a drink tonight?" Kit said. "We can tell him we're trying to find out whether Carolyn took Tommy out to the lake house. By focusing on Tommy, Hal won't know that we're aware of Carolyn's attendance at the poker games, or about Brandon's connection. How does that plan sound?"

"I hope everyone realizes that we're playing with dynamite," Ruth said. "We'd better be prepared for an explosion."

"Everything we're doing is dangerous, to hear Paul tell it," Kit said. "Let me check these plans with him." She rose and went to the phone. Ruth crossed her fingers as Kit explained that they wished to invite Hal over for supper and to discuss with him whether Tommy and Caroline had spent time at the lake house. Ruth uncrossed her fingers when the brief call ended. Kit dialed Hal's number, and Tracy stopped to listen to that conversation. It ended with a laugh, and Kit was still giggling when she turned to the table. "It's not hard to see why we all love Hal. He's a sweet-talker."

"I'm not sure we should trust sweet-talkers," Tracy said. "Do you believe everything he says?"

"What do you mean?"

"Just what I said. One minute he has me spellbound—I'm believing every word he says—and the next minute, I'm totally confused." She paused. "I do know better than to get involved with a married man who allows his mother to dominate his life. That's two strikes against Hal."

Ruth raised her eyebrows and nodded with a smile. Kit sat down and placed her arm around Tracy's shoulders. "Oh, Tracy, I've underestimated the trauma you're going through with Hal. I shouldn't have invited him for supper."

"It's alright. This is my payback for making bad decisions. I'll get over it and learn my lesson."

"Why don't you go upstairs and relax for a while? Ruth can help me with the salad."

"I do need time to make a couple of phone calls, if I may," Tracy said. "I'll hurry."

Upstairs she looked through the phone book and wrote down the number for the Oklahoma Attorney General's Office. She should have known the office would be closed. On the answering machine, she left a brief message reporting Carolyn's death and the fact that the teenager may have been raped at a university fraternity party.

Unsatisfied, she called the FBI. She had no idea what to expect when she dialed the number and was surprised when her call went through to the regional FBI office in Chicago. An agent named Russ Cameron answered, and Tracy repeated her report of Carolyn's death. She added information about the police chief's threats against her, and her belief that he was trying to scare her off the investigation of Carolyn's death. The agent asked why, and she explained that the death might be connected to Dr. Smeltzer's disappearance and to illegal activities at the ranch.

The agent listened until she finished, then told her that the FBI was already aware of the assault on Ruth. Tracy sat, numb, as he informed her that the FBI had been investigating pro-life activities in Pontotoc County for several months, because it seemed to be connected to a conservative movement out of Arkansas, where other clinics had been targeted. In fact, she and Ruth had been under surveillance since they arrived in Ada. He ended the conversation by insisting that she and Ruth return to a room at the hotel, where agents would contact her later this evening to take down a written report. Under the circumstances of the attack on Ruth, he felt that they should move back to the hotel, where they would be under constant surveillance in case of another attempt or in case Falco kept following her. He thanked her for calling, and the telephone went dead. Tracy sat looking at it, not believing what she had heard.

She needed to relay this information to Ruth and Kit, but she could hear Paul's car pulling into the driveway. Hal was due any minute. Dreading Paul's anger when he discovered she was setting Hal up for a broad interrogation, Tracy decided to stay upstairs until Hal arrived. She hurried through applying her makeup until the sound of masculine voices announced Hal's arrival. There was no time to change plans. She descended the stairs, smiling and apologizing for leaving the cooking to Kit.

"Don't give her all the credit," Paul said. "Grilling is what takes talent."

Kit had accepted three small pots of violets from Hal and was busy arranging them in a basket on the coffee table.

"Let's go do the trout," Paul said to Hal, handing him a drink and pushing him toward the kitchen door.

The meal was a pleasant mixture of good food and conversation. Tracy regretted that they had to retire to the living room to discuss unpleasant subjects, but Hal made it easy. He sat alone in a chair across from Tracy. "Now," he said, "tell me what mischief you've been up to."

Paul looked around in surprise. Kit coughed as her drink caught in her throat.

Tracy felt calm. She loved the power surge she got from interrogating suspects. Nothing could be more fun than having Hal Montgomery on the hot seat.

"We're concerned about why the police are dragging their feet on the investigation of Carolyn's death. Particularly how Tommy and Brandon might be involved."

"Where did you get the idea that the police aren't pursuing the case?"

"The chief called me into his office twice to suggest that Carolyn died from a coat-hanger abortion, yet the coroner's report specifically states that there is no evidence of injuries related to sharp instruments. The report said that the trauma to the uterus was similar to that left by rape or forced entry. Furthermore, while I was in the chief's office, he threatened to arrest me for being an outside agitator working for pro-choice groups. He asked me to leave town."

"That sounds kind of crazy. You talked to him this week?" Hal took his drink in both hands, placed his elbows on his knees, and leaned toward Tracy for an answer to his question.

"Yes. Twice. I didn't misunderstand him," she said. "He made it quite clear."

"The coroner was sure it was not an abortion?" Hal sounded relieved.

"The autopsy says she died from loss of blood. She was pregnant and lost the baby due to trauma to the uterus. That trauma caused the bleeding."

"Was it a miscarriage, or wasn't it?"

Tracy's voice broke, as she responded. "The loss of the fetus wasn't caused by a coat hanger. Carolyn was raped, multiple times."

Hal's body tensed. He gritted his teeth and his jaw muscle bounced to the applied pressure. "That's outrageous. Let me get in touch with Matt tomorrow. I'll handle this. You should stay out of it."

"Do you have any idea where this might have happened and who was involved?"

"How would I know?"

"We know Carolyn was out at the lake house the evening she died. She left with you about eight thirty. Where did you drop her off?"

"I took her home." Hal walked over to the sweep of windows that opened to a broad view of the lake. "She said Tommy was picking her up. She didn't say where they were going."

"So you're unaware that they went to Brandon's fraternity party?"

Hal walked back to his chair, no glimmer of expression on his face.

"I recall that she mentioned a party, but I didn't know Brandon was involved in it. I assumed it was high-school kids." He leaned back in his chair, pretending to be at ease, but Tracy suspected that his every muscle was poised to strike. "Would you mind telling me what your interest in this case is?" His voice was taunting, and Tracy felt her face warming under his stare.

"The same as everyone's should be," she answered. "Justice."

"We have a court system for that purpose, Tracy. I'm surprised you didn't learn that in your police training."

His condescending response angered Tracy. "I did. But of course, the courts can't respond to cases like this unless the police bring them evidence of a crime. For some unexplainable reason, Chief Mayfield doesn't believe there was a crime. I thought perhaps you could open his eyes."

Hal seemed tired of arguing. "I said I'd take care of it. What else are you asking me to do?"

"Help us follow Carolyn from the time you dropped her off at home."

"I'm sorry. I don't know where she went. As I said, all she told me was that she was going to a party. She didn't say where or with whom, and I didn't ask her."

Tracy felt the short hairs on her arm bristle. Hal had no reason to lie, unless he was protecting himself or Brandon. He was smooth, she thought, and he was aware of the potential consequences of this conversation.

"Have you talked to Brandon since Saturday night? Did he mention that Carolyn came over to the party?"

Hal's answer was too swift. "No. I haven't talked to Brandon. I've been busy following up on the auction sales. If I monitored every party Brandon attends, that's all I'd have time to do." The sarcasm was pointed.

"I guess you'll be surprised, then, to learn that Carolyn did go to Brandon's fraternity party and took part in the initiation rites for new members, which Brandon directed." Tracy's voice was strong and her accusations clear.

Hal straightened in his chair. "I'd be terribly disappointed," he said.

Tracy's voice softened. "We have evidence that Carolyn was gang raped by fraternity boys in an initiation rite in an upstairs bedroom at the fraternity house. That's evidently where she lost the baby."

Hal's face darkened and his eyes squinted almost closed, but Tracy saw no shock in his reaction. "You're prepared to name names?"

"I can't at this time, but I'm sure it won't be hard to collect them." She watched as Hal leaned back in his chair and tipped his glass to empty it. He stood and walked back to look out the windows. She rushed her next charge, expecting him to leave at any moment.

"Tommy brought Carolyn back to Ada and left her at her home, alive, but still hemorrhaging. Someone took her to the city park. We don't know whether she was dead at that time or whether she died later."

"I'm a little shocked that you seem to be pointing a finger at me." Hal's voice was razor sharp.

"I'm not, but I thought you might know who did do it, since she lives on the ranch."

"Sorry, I don't know. Why don't you ask her parents?"

"We did. They have not been helpful."

Hal relaxed.

"I have a few more questions," Tracy said. "Where were you Saturday night after you left the poker party?"

Hal pulled a handkerchief from his pocket and wiped his forehead. "Kit can answer that question for you. She knows I was in Tulsa Saturday night. I sent a bottle of wine to her table." He looked at Kit.

Tracy hesitated before deflating his alibi. "Kit says she didn't see you in Tulsa that night."

"I didn't say she saw me."

Tracy was tiring of the cat and mouse game. She sighed. "Just one more thing. We've been told that Carolyn went over to the lake house on Saturday nights to help with the gambling tables." The room became so quiet Tracy could feel her heart beat.

"What gambling tables?" Hal chuckled and handed his empty glass to Paul. "I guess we're not through here. How about another round?"

For the first time, Tracy was caught off balance. He was denying there were Saturday night poker parties at the lake house?

"There aren't any high-stakes gambling tables at the lake house," Hal said. "Friends show up to play cards, penny ante. Where did you get the idea it was more than a social night among friends?"

Tracy felt her face flushing with anger. "Carolyn described the games to her mother as high-stakes poker, with businessmen coming from all over the state. But then, what does a dead fifteen-year-old girl know?" She knew her tone was derisive. She might as well have been in a cage with a wild animal, deliberately poking him with a sharp instrument.

The beautiful eyes she had always loved filled with fire, and she felt challenged to ratchet up the stakes.

"Were Julie and Marge playing penny ante, also?"

Hal stood up and looked at Paul. "Sorry to break up the party, but I've got to go." He turned to Tracy. "I don't know who gave you the authority to butt into affairs in this county, or what you expect to accomplish with your innuendos, but we have a police department hired to keep the streets clean and peaceful. We don't need outsiders dumping horse shit around."

Tracy found it impossible to respond. He sounded a lot like the police chief.

Hal picked up his hat and moved across the floor. As an afterthought, he reached down and grabbed the basket of violets he had brought. He walked out the door, and everyone sat stunned as the flowers crashed against the far end of the porch railing. In the silence, they heard Hal's footsteps fade as he walked down the slate pathway to his pickup. The vehicle roared onto the road, and silence settled in the room like a suffocating cloud of anesthesia.

"I can't believe he reacted this way," Tracy said.

"We tried to warn you," Ruth said.

Paul rose, almost shouting. "How did you expect him to react? Those were damn pointed accusations."

"Maybe we did more harm than good?" Kit sniffled.

Paul stood up. "If he's guilty, I don't know what the advantage is in telling him what you know. Now he'll have time to find alibis to cover himself and Brandon."

"I didn't tell him anything he didn't already know, Paul. He's angry because I know it." Tracy leaned forward, resting her head on her clenched fists. "I wanted to see his reaction, and I did. He still thinks his alibi is good for Saturday night." She looked at Kit. "I think he was lying. I'm sure he talked to Brandon and knows what went on at the fraternity house. That's what he's trying to cover up. I contacted the state attorney general's office and the FBI, and they said they had been notified of the fraternity escapade. They're already involved in the investigation."

"You called the attorney general's office?" Paul asked.

"I left a message. And, yes, I called the FBI to report the threats the police chief made against me and the assault on Ruth. They know about the assault, and they are following up on it because of its possible connection to Nora's death. They asked that Ruth and I move back to the hotel, because it's easier for them to monitor the policeman in case he keeps following me."

"I don't understand why he's following you. It's like stalking," Kit said.

"Maybe I didn't tell you that the police chief planted several pro-abortion brochures in the magazine I was reading in his office. He accused me of leaving them there. He's setting me up as an abortion rights activist, visiting here to cause trouble. I guess his lapdog is following me to gather evidence of my participation in criminal acts."

Kit moved over to sit by Tracy. "It sounds like the police department is supporting the people who got rid of Nora. They're trying to get the investigation of Carolyn's death laid at the door of the abortion rights groups instead of on Brandon's friends."

Tracy took her hand. "I suspect they're worried that an investigation of Carolyn's death may lead to what's going on at the ranch, or maybe to the people who killed Nora."

"And what is going on at the ranch?" Paul asked.

"All we know is that there are poker games and a couple of prostitutes available to cheer up the losers or reward the winners. What the FBI suspects is that it's a money-laundering scheme set up to enrich Senator Fortenberry's campaign fund. That would be a federal crime."

"That's hard to believe. I'm sure Hal wouldn't be involved in something like that."

"If it had been a friendly poker game, he'd have invited you, wouldn't he? You weren't asking for favors from the senator."

Paul looked at Ruth, frowning. "Hal wouldn't invite me to a party where there were drugs and sex on the side. He knows how I feel about those things. I can't believe he's involved."

"It's happening with his knowledge, at the very least."

"He seemed out of control tonight. I'm worried about your safety," Kit said to Tracy.

Paul nodded. "You said the FBI was watching you and Ruth. Couldn't they do that here instead of at the hotel?"

"I'm sure we're small fish, and they can't waste their time babysitting us. Their primary interest is in finding Nora's murderer."

"I'm surprised they don't order you to get out of town," Paul said. "Then they wouldn't have to worry about you."

"They did suggest it, but they seemed pleased that I'm keeping the police focused on the Pittman case. That leaves them free to look for more evidence about Nora's death."

"I still think you and Ruth should stay here, now that we have Henley's men watching the place," Kit said.

"So do I," Paul said, and he began pacing past the windows, as Hal had done.

"Paul, please sit down. We don't need you to start throwing things," Kit said.

Tracy looked at Ruth. "I think we should head back to the hotel. Let's pack."

Paul turned to Kit. "You come with me. We'll follow them in. I don't want to leave you alone."

As he spoke, they heard a whine and scratches on the door. For a moment no one moved, then Kit rushed to open the door. Outside, Charley fell on his side, pawing with one leg and continuing to whine. Paul picked him up and carried him to the table on the back porch, where he spread a blanket over him. "Get my medical bag, and I'll need some hot water." Overcoming their shock, everyone rushed to help.

It took a half hour to wash and bandage the wounds. All four feet were bleeding and swollen. The dog's head was still swollen and seeping blood where the butt of the gun had knocked him out. A lariat tied around his neck had been chewed in two. Hanging to the ground, it had rubbed his neck and chest raw as he walked.

"They underestimated how smart he is and how much he cares for us." Paul said. "I'd like to find the other end of that rope. I'd use it to string up the bums."

"How far do you suppose he walked?" Kit asked.

"Hundreds of miles. His feet are raw. He's lost weight, but he'll be okay in a few weeks," Paul said.

"As far as Arkansas?" Ruth asked. No one answered, but everyone caught the connection between Charley's disappearance and the brutal death of Nora Smeltzer. Could her body have been transported to the farm in Arkansas in the same old pickup that carried Charley?

Tracy wiped tears from her eyes. "I didn't dream this would happen, or I'd never have gotten everyone involved. I'm so sorry."

Paul's face was grim. "It isn't your fault. Whatever led to this outrage has to be exposed. If Hal's involved in it, he has to be stopped too."

Surprised and relieved that Paul fully supported their theories, Tracy and Ruth collected their possessions and headed for the hotel. They insisted that Paul and Kit stay home with Charley.

Tracy handed her keys to the valet at the hotel, and he deposited their luggage with the bell boy.

"You're back," the registrar greeted them. He glanced at the registration book. "Room 203," he said, making notations. He handed the room key to the bell boy, and the women walked behind him to the elevator. Upstairs, as he left the room, the telephone rang, and Tracy's eyes widened.

"Hi. This is Russ Cameron with the FBI. We talked earlier. Glad to see you've checked in. Do you mind if I drop by with another of our agents to take your statement? We want to make sure you know who the good guys are from here on out. Room 203, right?" He didn't wait for an answer.

Tracy turned to Ruth, who was pulling her gown from the closet. "Keep your shirt on. Someone who claims to be the FBI is headed this way. Who knows if they pillage and plunder the homes of innocent young females?"

"Even if they do, you and I are safe."

"Not to worry. It's the agent I talked to on the phone."

She opened the door to a soft knock. Each of the men held out identification badges and tried to hide their amusement as both Tracy and Ruth took one and examined it carefully.

"Who's Cameron?" The one with dimples saluted with one finger.

Ruth covered the other badge from the second man's view. "And your name?"

"Harry Smith."

She looked at Tracy. "They can read and recite names."

"That's sufficient to pass a government exam," Tracy said and returned the badges. "What can we do for you fellows?"

"May we close the door?"

The women looked at each other and nodded.

"Our first mission is to get your statement of what's been happening, and the second is to convince you to leave town."

"Why do people keep suggesting that to me? It's as if I'm not welcome in my own hometown," Tracy said.

"There are better places you could be right now. We've had two murders in the last week, and for some reason, you're connected to both of them. When were you planning to leave?"

"In a day or two."

"The sooner the better. We have information that a van load of anti-abortion people will arrive here tonight from Arkansas. Their goal is to close the Women's Health Clinic for good. You don't want to be in the middle of that."

Tracy paused for a moment to consider what he was saying. "Are you willing me I'm creating problems for you by staying here?"

"I wouldn't wish to diminish your importance to this case, but we do have our hands full without having to guard you," Smith said.

"Good," Tracy said. "Because I don't want to be guarded. Sergeant Falco has been stalking me ever since I got here. Why don't you check in with him every day to get the low down on what subversive acts I've committed?"

Cameron chuckled. "We've been curious as to why the police are following you. You haven't been up to something we don't know about, have you?"

Smith looked at Cameron. "Maybe he just likes to follow pretty women. Some of us guys do."

Cameron's glare could have lit kindling.

"I repeat my question. Have you been up to something we don't know about?"

"I have not. I was unlucky enough to find Carolyn Pittman's body in the park on Sunday, and because of that, they have accused me of teaching women the fine art of abortion, which I know nothing about. Your guess about how they came to that conclusion is closer to the truth than mine would be."

"Then you don't have much imagination, Miz Hunter. Dr. Smeltzer is dead because she refused to take seriously the accusations made against her. Now, could we get your report in writing?"

"What do you need to know?" Tracy asked, and she spent the next twenty minutes answering their questions.

"Do you think there's a connection between her death and Carolyn's?" she asked as they closed their books.

"We have no proof at this stage, but we're looking into it."

"Umm." She looked at Ruth. "I guess we're still in business then." Her voice trailed off as she opened the door. "It's been nice knowing you."

Smith hurried out, but Cameron hesitated. "Maybe we should get together for lunch sometime. Exchange theories." Smith could be heard chuckling in the hall. Embarrassed, Cameron followed him and closed the door.

"I think he likes you," Ruth said.

"Please, no. I don't need another man in my life."

"At least this one wants you to leave town. That's an improvement." Tracy threw a pillow at her sister and dialed the Jordans' number. Paul picked it up on the first ring.

"Tracy?"

She laughed. "Do you have my line bugged, too?"

"No. Who does?"

"I don't know. I'm getting paranoid."

"Please don't do anything crazy, Tracy." Paul choked and struggled to breathe. Until now he had refused to admit, even to himself, that Tracy was his daughter. He had begun having nightmares about what might happen to their future relationship. What would a revelation of the truth do to Tracy's love and respect for her mother? Would he be able to convince her that it was his fault the affair happened?" Also, such an admission would create a number of problems in his immediate family, which he was not brave enough to face. Kit would have to be told, putting his marriage in jeopardy. How would his children react?

Tracy's delightful laugh brought his thoughts back to the present.

"Could you be more specific?" she asked. "Lately, everything I've done has been crazy."

There was a long pause before Paul replied. "I know it's futile to give you advice. Remember that we care about you. Try to stay alive. Here's Kit." He turned and hurried to his office upstairs. He needed to confess to someone he trusted. Perhaps he and Hal could share their problems.

Downstairs, Kit wrapped up her telephone conversation with Tracy. "Can we get together tomorrow to pare down our leads? We need to close this thing," she said.

"I agree. Let's meet at the hotel coffee shop. We will be within yelling distance of the FBI, and the hotel people can watch our every move."

"I'll be there at ten. And Tracy, stay safe. Don't open the door."
Tracy laughed. "Never?"
"You know what I mean. See you tomorrow."

SEVENTEEN

The next morning, Paul went to his office, wondering where to start digging for the truth about the Saturday night party. He decided to call Hal, who might know more than he had let on to Tracy. Besides, Paul needed to apologize for the after-dinner fiasco.

"This is Hal." The voice was quiet, much different from the jovial greeting Paul was used to.

"Hi, sport. I was hoping I'd find you at home. I have to apologize for what happened at the house last night. We need to talk about all this craziness. It's driving me out of my mind. What's going on from your end?"

"Paul, you don't want to know. You're a nice guy. Nice guys don't get involved in a mess like this." Hal's voice cracked.

"Hal, friends are friends, no matter what. We all have our problems. My theory is it helps to talk about them. Maybe I can help."

"How?"

"I don't know. You tell me."

"I don't think anyone can help. Brandon and his buddies screwed up big time. Muffy has been talking to the attorney general, and it looks like the boys could be facing murder charges. Brandon says it wasn't rape; Carolyn went into this deal willingly, but who's going to believe she agreed to screw every plebe in the fraternity? And it doesn't matter if she did. Everybody knows a minor can't legally give her consent." Hal snorted in disgust. "What a bunch of idiots."

Paul sighed as he switched the telephone to his other ear.

"What the hell is Tracy doing in the middle of this?" Hal added.

"I don't know how it happened, Hal, but the police chief gave Tracy the impression he'd finished his investigation into Carolyn's death. He was satisfied that Carolyn self-aborted her baby. Case closed. Tracy doesn't believe it, and neither does Kit, so they began investigating. That's when all the other stuff came out."

"By 'other stuff,' you mean what's going on at the ranch?"

"Yeah."

"It's not pretty, pal. And I don't want this passed on to Tracy or to Kit."

"Maybe I don't want to hear it either."

"I'd rather you heard it from me. I'm going to be blamed for the gambling, because it happened under my watch, but the truth is that old man Crosier, who sold me the ranch, is the one who's running the games. They started out as social get-togethers, but when I bought the ranch, Muffy saw the games as a way to launder big campaign contributions to her dad. Lobbyists were sent to gamble and lose, on purpose, to the senator's stand-in. Depending on how much they were willing to lose, his votes went 'yea' or 'nay' on legislation. The whole thing was underway before I knew about it. I tried to stop it, but my relationship with Crosier was, and still is, touchy. He gave me a good deal on the purchase price of the ranch, and he's still carrying the note. He's one of Senator Fortenberry's biggest financial supporters. Because the guys who were playing poker were using money their companies set aside for lobbying, the scheme didn't seem all that bad to me. I guess the IRS doesn't look at it that way."

Not to mention laws governing limits to campaign contributions, Paul thought, as he propped his elbow on his desk and rested his head on his palm. This was the information Tracy had been looking for, the reason Beatrice didn't want Carolyn's death investigated.

"What about the prostitutes?"

"Oh, hell. These women aren't running a business. They just come to party. They're dates."

"Not according to the scuttlebutt, Hal."

Hal didn't respond, and Paul heard a chair scraping against the floor. In his mind he could see Hal pushing away from his desk, ready to slam down the telephone receiver.

"I thought you called to cheer me up, pal," Hal said.

"God, I'm sorry. I did want to apologize for last night, but to be honest, I was also interested in what you knew about the fraternity party. Tillie is going crazy, worrying about Tommy's involvement. Do you know what part he played in all this?" Paul asked.

"Not really, but I think the bedroom stuff was limited to the initiates in the fraternity, like a rite of admission or something."

"Tommy wouldn't have been a part of that, and according to him, he didn't know it was going on," Paul said.

"What can I do to protect him?" Hal asked.

"I don't know. I had him talk to a lawyer, and she'll be with him if he's interrogated by the police or FBI."

"I was hoping you could help me with Tracy," Hal said. Silence hung between them, and Paul grew tense as he waited for Hal to continue. "Tracy and I go back a long way, and I had hopes we'd get back together. Seems like a pipe dream now." His voice regained its businesslike tone. "I told the police chief to lay off following Tracy, but I hope she'll get out of town. I don't want her around when the top blows off this mess."

"Hal, this woman isn't some kooky liberal out to change the world. She's been on the investigation unit of the Chicago Police Department for ten years, and she's incensed at the way the local guys are handling both Nora's and Carolyn's investigations. She and Nora were roommates in college, so she feels a special obligation to see that one through. I suppose you know she's questioning whether Nora came to one or more of the Saturday night poker parties. She's convinced there's a tie between what's going on at the ranch and Nora's murder. At first, I kidded her about playing Sherlock Holmes, but the truth is, I agree with most of what she's concluded."

"That doesn't bode well for Brandon and his friends, though I'll admit they deserve whatever they get. However, Mother wouldn't agree with that. I just wish Tracy didn't have to be in the middle of it."

"Hal I need to talk to you about Tracy, but not over the telephone. Can you meet me here at the office? Or I can come out there."

"Oh, hell. I have some people coming in this morning to buy some cattle. Maybe after five?"

Paul relaxed. "Five is fine. See you here." It felt good to have opened the door to a discussion about his problems.

Tillie knocked on the door and peeked in. "Patients are waiting," she said.

The day passed swiftly, and at five Paul hurried Tillie out the office door, hoping she'd be gone before Hal arrived. As he locked the door, he heard him calling from the back entrance. Settled into the office, they looked at each other, neither knowing how to start the conversation. Paul wondered if sharing problems was such a good idea, after all.

"So what's all this about?" Hal asked.

Paul shook his head. "I'm having trouble talking about it. I need to get something off my chest, and I thought you might be able to give me some advice. I figure if you're contemplating a future with Tracy, you have a right to know what happened a long time ago. Mostly, I'm going through hell, keeping secrets that may get out anyway, and if they do I'm afraid it will ruin my whole life." He paused and watched Hal frown and shake his head.

"What the hell? You know something bad about Tracy?"

Paul rose and began pacing near the windows. He stopped, his hands resting on the back of his chair. "It's more about me. I had an affair with Tracy's mother when I first arrived in Ada. Tracy was born nine months later."

Hal sat speechless, and Paul began spilling the whole story of his alcoholism, the death of his first wife and daughter, and his struggle with rehabilitation when he arrived in Ada. As his story ended, Hal's eyes wandered away from Paul, avoiding contact. He stared at the floor.

"Let me get this straight," he said. "You think you're Tracy's father?"

Paul nodded. "I'm afraid so."

"What's to be afraid of?"

"I'm worried about the consequences of telling either Kit or Tracy about my past. Imagine what a mess it will cause. I can't hurt Kit that way. I just can't do it to her . . . not to mention what it will do to my kids."

"Sounds to me like it's your own hide you're worried about."

Paul nodded. "You're right. I'm a coward, trying to justify hiding the truth. But it seems to be the best way to keep from hurting Tracy and my family. I need to know what to do next."

"I honest to God don't know, Paul. We all make mistakes we'd rather people didn't know about. I'd hate to see Kit hurt . . . or Tracy, for that matter." He scratched his head. "Why are you telling me about this mess? Tracy's the woman I love, and you tell me she's your daughter!" He stood, and slapping his hat against his thigh, he began to laugh. "If this is true and we got married, you'd be my father-in-law."

"That's not the real problem, and it's not something to laugh about either. Keeping the secret is driving me crazy. I need someone to tell me what the right thing to do is. Does Tracy have a right to know? How is it going to help her when, more than likely, it will do nothing but darken her happy memories of her mother? It certainly isn't going to help my family to know what I did back then."

Paul's angry voice sobered Hal, and he sat down. "I see your point. In some ways, we're in the same boat. I've made some bad decisions for sure, and I'm having to pay for them. It would have been nice to avoid facing all my legal problems by continuing to hide the facts. Unfortunately, I don't get that choice. I guess you do."

"Humm. Your comparison helps in some ways. If illegal activities are made public, the victims will likely find justice in the courts. In my case, I'm playing the role of judge. I have to decide whether Tracy and my family will be better off or worse off, if I tell the truth."

"You surely don't think I know the answer to that question."

"No. But talking about it helps me to see things more clearly. I'm coming to the conclusion that I can't play God with other people's lives. This is my burden, and I shouldn't dump it on everyone I love."

"Yeah, but if Tracy agrees to marry me, I'll have your guilt hanging over my head, too." Hal stood. "Thanks for sharing your load. If the shit hits the fan in my case, I'll return the favor."

Tracy awoke with a dull headache, which was no way to start the day. Ruth's bed was empty, and she hoped her sister had gone for coffee and rolls. Rummaging in her purse for a little tin of aspirin, she shook the contents and was startled to hear the sound of metal against metal. Among the handful of small items were chewing gum, lipstick, aspirin, and a high-school ring with tape around the band.

Tracy stared in disbelief. When and how had the ring gotten from her coat pocket to her purse? Her body began to quiver with chills. Whoever took the ring from her room had returned the stolen item when the purse was not in her possession. Why? The ring lay on the coffee table as if it were radioactive. The aspirin tin popped open and two tablets dropped into her hand. When Ruth arrived with the coffee, snacks, and a newspaper, Tracy's hand shook so that the coffee she gulped splashed on her nose and ran down her chin. She wiped it away.

"What's the matter with you, kid?"

Tracy pointed to the ring. Ruth sat on the couch, picked up the ring, and inspected it. "Where did you find it?"

"Someone put it in my purse."

"Are you sure you didn't?"

"I didn't."

"What do you suppose it means?"

Tracy shook her head. "Someone took it from my pocket and later decided to return it, hoping I'd believe I was confused about where I had hidden it. I'm not confused, Ruth."

"I'm sure you're not, but who would have done it? And why?"

"It had to have been taken from my coat while we were out of the room. Later it was dropped into my purse when I wasn't looking. I laid the purse on the floor by the piano last night, and Hal could have dropped the ring inside while we were in the kitchen. If it didn't happen that way, then someone came into our room last night while we were sleeping."

"I'd rather think it was Hal."

"I'm not so sure I would, but we need to show this to Tommy to make sure it's his. Then we have to ask whether he knows how it got to the floor at the lake house."

"What's that going to prove?"

"That Carolyn was in the bedroom with someone other than Tommy. The ring was dropped on the floor to hide it. There would have been no reason to do that if she was with Tommy."

"Okay."

Tracy looked at her watch. "Whoa. We're supposed to meet Kit in fifteen minutes. See if there's anything new in the paper about the murders while I'm dressing."

Kit was reading and drinking coffee when they arrived downstairs, Tracy with damp hair and no makeup.

"I'm sorry," she said. "It's not Ruth's fault we're late. I overslept and got up with a lousy headache."

Ruth pretended to be counting on her fingers. "This is only the second time in her life this woman has admitted something was her fault."

Tracy ignored her and told Kit to hold out her hand. Kit complied, and Tracy dropped the ring onto her palm. Kit's eyebrows raised in surprise.

"Where did you find it?"

"In my purse this morning"

"So it wasn't stolen after all."

"Yes, it was. I put it in my pocket. Someone took it out but decided to return it when I started making a fuss. The thief dropped it into my purse."

"You're sure?"

"I'm positive. And it could have been Hal, last night at your house."

Ruth picked up the list of questions. "It would help us to know why Hal wanted people to believe he was in Tulsa when Carolyn died."

Kit answered first. "Because he knew he could be linked to her from the time they left the poker party together. Maybe when he set up this alibi, he didn't know Carolyn went to the party with Tommy. He may have thought he was the last person to see her before she died. If so, it would be convenient to have an out-of-town alibi for the rest of the evening. The question is, where was he, if he wasn't in Tulsa?"

"We don't know," said Tracy. "Put a star by that question, and let's go on to the next one."

Kit took the paper back from Ruth and smoothed it in front of her. "Did anyone check to see if the ring has Tommy's initials? It could be Brandon's. Paul's been talking to Tommy, and that might be the best way to get to the truth."

"Yes. I cut off the tape. It has the initials 'TB' inside."

"Okay. Tell Paul to ask Tommy whether he and Carolyn went to the cabin together and also whether Tommy knew the ring was missing. If they didn't shack up there, then Carolyn must have been there with Brandon, Hal, or one of the men at the poker game."

"Yeah, more likely Brandon. Next, we need to talk to Mrs. Pittman again. Ruth, why don't you and I visit her?" Kit said.

"That's another clue we overlooked," Tracy said. "I reviewed the pictures with the pump heels, and there are also what look like flat moccasin prints in the dirt. Mrs. Pittman wears the only moccasins I've seen since I've been here."

"This suggests that both Tillie and the mother could have been at the murder scene that night, right?"

"Very likely."

"What else?"

"If they were in the park, they may have been involved in Carolyn's death or in covering the body or they may know who did."

"While I finish up at the clerk's office this morning, why don't you two dissect the alibis of those two?"

"Good idea, and let's meet at my house for dinner tonight to pool our findings," Kit said.

"Agreed," Ruth said. "I love your cooking."

EIGHTEEN

After leaving Kit and Ruth around noon, Tracy went back to the hotel and changed into sweats and running shoes. The snow had melted from the sidewalks, making it possible to run downtown to the clerk's office. Surely no one would try to kidnap her in public. Breezing out of the hotel, she hit the street running. The clerk's office was within a block of Paul's clinic, so she veered to the left, hoping to find him between patients. She would update him on finding the ring. Out of breath and sweating, not presentable for the front office, Tracy circled to the back door. Paul came out of his lab, distracted by papers in both hands, glasses resting low on his nose.

"You look busy," Tracy said, startling him.

"Never too busy to say 'hi' to friends. Hi," he said, and left her standing in the hall. Unwilling to be deterred, Tracy followed him, deciding to be straightforward. "I found the ring."

"Good. I thought you would. This should teach you to be more careful."

"I didn't lose it. It was stolen and returned."

Paul removed his glasses and stared at Tracy. "You're positive?"

"I'm positive."

"I guess that does make you a regular Sherlock Holmes."

"You're so perceptive."

"You're so transparent. You aren't the only one with a Sherlock Holmes kit, you know. I'll discuss this with Tommy."

"Thank you," she said and kissed his cheek.

As she reached the door, Paul called after her. "That will be five dollars."

"Put it on my account, Doctor." Tracy smiled and hurried out, hoping Paul would tell Hal that the ring had been found.

At the door of the county clerk's office, Tracy wiped the sweat from her brow and wondered if her smell would repulse those standing within five feet of her. There was no line, so she hurried up to Bonnie's window. A stranger came to help.

"Is Bonnie here?"

"No. She isn't in today. May I help you?"

"Oh. She was helping me with a special problem. Do you know when she'll be back?"

"No. She had a doctor's appointment."

"When will she be back?"

"I wouldn't know. She's sick."

Tracy gave up. Of course Bonnie was sick, but how sick? Would she be back next week?

Tracy dragged herself out of the building. What a bummer. If Bonnie was sick all week, the work on the birth certificate might be stalled forever. Maybe she and Ruth should go back to Tulsa until Bonnie returned. Wandering down the street, Tracy remembered that Chief Mayfield had said Nora's autopsy report would be ready today. She could go pick it up . . . unless Billy was also out sick. Hurrying down the street, she soon found herself at the coroner's office. Billy calmly went about his job in the same slow, methodical manner. Nothing seemed to fluster him, and the secretaries waiting for his services were more than happy to gossip while they waited at the counter.

After the crowd disappeared, Tracy gave Billy time to get a coke and sit down at his desk before ambling up to the counter, and with a shy grin, wiggled her fingers at him. He sprang from his seat and hurried to the counter, a little flushed.

"You're back," he said.

She nodded. "You run a busy office around here."

"Yeah. It comes in spurts. The last hour of the day is usually calmer than this. What can I do for you? Did Dr. Jordan find what he wanted in the Pittman report?"

"Yes, he did, and he was so pleased with my help that he sent me back. Could he also have a copy of Dr. Nora Smeltzer's autopsy?"

Billy paused, and then turned around and began shuffling through the file drawer, working much faster this time. He made copies and came back to the counter, holding them close to his chest.

"Thanks so much, Billy. Dr. Jordan will appreciate this." She reached out to take the documents.

Billy smiled, without offering to release the report. He leaned forward, as though they were sharing a secret. "Actually, I called Dr. Jordan after you left the other day, and he told me he didn't order that Pittman report."

Caught red-handed, Tracy wanted to melt right through the floor. Why hadn't Paul told her that Billy called? She was sure the punishment for lying to obtain government documents was a felony. A private investigator should know better than to get caught. Her fingers itched to reach out and snatch the Smeltzer report. Billy grinned at her.

"He told me what you were planning to do with the information. I don't let people around here know, but I liked Dr. Smeltzer, and I feel sorry for the young girls left without her care. My sister's one of them. Dr. Smeltzer was the only doctor they could talk to, except for Dr. Jordan, and a lot of them don't want to go to a male doctor." He pushed the report toward Tracy. "Do whatever you can to find the killers. Just don't let my boss know I slipped the report to you."

Tracy folded the document and stuck it inside her sweatshirt. "I promise you, Billy. This is just between you and me. It does get to the doctor, you know." They both smiled. "Thanks a million," Tracy said and hurried out of the building. With this kind of luck, she should be playing poker. It was scary to think her good fortune might not last until she got out of town.

Once outside, she headed toward the hotel, turning the corner from Main Street to Fourteenth. A larger than usual crowd of people gathered in front of the clinic, parading with signs and banners. Better instincts told Tracy to turn around and disappear, but that was not the instinct that led her into investigative work. Curiosity always got the better of her intuition. She crossed the street to watch from a safe distance. The noise from the crowd exploded, their angry shouts directed at someone coming out of the door. These must be the rabble-rousers the FBI was expecting from Arkansas, and Tracy was standing right where the agent had told her not to be.

Heat returned to her face, and her jaws clamped until her teeth hurt. What right did any group have to kill a doctor, even if they thought their cause was just? Plus, she believed these people were also indirectly responsible for Carolyn's death.

Tracy found herself moving across the street in order to see who was coming out of the clinic door. Falco was nowhere in sight. It was not surprising that he would not be where he was actually needed.

Pushing through the crowd, Tracy stood on her tiptoes. The shouts became louder, and just as she prepared to leave, Bonnie Heydt walked out of the clinic. Hecklers yelled that she was a baby killer. Without thinking, Tracy plowed forward to the door, pushing hecklers aside, bent on helping Bonnie exit the building. Once she reached the door, her friend escaped, but Tracy pitched forward beneath a blow to her head. Friendly hands pulled her inside and closed the door. She stumbled forward, shaking her head to clear her thoughts. "What's going on? Where are the police?" she asked the lady who had come to her aid.

The tall woman guided her to a chair. "Don't expect the police to arrest these criminals. They're all on the same side." The receptionist pushed a form toward Tracy. "Fill this out. We don't have time for any more appointments today, unless it's an emergency."

"Oh, I'm not sick," Tracy said. She sat frowning, listening to the yelling outside the building. "Does this go on all the time?"

"Usually worse than this." The woman's voice was surprisingly calm.

Tracy's own anger was churning. This was what one read about in the newspapers. Never before had she been in the middle of a demonstration. She rubbed the knot on her head, wondering if it was a concussion. Wait until Kit and Ruth heard about her adventure. Maybe they should keep it a secret from Paul. She looked around the office. Pamphlets similar to the ones the police chief had accused her of distributing in his office were spread on a table. They were similar to ones she'd seen from underground groups in Chicago, and Tracy was pleased that the local women had access to current information.

As she scanned the material, the noise outside magnified. The receptionist ran to the door, yanked it open, and pulled on the arm of a woman who was struggling to come inside. The newcomer pushed and kicked at the demonstrators, cursing like a trooper. Tracy ran over to help, as the woman pushed through the door, then stood upright and straightened her clothing. She was in her late twenties or early thirties. Her bleached blond hair, bright lipstick, and mascara contrasted with the unadorned receptionist. Her four-inch heels and mesh stockings seemed out of place. As she disappeared down the hall, Tracy was struck with an idea. Why wouldn't Marge and Julie show up as patients at this clinic? Maybe she could find their names on the patient list.

The receptionist returned to her desk and Tracy approached her.

"Hi. I'm trying to get in touch with a couple of your patients named Julie and Marge. I don't have their last names, and I thought you might be able to help me."

The receptionist looked at Tracy as if she were an idiot. "I'm sorry, I can't give out information about our patients. However, you can talk to the visiting doctor, if you want to wait." She pointed down the hall.

"I only need a telephone number."

The receptionist's eyes indicated that Tracy might be both a deaf and dumb idiot. Her monotone voice repeated the fact that they did not give out information about their patients.

Tracy gave up. Her luck had turned. It was unfortunate that one of her former classmates didn't work here. Maybe the doctor would be sympathetic. It was her only hope. In the meantime, she would pursue her other leads.

"Is there a telephone I can use?"

"There's a phone in the waiting room in back."

"Thanks." Tracy walked to the rear of the building. Maybe Mr. Pittman would answer the phone at the ranch. As strange as it seemed to have waiting rooms in the back of an office building, Tracy was happy for the privacy and assumed everyone who came to the clinic preferred to hide from the public. There was no one in the room, and she found a seat facing away from the door, where she would not be seen by patients arriving and waiting their turn to see the doctor.

The ranch telephone rang several times, and Tracy was beginning to think that no one would answer. She heard a click and recognized Hershel Pittman's voice.

"Mr. Pittman? This is Tracy Hunter. We need to get together again. I have more questions."

His voice sounded weary. "We buried my girl this morning, Miz Hunter. As far as I'm concerned, it's over." He dropped the phone on the hook, and Tracy shook her head. This did not sound like the man who had made an effort to talk to her before. She had assumed he would talk to her again. She replaced the phone. What had happened to close his mouth?

Her next call was to Kit, who answered on the first ring.

"Did you get to Mrs. Pittman this morning?" Tracy asked.

"Yes, after the funeral. Ruth and I stayed to help with lunch, and we talked to her after everyone left."

"And?"

"We know how Carolyn got to the park. Mrs. Pittman told us that after she got home Saturday night, Carolyn woke up and started crying. She told her mother that the fetus was buried in the park and they had to go get it. Mrs. Pittman tried to get her to wait until morning, but Carolyn threatened to walk to the park if her mother didn't take her. They drove to the parking lot and walked up the path to the place where Charley later found Carolyn's body, but they couldn't find where Tommy had buried the fetus. The mother said Carolyn sat down by a tree and wouldn't leave, insisting that her mother go home so her father wouldn't worry, and that she should come back when it was light and they could find the fetus. Her mother gave Carolyn her sweater and wrapped her in the wool blanket before she left." Kit stopped to blow her nose.

"I can't believe a mother would leave her daughter alone in the park under those circumstances," Tracy said.

"She said she didn't know Carolyn was bleeding. She understood why Carolyn was upset, but she didn't think about her needing a doctor. Mrs. Pittman had suffered miscarriages herself and hadn't sought medical treatment."

"Anything else?"

"This is where it gets weird. While Mrs. Pittman was at the park, Hal evidently went to their home and told Mr. Pittman that Brandon had called and said Carolyn left the party not feeling well. Hal wanted to make sure she saw a doctor if she needed one. Mr. Pittman told Hal not to worry about her, that Carolyn had gone to the park. He said Hal seemed relieved, thinking she was okay." Kit's voice slipped away.

Tracy ran the information through her mental processes, listing the possible outcomes from what she'd learned. "It looks like her mother may have been the last person to see Carolyn alive, unless Hal is lying. Instead of going home, he may have gone to the park and found her dead. If he covered her with leaves, it would look like a random murder in the park. The fraternity affair might never be reported."

"Hal wouldn't do that," Kit said. "He'd have called for an ambulance."

"I believe you're right, Kit. There has to be another answer. I'm here at the women's clinic. I'll bet if we could get hold of Marge or Julie, they could tell us more about what went on between Hal and Carolyn. I'm waiting to see the visiting doctor, hoping she can help me find one of the girls. I'll call you when I get back to the hotel."

"Ruth and I are on our way to Paul's office with the ring. Tommy is supposed to come in to identify it."

"Good. Then I'll meet you there as soon as I'm through here." Tracy hung up the telephone and leaned back in the overstuffed chair. Running had both exhausted and relaxed her. She pushed the chair to face the wall, cutting off the glaring light from the windows and reducing the noise from the hall. She propped her feet on the ottoman before picking up last year's copy of a *Life Magazine*. By page two, Tracy was fast asleep.

At five thirty, the telephone rang in the room where Tracy had dozed off. On the last ring, her eyes opened and strained to make sense of the strange surroundings. She could hear no human sounds. She rolled out of the chair and landed on her knees, then struggled to regain her seat on the ottoman. The solitude was broken by heavy footsteps running past the front windows. Inside, it was quiet, except for Tracy's heavy breathing. What if the staff had gone home and left her, unnoticed, in a locked building? What if the out-of-town agitators had returned to deface the building in the safety of darkness? Would it be safer to stay inside rather than trying to escape? Her training told her to call for backup, but whose life would she be putting in danger? Her friends, and even the police, would be of no help. The sound of running footsteps disappeared toward the front of the building, and Tracy hurried through the empty reception room to the back door. A large sign warned that the door was wired with an alarm which would go off unless a code was used to open the lock. It would do no good to call Paul and Kit if she could not safely open the door.

Tracy returned to the front office and rummaged through the desk. She knew from experience that women kept codes in an easy to find place. Sure enough, she lifted the heavy telephone and the alarm code was written on a piece of paper taped on the bottom.

Car doors slammed and motor noise receded down the street. She jotted the code down and headed for the back door, past two large wooden ⟨illegible⟩ the wall behind the receptionist's desk. ⟨illegible⟩ the drawers held the patient folders, and two of those folders could be for Marge and Julie. Her luck was not all bad. Without taking time to argue the merits of her actions, Tracy opened a drawer and started with the A's, searching for first names. She would worry about getting out of the building later.

Blackmer, Marge. Tracy pulled the file and noted that Marge listed the Lost Creek Ranch as one of her several places of employment. This had to be one of the prostitutes. Writing down the telephone number, she tucked the paper under her sweatshirt, along with Dr. Smeltzer's autopsy report. If Marge could be found, Julie wouldn't be far away. Smiling, Tracy headed for the back door, punched in the code, and pulled it open. An explosion knocked her to the floor. Flames licked around the edge of the door jamb as Tracy struggled to her feet. Diving out the doorway, she landed into the arms of Sergeant Falco.

One-half hour later from the jail, Sergeant Falco called Chief Mayfield. "Have Marvin pick up one of the girls and put her in one of the front cells. We've got a songbird."

NINETEEN

Paul sat in his office, watching Kit pace back and forth in front of the dark window. Ruth stood in a corner of the room, leaning on a file, trying to appear disinterested. Tommy had just left the room, crying after he identified his senior ring. Tracy had not arrived to witness the admission.

"I can't imagine where Tracy is," Kit said. "She said she'd meet us here." She looked at Ruth. "We got what we came for. We may as well go home. Tracy may have forgotten to come."

As the two walked out to their car and drove away, the telephone rang. It was Tracy.

"Paul, I'm in jail. I need a lawyer."

"Well, don't go anywhere," he said. "I'll call Vera Summers."

Tracy hung up the phone. "I get one phone call," she said to the jailer, "and that jerk has to joke on my time."

The jailer grunted. He'd heard the story before.

When Vera Summers arrived at the jail, Tracy was brought to the interview room. She held out her hand. "I should have come to see you when Paul told me to."

Tracy was dressed in a faded orange jumpsuit with "Pontotoc County Jail" stamped across the back. She couldn't remember a lower moment in her life. She looked up. "Thank you for coming."

"You're one of those people who prefer to learn lessons the hard way, I see."

"I can't believe I'm in jail." Anger sparked in Tracy's eyes.

Vera opened her briefcase and took out a pen and yellow pad. "What are the charges?"

Tracy looked at the lawyer, who was about Paul's age. She had a slight southern drawl, which was pleasant to the ear. Her iron-gray hair rose from her forehead into a pompadour, highlighted by a streak of pure white hair beginning at her widow's peak. It lifted one's eyes up and away from the worry wrinkles on her brow. Tracy wondered if this gentle family lawyer was competent to take on the police department, the demonstrators, and possibly the FBI, but Paul and Kit trusted her, so Tracy had no choice.

"Why are you here?" Vera repeated her question.

"Because I got locked in the Women's Health Clinic and had to break out."

"You broke out of the clinic?"

"I know it sounds silly, but I fell asleep in a chair in the waiting room in the back of the building. I had gone there to use the telephone. The staff forgot me. I had to get out, so I found the code for the back door and walked out." Her eyes lowered to the floor. "I guess you could say I was blown out."

"What did you take with you?"

"What makes you think I took something with me?"

"Paul makes me think you took something with you."

"That man's always a step ahead of me. I found Marge Blackmer's telephone number in the clinic's file. I hid it under my sweatshirt with a copy of Nora Smeltzer's autopsy report."

"What were you doing with an autopsy report?"

Tracy sighed, hoping she wasn't getting Billy into trouble. "I sweet-talked it out of the coroner's clerk."

"Don't tell that to anyone else. Who is Marge Blackmer?"

"One of the girls working at Hal's ranch during the poker parties."

"You've lost me, but we don't have time to go into that now." She stood and collected her notes. "I'll see what I can do to get you released."

"What are my chances of getting out tonight?"

"Not good. A judge has to set bond before you can be released, and the judges have all gone home for the day."

A chill left bumps on Tracy's arm. She knew what happened to many women in jail, and Sergeant Falco knew she was here.

"Hal Montgomery has lots of pull in this county," Tracy offered. "Maybe if you call him, he can help."

Vera shrugged. "I can try, but it seems to me you're asking for help from the people who want to shut you up. What makes you think he'll help?"

Tracy felt her face flushing again. "We're . . . we used to be friends."

Vera grimaced. "We'll see." She rose to leave, and an officer led Tracy to an empty cell. She heard the clanging of the door behind her, announcing the end of her innocent, carefree life. She rubbed her wrists, angry at the red marks the hand cuffs had left. She paced the cell, wondering what prisoners did to remain sane during incarceration. The bunk did not look inviting. Besides, she had just slept for hours at the clinic. She seemed to be the only prisoner within sight. She sat on the bunk, pulled her legs up to form a resting place for her arms, and hid her face from the world. An hour passed before she heard high heels clicking on the concrete floor. She looked up as an officer opened the cell across the hall and escorted an attractive, auburn-haired woman inside. Tracy grimaced. Why had she been forced to change into orange jail rags while this lady sported street clothes? And she did mean "street" clothes, the kind to attract men on the prowl. The lady pulled a pack of cigarettes from her blouse pocket.

"What you in for, honey?" The woman was leaning on the bars of the cell door.

"I don't know exactly," Tracy said, unwilling to put into words the horrible truth of what might be on her record. At the least, she would be charged with breaking and entering, and the district attorney would no doubt think of other charges, such as burglary.

"That figures. These two-bit deputies like to play cowboy. They pick us up just for the jollies they get out of searching us."

"It doesn't look like they searched you very thoroughly," Tracy said. "Why didn't they make you change clothes? And confiscate your cigarettes?" She realized she was whining at the inequity of their treatments.

"Oh, I'm a regular. My attorney will have me out in less time than it takes to undress. They know me here, so they don't worry that I'll hide something in my crotch."

"What are you in for?" Tracy asked.

The lady lifted her eyebrows and shrugged off the question.

Tracy's heart began to throb in her ears. She had difficulty keeping a smile off her face. This contact might be better than finding Julie's or Marge's telephone numbers. She looked down the hall to see if they were being watched. An officer at the desk was talking on the telephone. She moved closer to the corner of her cell, directly across from the woman, now lounging on her cot. She rested on one elbow and, in the opposite hand, held a cigarette between her thumb and forefinger, spreading her remaining three fingers outward with her blood red fingernails pointing at Tracy.

"So you don't know why you were picked up?" There was doubt in the lady's voice.

"I fell asleep in a back room at the Woman's Health Clinic. The staff left for the night and locked me in. I found the code to get out, but the door blew up in my face. A police officer was right there to arrest me when I came out."

The woman raised her eyebrows and flicked the ashes from her cigarette. "Good story. They didn't believe you, huh? Been drinking? Drugs?"

"No."

"I haven't seen you around before. New in town?"

"I'm visiting."

"Good. We don't need any full-time competition, especially from women like you."

"What do you mean 'like me'?"

"You look like one of them Junior League pussies. They draw all the guys with money."

Tracy flushed and assured her jail companion that they were not in competition for customers. She looked toward the guard's desk again. He was filling out forms, and seemed to be paying no attention to the inmates.

Tracy lowered her voice. "Say, do you know some girls named Julie or Marge?"

The woman's droopy eyes opened wide, and she let the smoke spiral upward from her nose until it disappeared. She coughed and cleared her throat. "What if I do?"

"I was in the clinic trying to find their addresses and telephone numbers."

"How come?" The voice revealed a certain degree of panic.

"I was a friend of Carolyn Pittman's," Tracy said. "The girl who was found dead in the park. I thought one of them might know her." Tracy watched the woman's fear dissolve into curiosity as she pulled one last haul on the cigarette before throwing it on the floor and grinding the stub with the toe of her red high heel.

"And if they do?"

"Carolyn's folks live on Hal Montgomery's ranch. I understand that Julie and Marge work the poker parties on Saturday nights. I think they might know who Carolyn was friendly with. Do you know how I could find them?"

The woman nodded. "I suppose I do. I'm Julie Smith. Yeah. I knew Carolyn. She was a sweet kid. I'm of a mind that the guys who did that to her should be strung up."

Tracy relaxed. Her arrest was giving her more information than she'd gotten from the Pittmans. "I suspect they'll get what's coming to them," she said, "if we can find the truth about what happened."

"Who you working for?" Julie's eyes squinted almost closed.

"Nobody. Some of us women talked it over and decided the police were dragging their feet on the case. So we started our own investigation. I'm a private eye."

Julie cackled and Tracy glanced at the officer. He raised his head and glared in their direction. Prisoners were not supposed to be having fun, she guessed. He went back to his paperwork, and Tracy looked at the woman. Her laugh was gone, replaced by a broad smile. "How long have you been in town, honey? Everybody in the county knows Matt Mayfield is in the pocket of the oil guys, including Hal Montgomery."

Tracy felt a pain shoot through her throat. Muscles tightened at the mention of Hal's name. She watched, without speaking, as Julie pulled out another cigarette, tapped it on the back of her hand, and propped it in the corner of her mouth. She flipped the lighter three times before it flamed. Julie sucked smoke toward her lungs as she snapped the lighter shut and placed it in her shirt pocket. Relaxed and smiling, she asked, "How well do you know Hal?"

"Since we were kids, but I've never been to one of his parties."

The woman stared, forgetting to smoke. "No, I guess not."

"I gather you have. Was Carolyn there?"

Julie nodded.

Tracy walked to the back of her cell to hide the tears in her eyes. She would rather not have gotten that answer. The bastards, she thought. And

Hal had to be one of them. Her teeth clenched, her face no longer beautiful, as the muscles around her mouth and eyes tightened. There were no
shining glints in her green eyes—only dark pools of anger. She walked
back to the front of the cell.

"Did Carolyn tell you she was pregnant?"

"Oh, sure. She asked me where she could get an abortion."

"Did you tell her?"

"Hey, look. I'm in enough trouble. The last thing I want to do is get
involved in that kid's death." She flicked ashes on the floor.

"Is that what you'd want her to say if you were the victim?" Tracy
gripped the bars of her cell so hard her knuckles ached.

The lady spit on her fingertips and pinched the burning end of her
cigarette. "Okay. I don't know how she got rid of it. I can guess. She told
us the doctor told her sex might cause a miscarriage. I had trouble believing that, but I guess she'd been spotting off and on. She was all hyper
Saturday when she came in. Said she was no longer worried. She'd found
a way to solve her problems."

"With an abortion?" Nausea pushed acid into Tracy's throat and she
spit into the toilet.

"No."

"Then how?"

Julie shrugged again, and Tracy snorted in frustration. "Did she say
who the father was?"

"She wouldn't say, but chances are good it was Brandon's. He
wouldn't leave her alone when her folks first moved to the ranch. He was
always bragging about how easy she was. I'm sure he slipped her a little
money on the side. Poor kid."

"How about Hal? Did he sleep with her? Could the baby have been
his?"

The lady cackled again. "Hal?" She shook her head. "No. That man's
impotent. He never has anything to do with us girls. Too bad, too. He's
a real good looker. We have tried to change his mind, but nothing works.
He brings us cigarettes and gets embarrassed when we call him our Marl-
boro Man. Won't sleep with us, but he's a nice guy."

Tracy was stuck on the lady's first statement. "He told you he was—"

"Im-po-tent. Didn't I say it right? He swore he couldn't get it up.
Hinted that that's why Muffy left him." With a flourish of her hand, she

bent over to loosen a strap on her sandal. She wet her finger with spit and rubbed a spot on the toe, then glanced in Tracy's direction. "How sad. He's got so much money, too."

Tracy began pacing around her cell. *Impotent! Another of his lies. Had he told them that in order to avoid sleeping with them, or was it true at one time?* She approached the bars of the cell. "Carolyn had bruises on her neck. Did she say how she got them?"

"Brandon, the little bastard. He tried that with me once. I bloodied his nose."

"Did Hal know Carolyn was going to the fraternity party?"

"No way. He threatened to kill Brandon when he heard about it. But Brandon is so spoiled, he does whatever he wants. I guess Hal can be blamed for that. But what kids aren't spoiled nowadays, with all the drugs and alcohol around? They should stick to safe sex."

Tracy resumed pacing. The ring. Carolyn was probably hiding it from Brandon when she dropped it by the bed. But who took it from Tracy's pocket? She might never know, and maybe it wasn't important to her mission. "One more thing," Tracy said. "Do you know who organized the gambling going on at the ranch?"

"Mr. Crosier started the parties when he bought the ranch, and he continued to run the tables for his friends after he sold out to Hal. Hal rarely plays. He doesn't like cards, and he mostly loses."

"I've heard that the players are paying for political favors by losing to Senator Fortenberry's staff. Are you aware of that?"

Julie looked at the ceiling, her mouth clamped shut. That was answer enough.

This girl is a gold mine, Tracy thought. Under oath, she would have to answer that question.

Two hours had passed and Vera Summers had not returned. It looked like a jail cell would be her home for the weekend, but she could not complain. If Julie kept talking, it would be worth the stay, assuming she was telling the truth. Tracy wanted to believe that Hal had not had sex with Carolyn, that Brandon was the father of her child, and that his fraternity pals might be guilty of causing Carolyn's death. What else could she learn? Maybe something about her informant, who would undergo stringent questioning in a trial.

"Do you get arrested often?"

"I try not to. It's not like jail's a weekend in Vegas. And besides, the ranch has a deal with the sheriff to look the other way as far as us girls are concerned—and the gambling, too, for that matter. I have no idea why I was picked up this time."

Tracy felt a chill cover her body. It did seem strange that the two women had been thrown into adjoining cells. Was it just a coincidence? She cursed under her breath. How could she have been so dumb? The two prisoners had been put within talking distance for a reason. The officer at the desk was too far away to hear them. She turned her back to his desk and let her eyes roam over the cell. In movies, the hero always found the hidden weapons, drugs, or microphones taped to the back of the toilet. Tracy clasped her hands behind her back and walked around the room. At the toilet, she cleared her throat and smiled apologetically as she indicated her intent to use it. Julie grimaced and turned her head. Seated, Tracy let her hands run behind the toilet bowl, over some adhesive tape and what felt like a mini-tape recorder. She groaned as if in pain, and watched Julie cringe and turn further away. She liked the privacy her ruse accorded, but decided it was good for only so long. She ripped off the tape and hid the recorder in her waistband as she heaved a contented sigh of relief and flushed the toilet.

Doors began slamming. Tracy smiled as she recognized Vera Summers standing by the front desk, while the officer examined papers the lawyer handed him. A gray-haired attorney standing beside Vera waved to Julie. The officer reached for a bag of clothing, but he was distracted by the ringing telephone. Tracy was unable to hear the conversation, but she determined that the clothes must be hers, since Julie still wore her street clothes. The officer replaced the telephone and headed for Julie's cell. "Your lawyers are out front," he said.

"Hot damn. I call that fast action," Julie said, and ran past him to the front of the office.

He led Tracy to the shower, where she dressed, tucking the recorder under her sweatshirt. At the desk, she grabbed Vera's arm, afraid the attorney might leave without her. "I didn't expect you. What happened?" she said.

"It seems your friendship with Hal worked wonders. He knows the judge and found him drinking at the club, in a good mood. Anyway, he signed your release." Vera was smiling like a lottery winner.

Tracy's fellow prisoner hurried away with her attorney. She turned and waved to Tracy. "See you, girl."

Tracy waved in her direction. "That woman is a gold mine of information. I don't know whether what she told me is all true, but if it is, it clears up a lot of things about Carolyn, Brandon, and even Hal.

"You realize the defense lawyers will shred this gal's testimony to bits," Vera said.

Tracy's high deflated like a balloon with a slow leak. Well, it was the best she could do. She reached under her sweatshirt and handed Vera the recorder. "You'll want to listen to this and copy it before the police discover it's gone."

Vera nodded as Tracy turned to meet Kit and Paul. "The gods may be with you," the lawyer said, "but don't push your luck."

Hal's Jeep was parked at the Jordans' when they arrived from jail. Hal stood at the pier, staring over the lake, with Charley keeping him company.

"I'll go get him," Tracy said, and hurried to thank him for his help in getting her released.

"Looks like the judge came through," he said, without looking at her.

"Yes. Thanks a million. I could have been sitting there all weekend."

"I'm sorry you got caught up in my problems, Tracy. I told you to stay out of it." Muscles began twitching on Hal's jaw, and the blue of his eyes disappeared behind lowered lashes.

"I'm not sorry. Someone has to stand up for Carolyn and Nora. And the jail stay wasn't a lost cause. One of the girls who works your parties was in the cell next to mine. She talked. I now know you weren't involved in Carolyn's death and that her baby wasn't yours."

"That's not news to me and it wouldn't be to you, if you had trusted me." He turned back to face the lake. "However, I am guilty of her death. I went to my lawyer this morning and confessed to her murder. He'll go with me tomorrow to the D.A.'s office."

Tracy laughed. "Hal, that's not true."

He turned, his face tight with anger. "It is true. I gave him a timetable to support it."

"Don't be ridiculous. It's obvious to me that Brandon is involved and that you're lying to protect him."

"I gave good reasons for what I did."

"Lies aren't good reasons."

Hal wrapped his arms around Tracy and kissed her forehead. "You never give up, do you?" he asked. "I've loved you all these years, and it makes me sick to think it's too late for us to make it together. If there was anything I could do to change what happened, I would. You know that. But there isn't. Things will get worse. If you love me, get out of here. Go home and remember the nice times we had. Or forget you ever knew me, while there's cash at." He wiped the tears from her cheeks. "I stopped here to say goodbye."

Tracy pulled away. "Hal, you've always tried to fix things for people, and maybe you can this time. But lying to protect Brandon is not the way to solve this case. You aren't doing him a favor by allowing him to get away with what amounts to murder. It's time to make him take the consequences for his stupid actions!"

Hal shook his head, and Tracy whirled around and headed for the house. Charley walked beside her, his head down, tail drooping. He stopped once and looked at Hal, then trudged on, falling behind Tracy.

Paul came out of the house and let Tracy pass him without speaking. He walked over to Hal's vehicle and waited until Hal arrived.

"Come on in. Supper's ready," he said.

"No. Tracy's too upset." His gaze followed her into the house. "She's something, isn't she?" He looked back at Paul. "It's beyond me how I've done such a super job of screwing up my life."

"You've said that before, and I'll repeat what I said. It'll all work out. Give it time."

"No. There's no way. She'll be better off without me." Hal climbed into the vehicle and left.

TWENTY

Saturday morning, Tracy woke up to the cooing of doves sitting on the window sill of the hotel room. "You fellows are a little late. The lovemaking is over." The cooing became louder, and she hoped the birds would leave before a fight began.

"Who are you talking to?" Ruth asked.

"Those lovebirds outside. I told them they were a little late. I'm going back to the clerk's office to finish up my birth certificate this morning. Then we need to get out of this place." She jumped into the shower and was soon dressed for action.

At the clerk's office, she stood in line to get to Bonnie's window. Bonnie took one look at her and turned to get her file, without speaking. "I found the school records, got an affidavit from the school superintendent, and called the minister, who agreed to mail a notarized letter declaring you were known as Tracy Hunter. That's all you need. You should fill out the application with the new name and the clerk will authorize the amended certificate. You can mail it to the Bureau of Vital Statistics. They'll mail you a new birth certificate in a few weeks." Bonnie was neither looking at Tracy nor smiling.

"Thank you so much," Tracy said. "I'm sorry I caused problems for you at the clinic. Are you okay?"

"You can pick up the documents here on Monday, or you can go back home, and I'll mail them to you."

"I'll pick them up on Monday."

"Fine." Bonnie turned from the window. Tracy bit her lower lip. Maybe Ruth could mend these hard feelings.

In the meantime, she needed to check with Vera to see where she stood legally. She retreated to the public telephone booth, where she dialed her attorney's number. Vera answered, jubilant. "I listened to the tapes. You've done a great job helping to resolve Carolyn's murder, and your being at the scene of the bombing has helped the FBI pinpoint the leaders of the gang who killed Mom Smeltzer." She paused. "Oh, I also talked to the district attorney. He has a campaign coming up in the spring, so he's walking on eggshells. He thinks the women's clinic won't insist on his filing charges against you since nothing is missing, and they won't testify against you if the district attorney is pressured to file the case. Judge Carson is laid back on the issue of the women's clinic—thanks to his wife's gentle encouragement—so your case could be kicked out at the pre-trial."

"Thank goodness," Tracy said. "What about Hal? Is he going to be charged?"

"I gave them the tape, and they say Hal has a pretty good argument that it was Crosier's gambling table, and that it was Muffy and his mother who were involved in the money laundering. If there were sexual favors being purchased, Hal is clean if his impotence defense holds up. He could be accused of running a prostitution ring."

"Really? That won't hold water, will it?"

Vera seemed reluctant to answer. "Well, the tape says he was impotent, and Julie's comments on the tape are pretty clear that he was, and that she and one other woman were hired to entertain the winners or losers at the poker table. He has the weak argument that he couldn't be described as a winner or loser, because Mr. Pittman played his hands. Also, any family donations to Senator Fortenberry went through Mrs. Montgomery's account, so none of his gambling losses were considered payoffs. His mother and Muffy will no doubt be issued indictments if the district attorney takes this to a grand jury . . . which he will. And any time you get a senator involved in criminal activities, it becomes a big political case. If the district attorney is successful in finding all of them guilty, he'll be running for governor himself."

"Do you think Hal will be indicted?"

"It's possible, since he owns the ranch and allowed the gambling and prostitution to take place there. However, he's so well-known and well-liked here they may brush his sins aside and go after bigger fish. The IRS will be trying to trace the gambling profits. However, these are not your problems, Tracy."

"Could Hal go to prison?"

"For the money laundering? I doubt it. However, Carolyn's death is a different matter. It's possible he could get a prison sentence if his plea bargain is accepted, but I doubt that you could find a jury here that would convict him, if it's left up to a trial. He wasn't at the fraternity party where it happened, and he certainly didn't arrange the party or the initiation rites."

"I'm sure he's lying about Carolyn's death in order to protect Brandon," Tracy said. "He thinks he's in deep shit already, and he can't be any worse off by taking on Brandon's problems. He'd do that for his mother."

"Well, Hal's problems are his," Vera said. "Don't worry about him."

"Do you know if they've found out who was behind Nora's murder?"

"That's another hot political potato. Weird as it may seem, Hal's mother knew that Nora was suspicious of the money laundering going on at the ranch, and she feared Nora was going to the FBI with what she knew. Nora disapproved of Senator Fortenberry's conservative voting record and would have been happy to see him lose his political power. Everyone's guessing that Mrs. Montgomery just used the anti-abortion crowd to get rid of Nora in order to throw the dogs off the rotten scent coming from the ranch. Nora was in the wrong place at the wrong time, and Hal's mother took advantage of it."

"It's so hard to believe, but thanks, Vera. You've done a great job." Tracy hung up the phone, trying to decide whether to be happy or to start throwing things. She compromised and called Kit.

"Are you still speaking to me?" she asked, as she heard Kit's soft voice.

"Tracy, of course. We've been worried about you, but I told Paul we had to let you work out your problems without our putting pressure on you. I talked Ruth into moving back out here until you leave. She said to tell you to check out of the hotel and join us."

"Okay, if you're sure you can put up with us again. Nora's memorial service is Sunday, and I want to stay for that. My birth certificate will be ready Monday. My arraignment is on Monday too. Vera will ask the judge to let me go home until the next hearing. Let's hope he does."

"Good. Hurry out."

At one o'clock, Tracy pulled into the hotel's basement parking lot, eager to pack and return to the Jordans' home on the lake. Puzzled, she watched as Sergeant Falco pulled his vehicle in behind hers, touching her bumper. She froze as he got out of his Jeep, his hand on his gun.

"Afternoon, ma'am," he said. "Miz Montgomery sent me to escort you up to her suite. She wants to talk to you." He nodded his head toward the door leading into the hotel.

Tracy sat in shock. The last thing she wanted to do was to follow Falco anywhere, certainly not to the Montgomery suite in the penthouse. What could she use as an excuse? She cleared her throat. "I'm expecting company to come by my room any minute. Let me go there first and leave a message."

"No, ma'am," Falco said. "They'll go away if you don't come to the door."

Tracy moved toward the hotel's back entrance. She puzzled over the secretiveness of Beatrice's message. Why couldn't Hal's mother have picked up the telephone if she needed to talk? The closer they got to the building, the more terrified Tracy became. If Nora was in the wrong place at the wrong time, maybe she was also. Or what if this was Falco's method of getting her into an empty room to assault her?

They reached the first floor, and while Sergeant Falco pushed the button for the penthouse elevator, Tracy searched the hallway for help. No one was there. Inside, the heavy smell of his cologne in the small enclosure caused her to sneeze. The elevator stopped and the metal gates opened, revealing heavy wooden doors to the apartment. Falco knocked, and a maid opened the door. They walked into a room large enough to cover a fourth of the hotel circumference. A number of seating arrangements were scattered near windows, in front of the fireplace, and beside tables.

Hal's mother stood near the window, posed like a movie star, dressed in a gold satin robe whose cuffs were covered with long silk feathers that waved in the air as she lifted a cigarette to her painted lips. She signaled for Falco to leave.

"Tracy." Her voice was low and hoarse from years of smoking. "Please sit down. I'm sure you must know why you're here."

"No," Tracy said, as she sank into a down-stuffed cushion.

"Let me inform you." Beatrice sat on the arm of a matching couch facing Tracy. She smashed her cigarette into an ash tray, making sure every spark was smothered. "Hershel Pittman has kept me informed about your little tête-a-têtes with Hal. Don't think I care, except for the fact that he hasn't been able to think straight since you arrived, and in his position, he can't afford to make mistakes."

She began refilling the decorative holder with a long cigarette. "Sergeant Falco has also kept me informed about your indiscrete contacts with . . . shall we say, 'ladies of the night'?"

She stood to assume a commanding position. "However, what makes me angry is the fact that you called the attorney general's office and reported an incident at the fraternity house where Brandon lives." Her hoarse voice cracked, and she coughed into a silk handkerchief.

Tracy's knees began to shake, and she picked up a small couch pillow to lay across her lap. Vera and the FBI had warned her of the Montgomery political power and the fact that Beatrice was the one who enforced it. Watching the woman operate in these royal surroundings, Tracy could believe it.

The raspy voice continued. "I can't imagine why you think it is your business to interfere in our affairs." She sucked deeply on the cigarette and watched Tracy through the smoke she exhaled. She waited for Tracy to respond.

"I found the body of a fifteen-year-old girl who died after attending a fraternity party at Brandon's school. Have you ever seen a fifteen-year-old girl covered in blood after she's been raped?"

Beatrice's lips pursed into an accordion circle. Angry sparks flew from her eyes.

Tracy continued. "She was a beautiful young woman who shouldn't have died. Those responsible for her death should be punished. You wouldn't suggest otherwise, would you?"

"Of course not. However, the police department is capable of determining how she died. Chief Mayfield tells me she died by her own hand, or from the botched work done at the abortion clinic your friend was running. If that's true, you will have done a great disservice to innocent people."

"Our justice system is set up to separate the innocent from the guilty. I have faith in that system." Tracy felt a heavy sinking in her stomach as she wondered whether the system would clear her reputation.

"You're very naive, child. Money separates the innocent from the guilty. We don't need the attorney general involved. It's obvious you don't understand politics."

"No, I don't. However, I do understand that I have a right to move freely in this society without being stalked. Why have you had your hench-man following me?"

Beatrice laid her half-smoked cigarette on the ash tray. This time she lost the movie-star quality of sophistication that had made her look so elegant when Tracy arrived. Instead, her lips pulled low on one side of her mouth, her eyes squinted, and unattractive wrinkles appeared around her eyes.

"Sergeant Falco is merely doing his job. This time it happens to coin-cide with my need to find out why you came back to Ada."

"Why does that concern you?"

"Everything my son does concerns me."

Tracy laughed and was pleased to note that her knees had stopped shaking. She laid the pillow aside. "That's a relief," she said and stood up. "You can stop worrying. Hal and I have decided to go our separate ways. And I'd appreciate it if you'd tell your hound dog to get off my tail. If he doesn't, I'll file for a restraining order naming you as the defendant." She turned and headed for the door.

"Tracy!"

She stopped and waited for Beatrice to speak. "You will call the attor-ney general office and inform them of your mistake concerning Brandon's fraternity. If you don't cooperate, the charges against you for interfering with the women's clinic will become felonies. I'm sure you understand the seriousness of that complication for your career."

Tracy faced Beatrice. "I'm beginning to understand a lot about the Women's Health Clinic, Mrs. Montgomery. Your fear that Nora would reveal what she knew about the gambling at the ranch, plus your neu-rotic need to protect Hal from women like her . . . and me . . . led to her death, didn't it? You just used the anti-abortion people as a cover." Tracy knew she was making charges that she couldn't substantiate—charges that might lead to her own death, in fact. Would she be able to get this latest development to Kit before someone found her body stuffed in a trash bar-rel in the basement of the hotel or in a cistern in Arkansas?

Beatrice picked up her cigarette. "Be careful what you suggest in the way of criminal activity, my dear. Dr. Smeltzer had no business setting up an abortion clinic in this part of the country. Her ploy to get Hal to support her efforts was foolish. The Montgomery political power is not for sale for love nor money. She should have known that, and so should you."

"I happen to know that what you are saying is a bald-faced lie. Money and sex have been buying Montgomery political power for a long time, via the poker parties. The FBI has proof of this, so getting rid of me or Nora will not save the owners of the Lost Creek Ranch nor Brandon from prosecution."

"I have no intention of getting rid of you. I just want you out of town. It's time for you to go back where you came from, and if you do, the criminal charges will be dropped."

Tracy laughed. "In plain English, Hal is still under your thumb, the way he was when we were kids. Is that the message you want me to get?"

The stiffness in Beatrice's face dissolved, and she became an old, unattractive bitch. "It's a shame things didn't work out between you and Hal. You're a lot like me. We might have gotten along famously, under the right circumstances."

Tracy's face flushed. "Thanks for the insult." She opened the door and walked out of the room into the arms of Falco. She pushed him away. "Your job is over, Bozo. Get lost."

Falco frowned and let his hand drop to his gun. Tracy entered the elevator, and Falco entered the apartment, answering Beatrice's call.

Tracy's heart raced. Why had she not realized that Hal's mother was the one who had the most to gain from making Carolyn's death seem like a random murder in the park? Such a finding would help to avoid the scandal for Brandon at the university, and it would protect the family fortune by absolving Hal of the crime. Furthermore, it would keep the investigation from leading to the ranch, where the FBI might find a connection to Nora's death and other crimes.

Trembling inside, she hurried to her room, finished packing, and took the elevator to the first floor, where she checked out of the hotel. She stood at the registration desk in a fog, listening for footsteps that might reveal Falco's presence. Her brain felt hot from overwork.

Now she knew why Falco had followed her. Beatrice had hired him to make sure Tracy did not interfere with the status quo of Hal's marriage. It was important that Hal not divorce Muffy, thereby breaking the political ties to Senator Fortenberry. Would it not follow that she had Falco hide Carolyn's body in order to protect Brandon's fraternity? Was it too far out to imagine that the sergeant and his cohorts, instead of the anti-abortion followers, were involved in Nora's kidnapping and death, and in

Ruth's assault? Julie, the jail informant, had said Hal Montgomery and Nora Smeltzer were close friends. Would Beatrice go so far as murder to preserve Hal's connection to Muffy and her father? The thought left Tracy dizzy. She shivered and nodded good night to the hotel attendant.

"Oh, ma'am! You had a call today from a Captain Carson in Chicago. He said it was urgent." He handed her a memo, which she tucked into her purse as she headed for her car. What possible trouble could await her in Chicago?

TWENTY-ONE

The sun sent brilliant sparks of light through the icicles hanging from the trees bordering the sidewalk leading to the United Methodist Church on Ash Street, as dozens of Nora Smeltzer's former patients, her relatives and friends from Chicago, and supporters of her clinic gathered to remember and honor her life. Paul supported Tracy, lacing her arm through his, as Kit, Ruth, and Tillie followed them into the sanctuary. Police Chief Matt Mayfield and Sergeant Jerry Falco sat in the back row, and unknown to the mourners, two FBI agents mingled with the crowd. Standing with latecomers, Hal Montgomery's eyes never left the scene of flowers surrounding the portrait of his friend, Nora Smeltzer.

The ceremony was short, just long enough to cover Paul's eulogy, statements from the clinic staff, and music by the church choir. As the crowd filed out of the church, they faced a small group of hecklers across the street, holding signs used earlier at the clinic. Chief Mayfield walked over to remind them that this was Sunday.

Monday morning at nine o'clock, Tracy sat in the courtroom with her attorney. She was living in a nightmare from which she could not imagine waking. Sunday's service had left her feeling angry and helpless, with no assurance that the evidence she had collected would be sufficient to find and convict Nora's killers, nor was she confident that she would be found not guilty for the charge of breaking and entering the clinic. For the first time in her life, she was glad her parents were not alive to witness this disgrace. She knew the legal procedure well, and sat beside Vera as she responded to the judge's questions, entering Tracy's plea of not guilty and waiving advisement.

The judge looked at Tracy. "Has your attorney explained the charges against you in such a way that you understand them?"

"Yes, sir."

"And are you knowingly and voluntarily entering a plea of 'not guilty' on those charges?"

"Yes, sir."

The judge handed the file to his clerk and told him to set a date for pre-trial. He picked up the next file, and Tracy walked out of the courtroom, while her lawyer approached the clerk to get the pre-trial date.

Paul, Kit, and Ruth met her outside. Paul smiled and said, "It's time you ladies closed shop. I think the police and the FBI can finish this. I'm going to the office."

"I have to run by the clerk's office," Tracy said to Kit and Ruth. "I'll meet you soon."

When Tracy arrived at the Jordan home, Kit walked to the kitchen counter and sorted through a pile of papers. "Let's see if we are ready to close shop. Here's the list. Our first job was to find out how the abortion or miscarriage happened. Are we in agreement that it happened at the fraternity initiation?"

"We are, and we can leave it to the attorney general's office to follow through on finding and convicting the guilty parties."

"Mr. and Mrs. Pittman. Have we found any evidence that they had a motive for killing their daughter?"

"No. They can't be voted parents of the year, but I didn't get a feeling that either would have harmed Carolyn," Ruth said.

"Hal. He has confessed to taking Carolyn to the park and covering up her body. I guess the courts will have to determine whether he's lying. That will be tied up with the fraternity charges, won't it?"

"We didn't find any evidence of his guilt, so we can drop his name," Tracy said.

"And Tommy?"

"He is a witness. If his story about the fraternity initiation is correct, and if he buried the fetus, he can be charged as an accessory to the crime."

"Tell us again what that means," Ruth said.

"He didn't do it, but he helped those who did."

"Tillie will die if Tommy's found guilty and loses his scholarship," Kit said.

"She needs to be told that losing the scholarship will be minor compared to his being found guilty of murder," Tracy said.

"Have we eliminated Tillie as a suspect?" Ruth asked.

The question hung in the air among the women, as the sun dipped behind a cloud and the room darkened. Kit picked up her coffee cup and moved to the kitchen counter. With careful concentration, she refilled her cup with the dark roast brew and lightened it with cream. No one spoke as Tracy followed the same procedure, and Kit moved to adjust the shade.

"We don't have any information on what Tillie did after Tommy got home Saturday night," Ruth said, looking at Kit, "yet you seem so sure she couldn't have been involved."

"Well, I've been forced to change my mind somewhat. She tells me now that when Tommy woke up Sunday morning after the party, he told her that he had buried the pillowcase in the park. She had no idea that Carolyn had gone back to find it, or that she was dead. I don't know what criminal laws they may have broken by not reporting Tommy's part in covering up the crime."

Tracy reached across the table and covered Kit's hands with her own. "I'm so sorry. That's what most people would have done under the circumstances. If the police find out who covered her body, it should clear Tillie and Tommy. And I have a hunch they will find that Sergeant Falco is the culprit, since he was working under Beatrice's orders."

"Besides," Ruth added, "it rained everywhere that night. Tillie could have gotten mud on her shoes anywhere, including her own home."

Tracy and Kit both nodded, and Kit drew a line through Tillie's name on the list.

"Finally, we have unanswered questions: who took the ring from your pocket? Who returned it, and why? Or does it even matter?"

"I don't think it does, unless tests show that the baby is Tommy's. Paul doesn't think that's possible, so the ring shouldn't be entered as evidence."

Kit folded the list of suspects in half and placed her hands over it in a final gesture. "If you girls have to go home this week, I can finish up. Paul talked to Chief Mayfield after the service yesterday, and he said that the protesters had been told to leave town."

"We'd better leave in the morning," Tracy said.

"Yes," Ruth said. "I do need to go home. My family may have discovered they can live quite well without me."

"Yeah. We know that's going to happen," Tracy said.

The three women grinned at each other and lifted their coffee cups in a salute.

"We did it!" Kit said, and they cheered.

"Here's to our memories of Carolyn and Nora, and to all the girls who find themselves needing a Dr. Sinclair." The room was quiet, except for Charley's breathing.

That evening the table sparkled with silver and candlelight, and the house smelled of pork roast and hot rolls when Tracy came downstairs, glowing in the silk blouse she'd purchased from the hotel boutique—a purchase she'd regretted making until tonight, when it seemed the perfect garment to reflect the candlelight on the table.

Paul whistled when Tracy came into the kitchen, where he was pouring drinks. Ruth was stirring gravy, and Kit was pulling hot rolls from the oven.

"Who are you trying to impress?" Paul asked Tracy.

"She didn't do it for you," Kit said.

The doorbell rang, and Paul nodded to Tracy. "Why don't you get that?"

Tracy frowned and felt her face flushing. She hadn't known that Hal was coming for dinner. She was glad the living room and dining area were dimly lit. Hal seemed embarrassed as he handed her a nosegay of violets. "I thought they would make less of a mess, if I decided to throw them."

"You wouldn't dare. They're perfect. And I'll keep them out of your reach, my friend."

She stifled her wish to stand on tiptoe and kiss him.

"Come on in and sit down," Paul yelled, "We're almost ready to eat."

"This is a real treat," Hal said. "I have been reduced to asking my own cook to sit down at the table with me for company, and she thinks that's somehow inappropriate."

There was no response to his statement, and he added, "I'll tell her to make enough food for five if you'll come out for dinner Saturday night."

"You bet. Paul and I never turn down a dinner invitation," Kit said. "Will you ladies stick around?"

"No," Tracy said. "I talked to Vera this afternoon, and she said I have been released to go home. She thinks the charges will be dismissed. If not, I'll have to come back for the trial, but it will be months away."

Ruth was nodding. "And Howard threatens to divorce me if I don't come home."

Kit looked at Paul, then Hal, and back to Ruth. "I think it's time to announce that we've been plotting to keep Tracy in Oklahoma." Her eyes moved to Tracy. "I'm thinking of running for mayor next election, and if I win, I'll be in a position to influence the election of a new police chief."

Tracy frowned and put down her fork. "No kidding." She looked around the table, picked up her fork, and resumed eating. After swallowing, she said, "You'll make a great mayor, Kit, and it's sweet of you to think of me, but I'm not sure Ada is the place for me. You know the old saying, 'You can't go home again'? I'm afraid it's true."

"Don't think of it as coming home," Paul said. "You're starting over in a new place. Why not here, where you have friends to support you?"

Tracy put a buttered roll to her mouth and nibbled on the crusty top before she spoke. "I didn't tell you I got a call from Captain Carson, my old boss. He wants me to return to Chicago. He made an offer that will be hard to turn down."

"Oh," Kit said. "That's great—I guess."

"I'm not sure I'll take it, but I need to go back and discuss the possibility. I can see that a private eye business will take some time to develop into a paying proposition."

The room was quiet until Kit rose and said, "Okay, guys, go to the living room while we clean up the kitchen, and you think of something pleasant to discuss to cheer us up. We'll bring in dessert."

It was late when Hal rose to leave. Tracy took his hand and walked with him to his Jeep.

"You'll freeze out here," he said, and wrapped her inside his coat. When she didn't pull away, he said, "Come home with me. Please?"

"Hal, I believe it was your idea for us to close this case and forget it ever happened. That's what I plan to do. It's unfair of you to suggest at this late date that it's not over."

"Closing the door on the present and pretending there was no past does not rule out the possibility of a future. To hell with Captain Carson."

Tracy pulled out of his arms, laughing. She tapped him on the chest. "I hate you, Hal Montgomery. I really hate you."

"Prove it," he said and pulled her lips to his for a kiss that was filled with promise. She pulled away and laid her fingers on his lips. "If you lose my telephone number again, you can always ask the Jordans for it." She turned and ran to the house.

In the kitchen, Kit and Paul were cleaning away all evidence of the meal. Paul cleared the table, Ruth filled the dishwasher, and Kit stored the leftovers.

"Why did you do this?" Tracy asked.

"Do what?" Kit and Paul responded together.

"Put me and Hal together again in a situation that looks so normal. You know it isn't."

"Who's to say what's normal?" Paul said.

"You and Kit are normal. Ruth and Howard are normal. Hal and I are aberrant. He's married. He's still a momma's boy. I plan to have a career. How can you think we have a future together? Besides," she looked at Paul, "you said you were glad that I wasn't in love with Hal."

Paul handed the last of the leftovers to Ruth before turning to Tracy. "My dear, you're like a daughter to me. No father wants his daughter to move as far away as Chicago."

"Look who's talking about being near his children. Your daughter's in California. And where's your son? Across the Atlantic ocean."

Paul sighed. "I know." He opened his arms and Tracy hugged his neck. "Somehow, my relationship with you is different. You've awakened memories of a part of my life that I've denied for years. I've found that accepting the reality of my past makes me feel whole. I don't want to lose that part of me, and I'm afraid if you leave, it will all seem like a dream."

"We would both like for you to stay, Tracy." Kit kissed her cheek.

"I love you for that, but I don't think my living here is in anybody's best interest. Hal makes a good friend, but I'm not sure he's good husband material as long as he's under his mother's influence and still tied financially, and otherwise, to a wife. Let's face it, I'm not great wife material either—busy starting a new career. Who knows? Maybe time will change both of us."

Paul and Kit looked at each other and shrugged, judging her comment to be a small victory.

"Be happy for me," Tracy said. "I came to get closure. I have it."

"I suppose you're being smart. Maybe even logical," Paul said.

Tracy flipped him with her dishcloth, then threw it across the back of a chair. "I have something to show you before I leave," she said, and ran upstairs. She returned with the application for her birth certificate and handed it to Paul. He sat down at the table to read, while Kit looked over his shoulder and Ruth stood aside, smiling. The name printed on the application was "Tracy Brigitte Hunter."

Paul rose from the table and squeezed Tracy in a bear hug. "Thank you, love. This is better than I deserve." Still holding her, he closed his eyes and saw Sarah walking across the yard in bare feet, slow motion. "We did good," he told her. Her smile became Colette's.

ABOUT THE AUTHOR

Maxine Neely Davenport's roots are in Oklahoma: she was born and raised in Ada and graduated from East Central State University. She completed her master's degree in American literature at Colorado State, before her growing family moved to Texas for ten years. She then graduated from Oklahoma University Law School and returned to Colorado Springs to work as a senior editor for McGraw/Hill's legal acquisitions and editing department, prior to opening a law partnership, Etheridge and Davenport. She practiced family law and pursued her interest in writing, as editor of *The Pikes Peak Writer's NewsMagazine*, a bi-monthly journal.

Following her retirement, Maxine began writing professionally. Unable to leave her love for Oklahoma behind, she published a book of short story fiction, *Saturday Matinee*, based upon childhood memories. In her current crime mystery, *Murder Times Two*, hometown Ada and the law both feature prominently.

Maxine is the mother of three children, grandmother of seven, and great-grandmother of two. She resides in Santa Fe, New Mexico, where she is working on two other manuscripts, *Rebel on Horseback* and *Sierra's Passions*, slated for publication in 2014.

ACKNOWLEDGMENTS

It is my pleasure to acknowledge the following friends and colleagues who helped to make this novel possible:

Critique members: in Colorado, Kate Curry; Sally Foley; Donah Grassman; David Huffman, author of *Summer Solstice*; and Karen Jenista. And in Santa Fe, Bethany Baxter, author of *Two Sons*; Reverie Escobedo; and Joyce Townsend.

Readers: Bob Keeton; Susan Smith; Michele Heeney; and Valerie Stasik, author of *Incidental Daughter*.

Editors: Jennet Grover and Mary Neighbour.

Book cover designers: MediaNeighbours.com of Santa Fe, Mary and Andrew Neighbour.

Interior design: Valerie Stasik and Mary Neighbour.